A FUTILE ATTEMPT. . .

Opal Wilder stood before the castle door to the Princess Suite, paralyzed. She had raced this far to rescue Toby Ferris from captivity and certain death. He was somewhere on the other side of this idiotic portal. She had no key to it. There was no way she could force it open. Therefore, in order to gain entrance she would have to push the buzzer. The door would then be opened by one of four people: Lawrence Whitehead, Alex Burnside, or one of the two gunmen she had seen enter the building. End of rescue mission.

She raged at her own impotence, her impulsive foolishness. She saw now that her only sane course was to go to the police. She had already wasted precious minutes. She turned —

The elevator doors opened silently. Of the five men who were on it, she knew three by sight. Terry Shields, built like a miniature tank, low and powerful, was first to emerge.

EMPRESS OF CONEY ISLAND

EMPRESS
OF
CONEY ISLAND

EMPRESS
OF
CONEY ISLAND

A Novel of Suspense

ROBERT GILLESPIE

PaperJacks LTD.

TORONTO   NEW YORK

PaperJacks

EMPRESS OF CONEY ISLAND

PaperJacks LTD

330 STEELCASE RD. E., MARKHAM, ONT. L3R 2M1
210 FIFTH AVE., NEW YORK, N.Y. 10010

Dodd, Mead & Company edition published 1986

PaperJacks edition published August 1987

This is a work of fiction in its entirety. Any resemblance to actual people, places or events is purely coincidental.

EMPRESS
OF
CONEY ISLAND

1

He called himself Mr. Whitehead. Lawrence White-head. He was a large man, dressed in a well-tailored dark suit. His manner was one of quiet affability as he methodically searched her apartment. Sarah Goode noted his extraordinary neatness: He left each closet, cabinet, and drawer in precisely the same condition in which he had found it. This frightened her more than his calm disregard of her protests and the sight of a strange man touching her possessions.

Several times he apologized for invading her privacy. "Just tell me where they are, and I'll go away," he said.

She said, "This is an outrage."

"I know," he said.

She said, "I'm only an accountant. What would I be doing with records like that? I don't even know what you're looking for."

He smiled sweetly. "Yes, you do."

When he moved from the bedroom to the room she had transformed into her office, she had a chance to phone the police. She didn't do it. She followed him.

She said, "I have many clients, Mr. Whitehead. Mr. Sammartino is only one of them. I assure you that all I do is keep his books and make out his returns. I deal in numbers and forms, not the sort of records you seem to be talking about."

Mr. Whitehead gave a delighted little laugh. "You keep his books—both sets?"

She said, "Mr. Sammartino is an honest businessman."

He gave her a wise look and continued searching.

Though she had graduated to the status of C.P.A., Sarah Goode still looked like the prototypical book-keeper. She had light brown hair that didn't shine, a pale face that didn't glow, a slender figure that would remain untouched in Attica, and a clubfoot. The heavy shoe that encased the foot was her secret weapon. She could disable an attacker with one kick. The trouble was, it was a one-shot weapon. If she missed, there was no second chance.

He stood before her. "They're not here, are they?" he said.

"That's what I told you."

"I'm afraid I'm going to search you," he said.

She gasped. "No way, Mr. Whitehead! It's obvious that I don't have any records or tapes hidden on my person. I couldn't possibly be hiding them."

"I'm not looking for them now," he said. "I'm looking for the key to your safe-deposit box."

"I don't have a safe-deposit box."

"That remains to be seen, doesn't it?"

Neither of them moved.

"I tell you what," he said. "We'll go back to the bedroom, and you can put on a dressing gown. That way you can preserve your modesty. Okay?"

"No."

He seemed to grow larger. She peered up at him through her rimless glasses and wondered if now was the time for the kick. She stood motionless.

He said, "Go."

She went ahead of him into the bedroom, her lovely

bedroom with the lovely double bed. How important was personal dignity? she wondered. To be forced to disrobe before him was a terrible affront to her integrity as a person. But how permanent was the trauma? After he left, she could take a long shower and wash away the stains of his gaze.

She took off her garments one by one and handed them to him until she was naked. She put on a flowered robe.

"The shoe," he said.

"No."

"Come on, Miss Goode," he coaxed. "And that'll be the end of it."

She hated to look at her disfigured foot and fervently hoped that it would repel this overbearing stranger.

He searched the shoe without looking at the foot.

"Please don't tear it apart," she said.

He found the small packet of bills. "Mad money?" he said.

She didn't answer.

He gave her back the shoe.

"Do you mind if I put it on?"

"Go ahead."

She put on the shoe and laced it. Sitting on the edge of the bed, she said, "It's time to leave, Mr. Whitehead."

"Not quite yet." He was leaning at ease in the doorway.

She jumped to her feet. "You said that was the end of it!"

"It was," he said. "No more searching. You don't have them." Then he said, "Tell me about Opal Wilder."

"God, this is too much! I'm going to call the police." She stood still.

"You've been seen with her. At her place in the Village, and here."

"Miss Wilder has nothing to do with it!"

"With what?"

3

"With whatever you're looking for."

"You two aren't crazy enough to try blackmail?" he said.

She edged closer to him. "Miss Wilder is simply a friend, that's all."

"She's a writer. The last steady job she had was at the *Herald-Courier*. That was years ago. She needs money."

"Everybody does. Are you going to leave?"

"Is she your lover?"

The kick came without conscious volition on her part. The four inches of hard leather smashed into his shin. His reflex actions were to raise the wounded leg and to step backward at the same time. They counteracted each other, and he fell heavily—outside the doorway, yet still blocking it.

She knew that her best chance of escaping him was to leap over him, get out of the apartment, and run until she was safe. But the foot that had felled him now prevented her from trying it.

She raced to the bedside phone and succeeded in dialing 911 before he stumbled forward and slammed a hand on the disconnect lever.

She whirled toward the doorway, but he now held her with one arm. He was incredibly strong. She peered into his eyes and saw the pain. She saw something else, and she moaned, "Oh, no!"

He held a tube that looked like a cigarette lighter under her nose. "Good-bye, Miss Goode," he said.

There was a hiss, something acrid stung her nostrils, then she was suffocating. Her throat was paralyzed. She tried to say something, but the blackness took her.

He let her fall to the floor and straightened up. "You try to be nice to them, and what do you get?" he muttered. A few particles of the nerve gas had gotten into his own nose, stinging it. He snorted to expel it.

His leg was bleeding. He could feel the trickle. He limped to the bathroom, pulled up the pant leg, swabbed the gash with tissue, found a Band-Aid in the medicine cabinet, and fixed it over the cut. The area of the wound was swelling, and he wondered if she had broken the bone. Since he could stand on it, he decided there was no break.

He flushed the bloody tissue down the toilet and looked around to make sure there was no other evidence of blood. He traced his steps across the bedroom carpet, but no drops had fallen there. He took a deep breath and expelled it. Now for the rest of the job.

He took two plastic dry-cleaner's bags from the closet where he had noted them earlier, tied knots in their tops to close off the openings, and put them aside on a chair.

Sarah Goode was barely breathing. Fine. He didn't want her to die of the nerve gas, though the traces of it in her body would be gone in a matter of hours. He took off her robe and the lethal shoe, laid her nude body on the bed, and covered it with the top sheet and blanket.

He hesitated a moment, then shrugged. He retrieved one of the plastic bags and put it over her head, tucking it around her neck so that no air could enter. He studied her, then pulled her arms out from under the covers and let them rest naturally on her stomach atop the blanket. Okay.

He limped out of the bedroom and made his way to her office. There he ran a sheet of her stationery into her word-processing printer, then turned on and entered her computer. He took a piece of paper from his pocket and placed it alongside the keyboard. Copying from the paper, he typed:

> We love each other and can't bear to be parted. His religion doesn't permit divorce, even though it is the only

thing that could save us. So we have taken this way—together for the rest of our lives, no matter how short, and for all eternity, God willing. We leave no one who will be hurt by our action. If anyone remembers us, remember only that we are happy, totally happy together. Together.

He scanned what he had written on the monitor, then signaled for it to be printed on the letterhead. A moment later he carried the suicide note to the bedroom, gently pressed Sarah Goode's fingers on it, then laid it on the bedside table.

He peered at her, saw that she was no longer breathing.

He went out to the living room to await the arrival of her partner in death. He had learned what he had come to find out. This Opal Wilder person was in possession of the records he sought.

2

A month later, Toby Ferris stood in the outer lobby of a Greenwich Village apartment and glared at the little black button to apartment 3H. The card alongside it identified the occupants as "B. McNeely," printed, and "O. Wilder," scrawled in ink. The silence closed in on him. He hadn't expected the silence, not in New York. Maybe the goldarn dingdong isn't working, he thought.

He put his finger on the button for apartment 1A, marked "Super," and hesitated. He hadn't prepared himself to confront a stranger; he had expected that the door would buzz, he would go in the elevator to the third floor, Opal would be standing in the doorway with that wide-eyed look of eager questioning partly masked by a reticence born of past disappointments, and he would say, "Hey, Opal." But the door didn't buzz. *New York was defeating him again.* Defying the thought, he jabbed the super's button as if gouging it from its socket.

Eventually a stocky man with gray hair emerged from a doorway across the inner lobby, scowled at Toby through the glass door separating the two lobbies, and, obviously muttering words that Toby couldn't hear, proceeded to the door with a sidling gait that reminded Toby of a crab. It was the arms, he thought; they were held away from the body as though his armpits pained him. He opened the door partway.

"Yeah?"

Toby marveled that one little four-letter affirmative word could carry so much menace, hostility, contempt, and negation. It was amazing, too, how the man could size him up so quickly. Toby knew he was wearing the raiment of a person deserving of, if not commanding, respect—a gray Brooks Brothers suit, striped button-down shirt, and plain Yves Saint Laurent tie—relics of his former stay in New York. No one ever said "Yeah" in quite that way to a Brooks Brothers suit. He concluded that it was his face and his posture that gave him away. The larger-than-average red nose, the watery blue eyes, and the excuse-me slouch of his six-foot frame were signposts bearing the legend: THIS MAN IS A RUMMY—KICK HIM. The fact that the label was terribly unfair was no consolation. He couldn't go up to everyone who set eyes on him and say, "Your impression of me is quite wrong, sir or madam, I inherited the nose and eyes from my father, and I've been a member of Alcoholics Anonymous for fifteen years, give or take a binge or two. The fact is, I'm as temperate as a Quaker and sober as a judge." The fact was, Toby Ferris never knew his father—or his mother either, for that matter—so he couldn't say for sure who contributed what feature to his unfortunate physiognomy.

He drew himself up to his full height and peered down the red nose at the truculent super. "Howdy, good friend," he said. "I'm looking for Miss Opal Wilder, and her bell seems to be out of order. I wondered if you might—"

"She not here."

The man started to close the heavy door.

Toby moved through the doorway past him. "I don't want to be a nuisance, but I've come a long distance to see her. Do you know where she might be?"

8

"She not here."

"Yes, you said that. But how do you know 'she not here' unless we take a look? It's important that I find her. She may be ill or something."

If the man's Latin face had previously been clouded, it now turned stormy. "How I know?" he said. He scampered to a table near the recessed mailboxes of the tenants. On it rested the magazines and parcels that couldn't fit in the boxes. It also held a disarray of regular mail. The man picked up a handful of letters and threw them down. "The mail!" he said. "She don't pick up the mail, she not here! Hokay?"

"A fair deduction," Toby said.

"Good-bye," the man said, trying to herd him toward the door. Toby asked more questions, learned that Opal's roommate "not here" either and that the man's name was Santiago. The man didn't know how long the mail had been piling up. He wouldn't let Toby touch it, but since the letters were scattered rather than neatly stacked, Toby saw at least six letters of his own written to Opal over the last month, lying there unopened like closed caskets.

Suddenly his nostrils were filled with the scent of death. A dizziness came over him, and he allowed himself to be nudged out the door. Opal Wilder was dead. The overly dramatic wail of Thomas Wolfe rang through his mind: "Oh, lost!" Oh, horse manure, he retorted; happiness continues to elude Friday's child, that's all, old buddy; it's only to be expected.

Thomas Wolfe was but one of the writers who went into the making of Toby Ferris. As an orphan in his native city of Jackson, Mississippi, he had had no parents to mold him, and he rejected the cast that his circumstances and surroundings had tried to force on him. Rather, he shaped himself out of his dreams, the movies he saw, his need for self-protection, and his books. He was Rhett Butler and W. C. Fields, Long John Silver and Mr. Micawber, Tom Swift and Bugs Bunny, King Arthur and King Lear, the Scarlet Pimpernel and Sam Spade, d'Artagnan and Paul Bunyan, Buck and Moby Dick, Huckleberry Finn and Hawkeye, Errol Flynn and Tyrone Power, The Shadow and Stan Laurel, George Washington and Robert E. Lee, and countless other heroes including his fellow orphan Oliver Twist and heroines such as Shirley Temple and Lady Macbeth. The combinations produced strange effects.

He learned early on that he was a skinny outsider with a large nose, so he became a comedian on the theory that if his contemporaries were laughing they would forget to beat him up. The comic thoughts came to him naturally; acting them out took all the courage he had. Eventually comedy became part of his facade. He discovered also that courtly manners, just the right mixture of courtesy and flattery, could also avert a beating, and they too became part of his facade, covering the swashbuckler within.

Some people thought he sounded more like W. C. Fields than anyone else, but that was all right. He had achieved the age of forty-five and he was still functioning, so what the hell.

He found himself out on the sidewalk of East Tenth Street, in the June sunlight, standing still. Opal wasn't there. The terrible-tempered Mr. Santiago had refused to open the door to her apartment. Something was wrong. In *Lives of a Bengal Lancer*, C. Aubrey Smith viewed an ominously silent outpost and said, "I don't like this. I don't like it at all." Toby didn't like the silence in the lobby, the door that didn't buzz, the unclaimed letters, the strange absence of Opal Wilder, the ponderous presence of New York City, the natives waiting in ambush . . . the helplessness he felt.

He turned around slowly, looking up at the forbidding face of the building, and saw the invisible handwriting: YOU'RE AN OUTSIDER. GO HOME, YOU MUTT. He shrank away.

What now?

He looked up the street, saw a policeman putting a ticket on his car. It figured. It was New York saying, NO PARKING, GET OUT. Actually, it wasn't his car. It belonged to his landlady down on the Mississippi Gulf Coast, an old woman with a foul tongue who had seen more adversity than Toby and had survived with all the good points intact. When he had hesitantly spoken of going to New York to look for Opal, she had said, "Take my old heap, Tobe. It farts somethin' awful, but it'll get you there. I'm mighty anxious to set eyes on that gal of yours. I'll teach her how to make a man happy."

Unfortunately, he had forgotten to take along her registration certificate, so he turned his back on the distant bluecoat, knowing that if he engaged him in conversation, the lack of registration could cause inconvenience if not incarceration.

What now?

"B. McNeely." Opal had mentioned her in her letters. She was Blossom McNeely, who owned a small, one-woman bookstore somewhere in the Village. Opal had never specified her age, but Toby had gotten the impression that she was in her late sixties, easily old enough to be Opal's mother. The name of the bookstore. It was something quaint and spinsterish. Something about tea. Toby dredged up the name. Tea and Books.

He strolled past the policeman, who was now ticketing another car, and walked down Broadway to Eighth Street scarcely aware that he was experiencing a rare occur-

11

rence in New York City—a nice day. The sky was blue and the sun was shining, and he was looking for a telephone. He found one with an Out of Order sign on it and a Manhattan directory in its slot. Tea and Books was in the South Village near Houston Street.

It turned out to be one of those grubby storefronts four steps below sidewalk level. It was closed. To Toby, it looked terminally closed. He went down the steps and tried the door. It opened. He backed away, tripped on a step, scrambled to the sidewalk, and went into the Italian delicatessen next door.

The owner said, "No, Miz McNeely ain't been there for weeks, Mac. She does that once in a while. Saves up and goes on a tour. Last year it was Mexico. This year she was talking about Egypt. That's where she is, you can bet on it."

"Did she tell you she was going? Ask you to keep an eye on the store or anything like that?"

"She generally does, but this time she didn't. She does that sometimes too. Was there something else you wanted? Pastrami maybe?"

Toby let him slice a half-pound of pastrami. He said, "Does she generally leave the door unlocked?"

"You're kidding! She didn't lock up? These old ladies," he said, shaking his head.

He accompanied Toby to the shop next door. They entered, found the switch, and turned on the light. Two tearoom tables were in the front of the shop; the rest was the typical jumble of secondhand books one finds in such stores. And yet there was an order to the disorder that didn't appear to be disturbed.

The man went to the cash register and opened it, saying, "Nobody in their right mind leaves money in the store at night—yi, I take it back. Miz McNeely forgot the money. Just like her. She's what they call absent-minded. Oh, well, no harm done."

12

Five minutes later, Toby stood alone outside the deli with a half-pound of pastrami in a bag, breathing deeply to keep down his panic.

A name came into his head. Ralph Simmons, patron saint of misfits.

3

Ralph Simmons had brought Toby and Opal together. At the time he was director of advertising and promotion at the *New York Herald-Courier*, the distinguished morning paper perennially struggling to stay alive in a changing world. Since the paper could barely afford to pay guild minimum wages, the turnover of copywriters was rapid, with the good ones leaving and the journeymen staying on. Simmons optimistically continued to seek out good ones.

It was ten years ago that he peered at the red nose and watery eyes of the then thirty-five-year-old man who fidgeted in the chair across the desk from him.

"Are you *the* Tobias Ferris?" he asked.

The man shrugged. "The only one I know," he said. The native Southern accent had Fieldsian overtones.

"Are you the author of *The Flood?*"

"Are you the one who read it?"

"It was a hell of a book. I loved it."

"You're the one. Very happy to meet you."

Despite Toby's age and inexperience—thirty-five was an advanced age to start as an apprentice copywriter—and despite the danger signs written on the face, Simmons hired him. On Toby's first day at work, Simmons

14

took him to lunch at the Ink Spot, the seedy bistro at the rear entrance to the Herald-Courier building.

Simmons said, "I'm gonna have a martini. What'll you have?"

"Bourbon and branch without the bourbon," Toby said.

Simmons took him to lunch several more times in those first weeks, and each time Toby chose a nonalcoholic drink and Simmons was satisfied. Meanwhile he became enchanted by Toby's comic observations which, when they weren't self-deprecatory, were put-downs of the pompous and the hypocritical. Toby noted, for instance, that the august and disdainful bartender wore a wig.

"I know how he feels," Toby said. "With it, he's monarch of the Ink Spot. Without it, he's Old Baldy, and people would be rubbing his head for luck."

"Do you have a wig?" Simmons asked.

"Of course. Everybody does," Toby said. It wasn't until a long time later that Simmons decided that Toby's wig was the comic facade he put up to hide his nakedness.

Toby seldom talked about his past life, and when he did it was often hidden in hyperbole. "Penicillin isn't the wonder drug, Ralph," he once said. "Money is. It makes you taller and stronger and better looking. It makes you superior to the common run of man, it makes your thought processes infallible, and people bow to the brilliance of your decisions so that you have to call on your monumental modesty to meet the flattery. By God, it makes you a *philanthropist*, that's what it does! . . . But don't ever try to marry into it, Ralph. It doesn't work that way. You have to be born into it, or else you're an interloper."

"Is that what you were, Toby?" Simmons asked.

"An interloper? No, sir, you have to have a large helping of arrogance to be a true interloper. What I was was a

15

country boy from Mississippi who had wrote me a book, the best goldarned book in the world, and got me a swelled head, so big that it hurt, and got me a rich wife, which was only my due for being such an immensely talented fellow. Is that arrogance? No, that's not arrogance, it's damn-foolery of the first magnitude—with, okay, maybe a touch of arrogance. I mean, I was only twenty-three and the writer of a hardcover book I had thunk up out of my own headbone, and one drunken reviewer, he must have been drunk, called me the successor to Mark Twain. Are you listening to me, Ralph, I was the reincarnation of the great Mark Twain! ... To the Richmans I was their daughter's mistake."

Over the years, Ralph Simmons pieced together a sketchy outline of Toby's story. Ferris was the name of the woman who found the infant in a trashcan behind a seafood restaurant in Jackson, Mississippi. She called him Tobias after the apocryphal youth who expelled evil spirits and cured blindness with the entrails of a fish. Later the foundling preferred to identify himself with Toby, the dog in the Punch-and-Judy show. He was not a handsome child, and whenever would-be adoptive parents chanced to view him he was likely as not ill with some unattractive childhood disease or other. He spent most of his life to his eighteenth birthday in a Baptist orphanage, which apparently treated him well enough to allow his natural intelligence to develop, though he later alleged that it was administered by Mr. Bumble and Mrs. Corney.

He worked his way through the University of Mississippi, near Oxford, in a variety of part-time jobs, the most lucrative of which was as cesspool cleaner in outlying areas. He cleaned up enough, he said, to give himself time after graduation to write his book. The hero of *The Flood* is a parentless boy, not unlike Huck Finn, who is

16

swept willy-nilly in his skiff on the floodwaters of the Mississippi River from one picaresque adventure to another in the vicinity of the river town of Pleasantville. The waters act as a willful god, returning him to scenes of earlier action so that the several subplots can be resolved.

The book won amazingly good reviews, but apparently the reading public wasn't in a comic mood that season, for the book sold poorly. Before the results were in, however, he met a Bryn Mawr student who was bowled over at meeting a real author, and they got married. Unfortunately they went to live in her family's home in one of those strangely named towns outside Philadelphia.

Toby scarcely ever spoke of his two-year hitch on the Main Line. He tried to draw his wife away from there but failed. The family didn't consider Ole Miss a true institution of higher learning. They induced Toby to take a position in one of the family enterprises, their real-estate holdings in South Philadelphia. He lasted two weeks and then took up drinking as a vocation. He called them slumlords. That did nothing to bridge the culture gap. His wife became pregnant and brought forth a male child, who was called Franklin.

He wrote what he thought was a comic novel about the snobs of Philadelphia, but although C. K. Dexter-Haven was one of his heroes, particularly as played by Cary Grant, Toby Ferris was no Philip Barry. He didn't understand the people he was lampooning, and the book was rejected by his publisher.

The divorce was a quiet one, for he was a thoroughly beaten man and an alcoholic. Yet the swashbuckler was still alive within him, and instead of returning to Mississippi, he dared to seek his fortune in the most challenging arena in the world, New York City. Naturally, he lost.

The early years in New York are hazy. The job he held longest was night clerk in a fleabag hotel. Beaten in Phila-

17

delphia, he was put to rout by New York. At his lowest point he did a stretch on the Bowery.

He was saved by the Salvation Army, not the real outfit but a rerun of the movie *Guys and Dolls*. He was particularly taken with Stubby Kaye's rendition of "Sit Down You're Rockin' the Boat." He saw the movie countless times in the course of a week, and he decided to stop throwing his life away. Just like that, cold turkey. When the tremors ceased, he got a job putting together a labor-union house organ, a job he held for two years until the day he cropped the union president out of all the photos in the belief that it was time to play up the other members. It was at this point that he applied for the job at the *Herald-Courier*.

When Opal Wilder applied for a job several years later, she was in revolt against everything conventional, including the grand old paper she wished to serve. She was born in 1949, the tail end of the postwar baby boom, raised in a comfortable middle-class home in Teaneck, New Jersey, and graduated from Stuyvesant University with a B.A. in English magna cum laude. She was idealistically caught up in the student revolt of the late 1960s and romantically caught up with one of her fellow rebels. They were married in Stuyvesant Park across the street from the university and recited their own poetic vows to each other.

The marriage didn't last long. Her young groom soon demonstrated that he regarded the revolt as a lark, and now that that was behind him he was going on to law school and to his father's law firm, which dealt in corporate law. He considered the wedding as part of the lark and wanted them to get married again—properly—in an Episcopal church. He was shocked to find that Opal really believed the malarkey they had been preaching. He was also shocked by her passionate lovemaking.

Opal left him, cut her hair short, moved to Greenwich Village, and supported herself with free-lance editing jobs for the big book publishers, poor-paying but adequate for a single woman's needs. She was twenty-seven when Ralph Simmons hired her on the basis of articles she had written for the college paper.

On her first day on the job, Simmons, following his custom, took her to lunch. They were accompanied by Simmons's regular lunch partner, Toby Ferris. The three misfits found each other most congenial. Ralph Simmons counted himself a misfit, and throughout his career he claimed he was delightfully surprised that there was a place for him in the commercial world in which he would be paid, actually paid, for doing something he enjoyed. Few men were so lucky.

And so the three became regular lunch companions, sometimes going to the Ink Spot, sometimes to the Stuyvesant Club, more often to an inexpensive Mexican restaurant, called The Chihuahua for some reason known only to the owner. The three took to calling it The Chili Dog.

Toby and Opal were more deeply wounded by their early marital misadventures than they realized. They each subconsciously were determined never again to get emotionally involved with another person. Thus they regarded each other as buddies rather than susceptible man and woman. Their looks facilitated this arrangement, he with his less than classical masculine beauty and she with her short hair and sharply cut features to which she applied no makeup except a black outline around her eyes. Her tailored clothes completed the disguise. They liked each other too much to risk getting serious and spoiling the relationship.

Toby fell off the wagon just once that Opal was aware of—until the end, that is. The triggering event had some-

19

thing to do with the son he was never permitted to see. The family was sending young Franklin to the snootiest private school in the Northeast. Toby disappeared from the office, and Opal found him, hours later, nearly incoherent at the Ink Spot bar.

"They're turning my boy into a Richman," he told her in a voice that quavered with suppressed sobs.

"What's wrong with being a rich man?" she said, deliberately misunderstanding.

"Rich men can't . . . get to heaven," he said.

"Bull," she said, and took him home in a taxi.

He was out for three more days, and on the fourth day he arrived back at the office pale and apologetic. Even his nose was pale. "Thanks, buddy," he said to her.

About a year after they first met they ceased being buddies and became lovers—for one night. It was a night when they had to work late. Toby was feeling low. The publisher had criticized in contemptuous language an ad campaign that Toby had labored over for weeks. When they finally quit the building, Opal saw Toby's state and said, "Let's take a cab." Since they both lived in the Village, a half-mile apart, Toby agreed.

When the cab halted in front of Opal's building, a row house converted to apartments, Toby absentmindedly got out of the cab with her and paid the driver. He stood on the sidewalk. She said from the stoop, "What did you do that for?"

He said, "I'll walk home. I need the exercise." But he just stood there. A moment later he became aware that she was still on the landing looking down at him. "What are you waiting for?" he said. "Go on in. It's a gentleman's duty to see that the lady gets safely into her home."

She came down to him. "I don't think you're capable of walking home."

He looked up at the opaque sky and said in a small voice, "This goldarn city is my windmill, Opal honey, and my lance keeps getting caught in the vanes. Right now I'm dangling fifty feet in the air and going around. It'll bring me back down in a minute, then I'll go home."

She said, "Stop dramatizing. Come on up, and I'll make you some hot buttered apple juice."

"Hot diggity damn!" he said. "I've always wanted some of that."

Inside her apartment door, he looked at her and said, "Hey, Opal."

She said, "Hey, yourself."

He said, "Let's give it a try."

She said, "I'm punky."

He said, "So am I, so we're even."

She said, "We can splash ourselves with cologne."

"Good idea. How long does it last?"

"It'll be gone by the morning."

She led him to the bedroom.

He said, "About the cologne, what do you say I put it on you and you put it on me? Is that a good idea?"

"Why don't we try it and find out?" she said.

The kiss started in introductory fashion, the lips testing texture and resiliency, and suddenly their bodies were caught up in an embracing fit of passion, pressed desperately together from knee to nose.

"Great heavens to Betsy!" she said.

He said, "Let's get out of these goldarn clothes!"

The anointing ritual worked almost too well for people all wound up and ready to spring. The hands applying the cologne shook, and the parts to which it was applied tightened.

They stood apart for a moment, gazed at each other's body, and approved. His was gangling, wiry rather than skinny. Hers was firm, with somewhat larger breasts than her mannish clothing had led him to assume. "Classic modern," he said.

Their lovemaking was brief but intense, foreshortened by the lingering laying on of hands. The second time around was better. They fell asleep, side by side.

In the morning she said, "It's not love, is it?"

He laughed nervously. "Of course not. Just a little fun and games."

So they played the game one more time and had fun.

He said, "Suddenly we're playing in a different ballpark. Maybe we better not do this again."

She said, "I'd rather keep you as a friend than lose you as a lover. Does that make sense?"

He said, "I think we're not ready. Tell me when you're ready."

"You too," she said, moving away from him.

And so they remained friends.

The competitive situation of the *Herald-Courier* continued to deteriorate, and Ralph Simmons's department couldn't work the miracles needed to stop the downslide. He was promoted to a new position with the title of Director of Research and told to find new ventures. He knew that nobody expected him to come up with anything, so he spent his time tending to his first wife, who was slowly, grudgingly dying of cancer, and submerging his sorrows at the Stuyvesant Club bar. A year later the position was abolished and he was given early retirement at the age of sixty.

His successor in advertising and promotion was a suave, fast-talking young man from Madison Avenue, and one of his first acts was to fire Toby Ferris, who had once again fallen off the wagon. Toby didn't even bother to take his case to the Newspaper Guild, which nevertheless made sure he at least received his severance pay. Thus he was again without a job in New York City.

Opal marched into the new boss's office and threw coffee in his face. The Guild was unable to get severance for her. She went back to her apartment and in a frenzy of antiestablishment rebellion, banged out a scandalous novel, called *Flat On My Back*, about the sexual mores of Greenwich Village. She wrote it in the first person, as if the mind-boggling variations on the theme were hers. In actuality she had experienced firsthand only one of the kinkier episodes; the rest came from hearsay and imagination. The book was published by one of the fringe publishing houses, and like Toby's book it was a critical success and a financial failure—too raunchy for the general public and not raunchy enough for the seekers of pornography. Her literary agent obtained free-lance editing jobs for her, and she survived.

Meanwhile Toby had disappeared, too proud to accept sympathy from his friends. Apparently the pickings for him in New York were poor. He surfaced briefly to borrow a hundred dollars from Opal and two hundred from Ralph Simmons. He was not heard from again for two years. Finally she got a letter from him, postmarked Pascagoula, purporting to relate his adventures since last she saw him. They were hilarious, scatological, and totally unbelievable.

He enclosed a clipping from the local newspaper. It was a humor column, headed "The Ferris Wheel," containing exaggerated accounts of local doings. He wrote: "You can see that I have finally found my niche—small-town Official Comical Person. Don't laugh, or rather, *do* laugh. Remember that Art Buchwald started in a place called Paris, and Erma Bombeck first wrote about Centerville, Ohio. I'm being syndicated to places as far away as fifty miles, so there!"

About her book, he wrote that he had identified with all of the male characters and two of the female. "I'm using it as an advertisement for myself among the nubile natives of Pascagoula, but not too many of them can read. When I read it to them, they punch me in the nose."

Their correspondence started out as mere entertainments but got increasingly more intimate. She wrote that she could no longer afford the rent on her apartment and had moved in with her bookstore friend, Blossom McNeely. He wrote that in order to make ends meet he worked part-time as a waiter in a seafood restaurant. "I keep looking in the garbage cans to see if I'm there," he wrote.

Then two months ago he wrote: "I told you I would tell you when I'm ready. Hey, Opal, I'm ready. Son of a gun, I think I'm ready! Did I say I was ready? I'm as ready as a randy rhinoceros, a ravenous rabbit, or a rutting razorback, take your pick.

"I finally got the Philadelphia monkey off my back. In my aging years I think I finally understand the person I married, and I say the hell with her. The boy Franklin is now a man, and I don't have to worry about him anymore either, fat lot of good it did me—or him. Can you imagine naming a boy of mine Franklin? But enough of that.

"I feel like a red-faced schoolboy, saying if it's okay with you I would like to spend some time with you, like the rest of my sorry life. I've been told I'm not easy to live with, but the truth is I'm the most companionable of persons, as cuddly as a barrel of pussycats. Hell, you've seen me at my worst and at my best, such as it is. Do you think you could bear to spend some time with me? Tell me if you're ready."

She wrote back: "Why not? We're both edging further and further away from adolescence, and you'd be more amusing to have around than old Blossom. She's a dear old soul, but she rambles. I'm as ready as I'll ever be, possibly because I love you, you randy old rhinoceros. But being a practical-minded young girl, may I ask what you

24

have in mind to use for money. After all, neither one of us has a teapot to tiddle in."

He responded that he could practice his art in any locality, and besides, he was an expert panhandler. He went on to give a dissertation on the science of panhandling.

When he received no reply, he continued to write, alternately saying that he loved her and couldn't live without her and that he was only kidding and didn't want to lose her as a pen pal and a buddy.

After a month without word from her, he dashed off some advance "Ferris Wheel" columns for his local paper, borrowed his landlady's car, and lit out for New York, knowing that his words were true: He couldn't live without Opal Wilder.

By the time he got to New York, he was one of the great tragic lovers in all of history. His self-deprecatory wit spoiled the image somewhat by dredging up Cyrano de Bergerac. So be it, Cyrano was a noble character. Toby didn't mind being Cyrano for a while. But now his Roxane had disappeared, and Cyrano was left without a rhyme.

4

He said, "Bless my soul," to the woman who opened the door of Ralph Simmons's house, giving her an embarrassed hug. He wasn't looking his best, he knew. He had lost his way. Though he had been to Ralph's house a number of times, he had always come by train or in Ralph's car. This day he had roamed Long Island by car for hours looking for the elusive Savage Point, the community where Ralph lived, finally arriving at six P.M., unannounced, bleary, dog-tired, and in a high state of anxiety. The presence of Lillian Caplin further befuddled him.

Lillian Caplin had been Ralph Simmons's secretary for fifteen years. Now it appeared that she was his wife. Well, well, he hadn't known that. She was a short, bouncy, rather rotund person in her midfifties with an oval face, happy blue eyes, and gray-blond hair. She spoke in clichés. "Hey, Ralph," she called. "Look what the cat dragged in!" Toby cringed, knowing that her choice of words was only too apt.

Simmons greeted him warmly, bawled him out for not calling, observed it was the cocktail hour, and asked what he would have. Toby said he would have "sparkling seltzer on the rocks in a frosted glass."

Settled on the living room sofa, Toby blurted out his

reasons for coming. One, where's Opal Wilder? Two, could they bunk him down for the night? Three, to repay the two hundred dollars.

Ralph said, "By all means," to the second and pooh-poohed the third, but he accepted the money, knowing that Toby would be insulted if he didn't.

"Have you seen Opal?"

Lillian said, "That was some book, wasn't it? Ralph and I had to take cold showers for two weeks."

"Together?"

"Of course."

"Chapter fourteen," Toby said.

Ralph said, "We held a literary lunch for her when her book came out, just the three of us, and I've had lunch with her several times since, but not recently." Then he said, "What's up, Toby?"

Toby's shoulders slumped. "I can't find her," he said in a voice that was nearly a wail. He told about the abrupt cessation of letters, the pileup of mail, and the strangely vacant bookstore with the door unlocked and money in the till.

Ralph's round face showed concern. "It's probably nothing, and we'll both be embarrassed when we force the super to open the apartment and find everything normal. We'll do it tomorrow. Right now, we eat."

Toby tried hard to be an amusing guest, but his attempts at humor fell away midstory as his thoughts kept homing back to Opal.

Lillian said, "You're in love with her."

"I think you're right."

"What took you so long?" she said.

In the kitchen, where Toby insisted on helping to clean up, Lillian said, "Marriage is a big step. It's possible Opal just went off by herself to think it over. Women get cold feet too, Toby."

When Toby's restlessness became unnerving, Ralph took him for a walk along Shore Road. Savage Point was on a small peninsula that jutted into Little Neck Bay on the North Shore of Long Island. Ralph said, "You're in good shape, Tobe. How do you do it?"

"Down home I don't have a car," Toby said. "I ride a bike. You see more when you're wobbling along on two wheels than when you're tooling along on four."

Ralph ruefully patted his paunch. "Too many potholes around here for bikes. Hence, too many pots."

It was a typical midspring evening in New York—clouds overhead and a nip in the air coming off the dark water of the bay. Ralph pointed out some of the houses on the inland side of Shore Road, most of them belonging to newly rich newcomers.

He pointed to a structure larger than the others. "Old money," he said. "Not as old as what you married into and not as huge, but enough to make the owner a philanthropist, if you'll pardon the expression."

"That word always makes me want to pee."

"Roger Meuwssen," Ralph said. "I don't think he ever worked for anything but charities—at a princely salary, of course. Guess what he heads up now."

"The Ford Foundation."

"No, the New York Casino Control Agency. It was bound to come, and it finally came. You didn't know that, did you?"

"What?"

"Casino gambling. It's finally here, but they needed someone above suspicion to head it up. So they picked Mr. Clean, Roger Meuwssen, the noted philanthropist. What are you doing?"

"Watering his shrubbery. Do you think he'd mind?"

"I have an awful urge to join you."

"You take that one. This one's mine." He gave a satisfied sigh. "Ah, one of the simple pleasures of the poor," he said in the grand manner of royalty.

At nine the next morning Ralph found a parking garage five blocks away from Opal Wilder's apartment building. Having gotten a good look at Toby's car in daylight, Ralph had insisted on driving his own car, a red VW Rabbit, and Lillian had tagged along. Toby darted through traffic and then waited, practically dancing in place, for Ralph and Lillian to catch up.

Ralph Simmons, amiable-looking, mild-mannered, and overweight, was no more commanding a figure than Toby Ferris, but he took the initiative when the scowling superintendent opened the foyer door. "I'm Miss Wilder's father," he said.

"And I'm her mother," Lillian said. "I may not look old enough, but—"

Ralph interrupted her and sternly demanded that the super permit them to view the apartment. "Or must we call the police?" he said.

Apparently the super had no desire to have police on the premises, for, growling and grumbling, he produced a key and led them in the slow-moving elevator to the third floor.

In the third-floor hall the smell was only a faint unpleasantness. The door to apartment 3G opened, and a woman in a dressing gown and hair curlers said to the superintendent, "Are you finally doing something about the smell?"

Santiago walked past her. "I no smell anything."

The woman pulled a can of Lysol from behind her and sprayed it at his retreating figure. "Maybe it's you," she said, and slammed the door.

As he used his key to open apartment 3H, he grumbled, "That lady, she's a crazy lady."

The door opened into a darkened living room. Santiago flicked on the light. "There! You hoppy now?" he said.

It was a cluttered room with an eclectic selection of objets d'art, paintings, statuettes, a Mexican blanket on the sofa, and a Mexican travel poster on the wall. Built-in bookshelves surrounded the two small windows floor to ceiling. The odor was stronger in here.

"Don't you recognize it, you silly fellow?" Toby cried. "The smell of death!"

He rushed to one bedroom door, then to the other, and stopped. "Oh, my God!" he said in a strangled voice, and went in.

Ralph said to Lillian, "Stay here," and he followed Toby.

A figure in a nightgown was sprawled on the floor near the doorway to the bathroom. The disheveled hair was gray. An outstretched hand held a druggist's prescription bottle from which some white pills had spilled on the bathroom tile. The flesh seemed to have fallen away from the hand, exposing the delicate bones.

Ralph's stomach rebelled. Unable to go past the body to the bathroom, he rushed back past Lillian to the living room window, where he snapped up the shade, tugged the window open, leaned out, and heaved. Only after the paroxysm subsided did he notice with relief that he had tossed his breakfast not on the sidewalk in front of the building but in a rear alley. "Sorry," he muttered.

Toby shouted, "It's not Opal, thank the Lord God! It's not her, Ralph!"

The superintendent stood in the middle of the room in a pugnacious pose, as if expecting to be assaulted.

Ralph called the police.

Toby's emotions were in a turmoil. This was where Opal had lived. He went into the empty bedroom. The closet was bare of clothing. The bureau drawers held

30

nothing. There was no sign of her. He wandered back to the living room, glared around at its contents. Nothing of Opal's. Everything he saw belonged to her roommate. It was as if Opal had never lived there.

A shallow alcove contained a desk and a chair. He pulled open the drawers and lifted out office supplies. Anonymous.

Santiago said, "You no do that!"

Toby said, "Go to hell, my friend."

There was nothing of Opal's in the desk. She always used a typewriter, an Olivetti portable. It wasn't there. The wastebasket in the well of the desk was empty.

He studied the chair. It was the size of a stenographer's chair but sturdily built and comfortably padded. Opal had had just such a chair in her old apartment. Anyone who spent her working days in front of a desk needed a comfortable chair to keep from getting housemaid's knees on her rear end, also support for her back to avert fatigue. It was Opal's chair, he was sure of that. But he had no way of proving it.

Still, the chair soothed him; it showed that his beloved Opal had indeed been here. But she had cleared out before whatever happened to the poor woman in there happened. Undoubtedly laden with luggage, she had been unable to take the chair with her. It had not been a normal move. It had been done in haste, or else she would have taken the chair with her. That was the soothing thought. Opal had escaped the fate of her dead friend, Blossom McNeely.

Other, more disquieting thoughts intruded, but he pushed them away. He sat in Opal's chair, saying firmly to himself, She's alive, she's okay. But where? She couldn't have known that her elderly roommate was dead, for she wouldn't have just left her there quietly to rot. Maybe Lillian was right, she had gone off somewhere

31

to think it over. The prospect of life with Toby Ferris had to be disturbing. He never should have upset their friendship by proposing marriage. Yet, she was thirty-five, and if she was ever to have children she had little time to waste. Toby brought his thoughts up short. He didn't even know if she wanted children! He groaned. There was a lot he didn't know about Opal Wilder.

The police arrived. Toby, Ralph, and Lillian went down to the lobby to wait. There was no place to sit, so they sat on the steps. Lillian's eyes were swimming in tears. She kept referring to the dead woman as "the poor thing."

Toby said, "What do you think, Ralph?"

Ralph said, "I don't know. It looks like she was trying to take some medicine and passed out."

"I mean about Opal."

"Lord, I don't know, Toby," Ralph said irritably. "It appears that she moved out."

"What do you mean, 'appears'?"

"It's possible someone else moved her things."

"I wish you hadn't said that."

Ralph squeezed Toby's shoulder. "Don't worry, we'll find her. Or if she's on the run, maybe she'll find us. After all, she can't be very expert at—"

"On the run!" Toby said. "Holy Christ, what makes you say that?"

Ralph sighed. "I'm just speaking of possibilities, and they're probably all wrong. Forget it. Let's just take one thing at a time. Like the police."

A uniformed cop stood over them and politely invited them to see the lieutenant in apartment 3H. In the third-floor hall they passed a black plastic bag being wheeled to the elevator.

Inside Opal's apartment, a bald-headed man with polite manners identified himself as Lieutenant Greenberg and apologized for having them reenter the apartment of death. "Unless you would prefer to come down to the station house," he said.

Toby stiffened, and they all said no.

They told their straightforward story about seeking out Opal Wilder and finding instead the remains of old Blossom McNeely. Ralph and Lillian were invited to explain why they had posed as Opal's parents, which they did, Lillian adding, "Nobody in their right mind would believe I was the mother of a thirty-five-year-old woman." The lieutenant, with a little smile, agreed.

He said, "I'd like to have a word with Miss Wilder too. When you find her, tell her that, please." He gave Ralph the phone number to call.

Toby sat tensely on the sofa.

Ralph said, "Was it—was it a natural death?"

The lieutenant peered at him. "That's the theory we're going on," he said. "Do you have reason to think otherwise?"

"No. Oh, no. Just asking."

"There'll be a postmortem, of course," the policeman said. "But the condition the deceased was in . . ." His eyebrows expressed his doubt that much would come of the examination.

"What were the pills?"

"The M.E. said they were nitroglycerin."

"For heart victims."

"Angina."

"So she was going for her pills and didn't make it."

"That's what it looks like." Lieutenant Greenberg frowned. "One reason I'd like to talk to Miss Wilder is to ask her about her friend's injury."

The three stared at him.

"It appears that one of her fingernails was nearly ripped off shortly before her death." The detective

33

looked uncomfortable. "Those things happen, you know. I nearly lost one in a car door. We'd like to know more about it if we can, that's all."

Toby Ferris jumped to his feet. "May we go now, sir? We came to find Opal Wilder, and we'd like to get going." He fidgeted. "Sir," he added.

The lieutenant looked at him in surprise. "Is there something you ought to tell me before you go, Mr. Ferris?"

"No . . . Yes . . . Can you tell if the old lady was being tortured when she had her heart attack?"

"The thought occurred to me," Greenberg said slowly. "But why would anyone want to torture an old woman like that?"

Toby spread a spastic smile on his face. "No reason. It was just a dumb question. But little old ladies don't generally go around doing things that'll tear off a fingernail. Carpenters do it. Garage mechanics do it. But you're right, it was a dumb question, sir."

"No, it wasn't, Mr. Ferris," the policeman said. "However, we'll have to see what the Medical Examiner says, won't we?"

Down on the street, Toby's agitation took hold of him. His hands trembled, and he had trouble speaking clearly. "Someone was *torturing* that woman, I swear to God! Even if she died of a heart attack, that's—that's *murder!*"

Ralph said, "Now, Toby."

Toby started up the street at a fast pace.

Ralph trudged after him. "Where're you going?"

Toby stopped and turned, a lost look on his face. "I don't know."

"Well, let's go rescue the car," Ralph said. "I know a place to start."

5

It was lunchtime when they arrived at the Stuyvesant Club in midtown. Toby said, "I'd rather eat at the Chili Dog."

A sedate brass plaque beside the front doors was the only external identification on the blank-faced building. Ralph pushed him through the doors, saying, "Opal isn't a member of the Chili Dog. She is a member of the Stuyvesant Club."

"But it's so goldarn Ivy League," Toby protested. "It's moldy with age, and snooty to boot. I don't know how you stand it."

Dark-suited members, standing in the entry hall waiting for business-lunch companions, were all over six feet tall. Toby slouched through them. "I feel like clutching my forelock," he muttered.

Ralph led them to the canopied bar at one side of the cavernous dining room and seated them on red leather barstools. He said, "You've always sold yourself short, Toby. You come on like a rube. That's a pose as phony as the soft-voiced superiority of these stuffed shirts. Look at it this way, you're the funniest man in the room. Isn't that something?"

Toby clutched his forelock. "Yes, sir, boss."

Ralph frowned. "Why do I stand it? I told you long ago. It makes me feel important. I'm part of the power elite for a few hours. Besides, Keito makes the best drinks in town."

Lillian said darkly, "It's a luxury we can't afford."

"Why Opal is a member is something else," Ralph went on. "There's a little bit of snob in all of us, but that's not the reason. I think she loved Stuyvesant despite her rebellions, and she graduated magna cum laude. Most of these phonies barely squeaked through. I think she joined the club mainly because there are so few women here. It wasn't too long ago that it was all male. Joining is her way of thumbing her nose at them."

Toby said, "Boss, did anyone ever tell you that you talk too much?"

"Plenty of people. At length."

Keito, the imposing gray-haired bartender, greeted Ralph and took their orders. Toby said he wanted a Hail Mary. "That's a Virgin Mary with a dash of holy water over hailstones—in a frosted glass."

"Just say a prayer over it," Ralph said.

When Keito brought the drinks, Ralph asked him if he had seen Opal Wilder.

"Two weeks ago," Keito said. "She was looking for someone. She didn't stay long. She had her usual, then asked me to cash a check for her. She said, 'You saved my life, Keito.' I don't know if she was talking about the drink or the money."

"Who was she looking for?"

"She didn't say. I thought maybe it was you. She was in a rush."

Ralph sighed. "Did she say where she was living?"

"No."

"Damn."

"She wrote it down. She said it was possible the check

would bounce, and she didn't want me to be stuck with it. She asked me to let her know if it did." He took out his wallet and extracted a folded bar stub. "She told me to keep it a secret, but you're a friend of hers, so I guess it's all right."

"We think she's in trouble," Ralph said. "We're trying to find her."

Keito nodded sadly. "Tell her the check went through."

Toby grabbed the slip of paper. "Where in blazes is Atlantic Avenue?" he said.

"Downtown Brooklyn," Ralph told him.

Toby groaned. "Terra incognita," he said.

"Not to two million people. Shall we grab a bite before we go? My stomach is empty."

Lillian said, "We know."

Toby said, "I'm not hungry." He drained his drink.

Ralph and Lillian refused to be hurried. "Five minutes," Ralph said.

A newcomer to the bar bumped Ralph from the rear. Ralph turned and exclaimed, "Well, if it isn't the Lord of the Gaming Tables! How are things on sinful Coney Island?"

Roger Meuwssen was tall and slender, with flowing gray hair and an aristocratic beak on a bony face. He was dressed in a dark three-piece suit, the vest of which was a royal red. He gazed down at Ralph without amusement.

"Oh, Simmons," he said in a tone that would have infuriated any other man, but Ralph took great delight in poking needles in the man, and he was secure enough in his self-esteem not to be bothered by the man's lofty contempt.

Lillian, who had met Meuwssen but once, briefly, at the Savage Point Club, said, "Hiya, Roj! What's a classy guy like you doing in a dump like this?"

37

Meuwssen barely nodded to her and said to Ralph, "I do wish you would stop joking about it, old man. It's not funny." He started to turn back to his companion, then apparently thought better of it. It wouldn't look good for him to snub a neighbor, even one as inconsequential as Simmons.

Coldly he introduced the man next to him. "Alex Burnside, this is a neighbor of mine from Savage Point, Ralph Simmons, and his lovely wife—"

"Lillian," Ralph supplied.

She beamed and said, "Pleased to meet you, I'm sure."

Ralph introduced Toby, who appeared to be backing away. "One of the Ferrises of Mississippi," he said. "He writes the syndicated humor column 'The Ferris Wheel.' You must have read it."

"Really," Meuwssen said. Momentarily not master of the situation, he talked on while he regained control. "Mr. Burnside is the operator of the first licensed casino on Coney Island. I'm afraid your jokes have offended him, Simmons. I daresay there is more sinning going on in Savage Point than there is in Coney Island today. It's clean, Simmons, you might say squeaky clean."

Burnside said, "It all depends on what sins you're talking about," and he laughed. It was the melodious laugh of the Caribbean that Ralph considered one of the unsung attractions of the area. Alex Burnside was a bulky black man garbed in raiments that were nearly the duplicate of Meuwssen's, except that his vest was yellow instead of red. His face was round and glistening and exuded good humor. His Afro haircut was short and neat.

"Casino?" Ralph said. "Not the Empress of Coney Island?"

"The very same, Mr. Simmons," the black man said, chuckling.

Lillian said, "Is it really as swank as the papers say? Do

all the rooms have water beds? I'd like to spend a month in one of them." She hugged herself at the thought of such luxury.

"No, we find that some people get seasick, so we provide other beds as well—equally swank, to use your word."

Ralph said, "You're from the Virgin Islands. St. Thomas, I'd guess."

"St. Croix," Burnside said. "But really I thought I had gotten rid of my accent."

"You can change your accent, Mr. Burnside, but you can't change your laugh."

Meuwssen intoned, "It's been a pleasure having this little chat with you, Simmons. I expect I'll be seeing you around Savage Point." He turned his back.

Ralph said to the back, "What does one have to do to pass inspection by the Casino Control Agency? I gather that no one from Las Vegas or Atlantic City has met with your approval yet."

Ralph heard the insulting sigh before Meuwssen turned to face him. "The operators must have experience, they must have money, lots of it, and they must have a history untouched by scandal. And they must be American citizens. Take Alex, for example. As you pointed out, he's from the Virgin Islands. That makes him a citizen. But he has spent much of his life in Jamaica and some of the other islands, running casinos there. Our investigations show that he is scrupulously honest, he has never had any ties to organized crime or involvement in drugs, prostitution, or racketeering of any sort."

"And he has the money," Ralph said.

"He and his associates, yes. Now if—"

"And his associates passed the same test," Ralph said.

Burnside peered around Meuwssen. "With flying colors, Mr. Simmons," he said, smiling. "You and your

39

beautiful Lillian must come out and see us. You too, Mr. Ferris. I guarantee you'll have a lahvely time."

Toby Ferris was fidgeting with impatience. He said, "Opal. Remember Opal? Drink up, for God's sake."

Meuwssen stared at him frostily. "I beg your pardon," he said.

Toby flushed. "I was talking to Ralph. I was just saying we have to find Opal Wilder. That's a friend of ours. Sorry."

After a moment Meuwssen turned back to his luncheon guest.

In the car going down the FDR Drive toward Brooklyn, Ralph said, "Don't mind that bastard, Toby. It's all my fault. I just love needling him, he becomes so completely obnoxious. Lillian, you were wonderful. 'Hiya, Roj!' Great! 'What's a classy guy like you doing in a dump like this?' Terrific! I could see his ulcers kicking up."

Lillian said, "Yeah, but what was a classy guy like Burnside doing with a bum like Meuwssen? He seemed like a nice guy."

"Even nice guys have to butter up bums once in a while," Ralph said. "What Roger giveth he can also taketh away."

Toby, perched tensely in the back seat, said, "Pass that goldarn speed merchant, Ralph! Look, he's wearing a hat! Old men are the worst drivers in the world. They wear hats, take up two lanes, and think they're tearing up the road at fifteen miles an hour. We'll never get there! Pass him!"

Ralph swung into the speed lane and passed the old Buick.

"We were talking about the Casino Control Agency," he said. "All this happened while you were away living it up on the Gulf Coast. The Devil took the Mayor and the

Governor to the top of the World Trade towers and pointed to Las Vegas and Atlantic City and said, 'All this can be yours if only you'll bow down and okay casino gambling.'

" 'What's the bottom line, Nick?' they asked.

" 'Would you believe five hundred mil?'

" 'No.'

" 'Believe it,' said the Devil. And they did.

"It had to come, Toby. The cost of government kept going up, and the ultimate was in sight—the hundred-and-one-percent income tax! So naturally everybody went for the five hundred mil. That set a whole mess of things in motion. The legislature had to pass the referendum measure, and after it was approved by the voters—by a close vote, believe it or not—the machinery had to be set up.

"First they had to pick the site where casinos would be erected. A lot of places were proposed. There was Fort Totten out near Savage Point. The federal government put the kibosh on that. Then there was the South Bronx, where demolition was no problem. But someone pointed out that it wouldn't do to have the muggers waiting outside the perimeter to relieve the gamblers of their sporting money. So they settled on Coney Island, which, when you come down to it, is more famous the world over than Atlantic City. That set the land packagers to work buying up land from the people who lived and worked there.

"The big job was to keep out the criminal element. That's where our amiable friend Roger Meuwssen comes in. His agency was set up to control the casino operators, issue licenses, and keep everything squeaky clean. The first and only one approved so far was Lillian's nice guy, Alex Burnside. I haven't been there, but I've read that the Empress of Coney Island is on the oceanfront near where Steeplechase used to be ... And here we are humming

41

through the Brooklyn-Battery Tunnel. We're practically there, Toby, so sit back, damn it, and relax."

After going through the toll booths, Ralph looped back onto the Gowanus Parkway and exited at Atlantic Avenue. It turned out to be a broad, unlovely street flanked by dingy old buildings, many of them lofts converted into tenements. The only semblance of gaiety was in the storefronts of the Middle Eastern shops that had congregated in the area. The address Keito had given them was an old red-brick structure that looked more like the habitation of rats than of humans.

"Opal always liked exotic surroundings," Toby said. "Let me out."

"Stay with us," Ralph said.

He found a parking space two blocks beyond the building and silently prayed that the car wouldn't be stripped before they returned.

Enticing odors were in the air, and Lillian said, "I'm hungry."

Toby strode along with his head held high. "Pay no attention to the natives and they won't harm you," he said.

At Opal's address an opaque glass door opened into a vestibule containing six mailboxes with identifying cards in Arabic and English. One card slot was empty. Ralph pushed the button beside the empty slot. He pushed it again, then said, "Let's find the owner."

Toby said, "Doesn't that smell like hashish?"

Ralph said, "Oh, for Pete's sake!"

Lillian said, "It smells more like wet overcoats."

Toby said, "They served hashish to the Assassins, you know."

They entered the ground-floor shop, which was filled with all sorts of brass objects, fixtures, receptacles, and ornaments. A young man with a magnificent Semitic nose greeted them. In his soft, obsequious voice, he said he was the son of the owner.

"Ah, yes, Miss Wilder," he said in answer to Ralph's question. "Are you here to pay the money she owes us?"

"I'm her father," Ralph said. "If she owes you money, I'm sure she'll pay it."

"But no, sir," the young man said. "It appears that she skipped out on her rent. That is not honorable." He said she had taken all her possessions and left, he didn't know where. "I think she is what is called a deadbeat," he said.

Toby demanded to see the apartment in which Opal had stayed.

"I would very much like to show it to you," the young man said. "But my father would be very unhappy if I permitted someone to enter without payment of rent in full. Unlike Miss Wilder, my father is honorable, and he would insist, I believe, on being paid his honorable eighty bucks."

Ralph took four twenties from his wallet and gave them to him. The young man bowed, put the money in his pocket, and led them through the entryway next door, up two flights of uncarpeted wooden steps to Opal's apartment. In Greenwich Village it would be called a pad—an elongated, oddly shaped room furnished with a minimum of threadbare pieces. En route, they learned that the young man's name was Ibrahim.

The only sleeping arrangement was a single daybed placed close to one wall. There was a wastebasket near the foot of it. The basket was empty. There was no sign of Opal's occupancy. "I keep everything clean," Ibrahim said. "Empty the baskets every week."

Ralph asked if she had had any visitors.

"No visitors. One man asked about her, that's all. He went away."

"Oh? Tell us about him."

Ibrahim shrugged. "There's nothing to tell. You must know him, of course. He said he was her cousin. A very pleasant man."

Toby, who had slumped onto the daybed, was once again standing up. "Her cousin? It must be Harold. A fat fellow with glasses. Big red lips. A scar on his neck where he had the thyroid operation. Was it Harold, sir?"

"I think not," Ibrahim said with a smile. "This was a large man who looked like an American football player. I only saw him for a minute. It was the middle of the afternoon. I said if he wanted to leave a message I would give it to her. But he said he wanted to surprise her. Then he left."

"It must be Cousin Jim from Muscle Beach, Ralph," Toby said. "How long ago was it that he was here?"

"A week, maybe a week and a half ago, just before Miss Wilder took it on the lam."

"On the lam?" Ralph said.

"In a manner of speaking, sir. Look, I really must get down to the shop."

Toby said, "Cousin Jim has dark, bushy hair. Did this visitor have dark hair?"

Ibrahim laughed. "Far from it. His hair was so light it was almost white, and it was cut short. I suspect he wasn't a cousin, don't you?"

Toby drew himself up to his full height. "What are you implying, my good man?"

"Nothing. Nothing at all. I just saw him for a minute. You really must leave now. I must get back to the store before my father returns."

Ralph, taking one last look around the vacant apartment, crouched and peered under the bed. "Ah-hah!" he said. He reached under and pulled out a folded slip of paper with curls of dust clinging to it.

Ibrahim said, "Whatever it is, it's yours. Now, let's go, please."

Lillian looked at the dust and said, "Some cleaner!"

They followed the young man down the staircase to

44

the street and observed him being greeted with Arabic expletives by a rotund elderly man, who bounced up and down with rage. Toby was fascinated by the scene and watched until the two disappeared into the shop. The last thing he saw was the old man swinging at Ibrahim's ear and missing.

As the three walked up the street toward their parked car, Toby said, "What was the most interesting thing about that encounter? I'll tell you what the interesting thing was. Here was the old man bawling the daylights out of him, calling him a thousand variations of camel dung, and not once did friend Ibrahim attempt to pull out the honorable eighty bucks, which surely would have assuaged the old man's righteous anger. I'm betting right now that Papa never gets a smell of the son's windfall profit. Not only that, it's fifty-fifty that he's not the old man's son at all. Papa had a small marshmallow of a nose while the kid had a banana. Now, unless the mother . . ."

Toby excitedly expounded on the ramifications of the observed encounter until they arrived at the Rabbit and were seated inside.

Ralph groaned. "Now who's talking too much?"

"The difference between you and me, Ralph," Toby said, "is that what I say is goldarn brilliant and leaves the listeners both edified and enthralled."

"And what I say puts them to sleep."

Lillian said, "Cut it out, you two."

Ralph handed Toby the slip of paper. "Here's something that may edify and enthrall you. Then again, it may not."

Toby unfolded it and saw that it was a receipted bill garnished with a royal crest, the name of the establishment set down in royal script: *Empress of Coney Island.* Dated five weeks before, it acknowledged receipt of $137.50 for a one-night stay by Opal Wilder of N.Y.C.

There was no address. The initials at the bottom were indecipherable.

Toby said, "Well, shut my mouth!"

Lillian examined it with a puzzled look on her face. "I don't get it," she said.

"It's what's called a funny coincidence," Ralph said. "It appears that Opal Wilder, who is not a known gambler, spent a night at a glittering gambling palace and within the next four weeks hastily vacated two residences, the first containing a dead roommate, the second after a man big enough to be an American football player inquired about her. That's one way of looking at it. And when you look at it that way, it would seem that the young brass salesman was right. Opal is on the lam."

Lillian said, "From what?"

Ralph sighed. "What do you think, Toby?" he said.

Toby Ferris looked as if he were peering into the bottom ring of hell. "I think we should pay this here Empress a visit," he said.

As Ralph hesitated, Lillian said, "It's three-thirty. It won't do any harm to have lunch there, will it?"

Ralph started the car.

Halfway down the avenue behind them, the driver of a gray Volvo parked by a fire hydrant spoke into a car telephone. He was a pleasant-looking man with ash-blond hair. "Looks like they're about to move off," he said.

The voice on the phone said, "Stick with them until you can get one of your boys to take over. Did they find anything?"

"A piece of paper," Lawrence Whitehead said with a laugh. "These poor folks don't know what they're doing. There's no way they're going to catch up with the elusive Miss Wilder. Still and all—"

"Still and all nothing," the voice said. "We've run out of leads. They're our best chance at the moment."

46

"I know. I'll stick to their backsides like a Band-Aid. Hi ho, they're moving. I'll keep in touch. Goom-bye."

He had a good-natured smile on his face as he watched Ralph's red Rabbit make a U-turn and head back toward the Belt Parkway. Even the car was funny. It looked small enough to squash with one foot, blood-red all over. He rolled unseen in its wake.

6

Coney Island has had as many ups and downs as its most famous ride, the Cyclone. From the time the first trolley car clacked across open grasslands to the sandy, windswept playground, it has had a honky-tonk air. Unlike Atlantic City, which attracted mostly middle-class sun-seekers, Coney Island was only a nickel ride away from the sweltering slums, and on July weekends people from all backgrounds, foreign and domestic, poured onto its beaches by the millions to sport more joyously than the rich folk did on the meager beaches of the Mediterranean and to lunch sumptuously on Nathan's Famous hot dogs and a variety of marvelously colored drinks.

Luna Park was the first to go, replaced by stodgy apartment buildings; then Steeplechase the Funny Place, where rides were cheap and kids could go through the Barrel of Fun all day for nothing. The Half Moon Hotel, where the Murder Inc. witness, Abe "Kid" Reles, somehow fell out of an upper-story window, was the tallest structure for decades until it was dwarfed by the parachute jump erected on the Steeplechase grounds.

"All gone," Ralph Simmons said sadly as he drove along Surf Avenue. "At least the parachute jump is still here even though nobody uses it. Do you know it can be seen from forty miles out at sea? It has a special place in my heart, and I'll tell you why."

"Lord have mercy," Toby muttered.

"I was coming home from Europe on a Liberty ship after the war and—"

"What war, Daddy? Was that the First World War, Daddy?"

"I was sick as a dog," Ralph went on. "I used to get sick on a roller coaster when I was a kid, and being jammed in this little ship with a bunch of smelly guys and going up and down with the swells was like being on a roller coaster to me. Anyhow, I was leaning on a rail, afraid I was going to live, when someone pointed out this silly thing on the horizon. We were under cold clouds, but the sun was shining on that dopey Erector set. I tell you, it was a comforting sight. And then coming up the harbor, there was no Verazzano Bridge then—"

Lillian said, "That's enough, Ralph."

Ralph was hurt. "You don't want to hear about the Statue of Liberty?"

"That's the Empress on the right, Ralph."

The facade of the fourteen-story edifice was apparently intended to be a royal escutcheon with purple-tinted glass panels topped by a golden female crown—rounded rather than pointed—the whole bordered by simulated plush theatrical curtains, drawn as if by a tie at the upper corners and allowed to fall in free folds at the sides, all in rich purple.

Toby said, "Hot damn, you can't get any classier than that!"

Lillian said, "It looks like a Carvel ice cream cake."

There was valet parking, and Ralph reluctantly surrendered the Rabbit to a young attendant in a purple uniform. A long aisle, carpeted and canopied, led to the palace doors. Toby muttered, "If it were a book, this would be called a purple passage."

You can't very well make a slot machine look like anything else but a slot machine, so no attempt was made. Platoons of them nearly filled the area immediately inside the doors, while the purple passage circled around them on either side leading to the main gambling salon, where the royal purple once again took over.

It was midafternoon of a springtime workweek, yet the gaming tables were surprisingly busy. More than half of the gamblers were women. Lillian said, "I read that they have a play area for children. The mothers just wheel them in and check them at the door."

"Where the hell's the coffee shop?" Ralph said. "I don't want to go to the main dining room."

"Maybe they've got Frank Sinatra singing," Lillian said.

"At this hour?"

Toby said, "The heck with food. Let's find out what we want to know."

He marched to the registration desk, which was in a corridor leading off to the right.

A handsome young black man eyed him disdainfully.

Toby stood erect. "What's Miss Wilder's noon rumber, my good man?"

"Her what?"

"Her room number. Miss Opal Wilder. What's her number?"

The man made a show of checking the register. "Is that with a W, sir?"

"Of course! She's expecting us."

"There must be a mistake. There's no one here by that name."

Toby flourished the receipted bill. "She was here five weeks ago. Please check again."

The clerk glanced at the bill. "Five weeks ago was five weeks ago. Today is today. She's not here."

"Maybe under a different name."

"That's possible ... Now, did you wish to reserve a room?"

Ralph stepped forward and took Toby by the arm. "Perhaps some other time," he said. "Where can we get a bite to eat?"

"Only in the main dining room. The coffee shop is closed at this hour."

Toby pulled away from Ralph. "We were invited here by Mr. Burnside. May we see him, please?"

The clerk shrugged, picked up the phone, mumbled into it. He said, "Mr. Burnside is not here. I'll tell him that you asked for him. Whom shall I say?"

Ralph said, "Tell Mr. Burnside we'll come back. We'll be in the dining room."

Away from the desk, Toby let his shoulders slump.

Ralph said, "Don't worry. At least we know she's not here."

"Under a different name?"

"The Opal we know can't afford to stay here even for one night, okay?"

"Maybe she came into some money."

"Maybe we ought to eat."

The dining room was a mammoth arena rising in circular tiers from a small stage. They entered at the top tier. The place was empty.

A waiter appeared at their side. "Will this be all right?" he said, indicating a nearby table.

Lillian said, "Do we have a choice?"

"Yes, ma'am."

"I want a ringside table," she said.

Ralph said, "There's nothing going on!"

Toby said, "Let's go get a hot dog."

They sat at a table on the bottom tier immediately in front of the stage. Toby looked around uneasily and muttered, "I've never felt so ridiculous in my life."

Lillian gazed expectantly at the stage, perhaps seeing and hearing in her mind the one singer in her life, Frank Sinatra.

Ralph peered into the upper reaches of the amphitheater, and although no one was there he felt that he was in a spotlight and many eyes were looking at him. He tried to joke about it. "Bring on the dancing girls," he said, but he couldn't shake his disquietude.

Two sets of eyes were looking at him.

Alex Burnside turned abruptly away from the rectangular window in his office that overlooked the dining room, and he sat down at his desk. "Come away from there, Whitehead," he growled.

Lawrence Whitehead glanced at him with an amused look on his face. "Why? Do you think they might see me?" he asked.

"I know they can't see you," Burnside said. "I just don't like people spied on from my office."

"You do it all the time."

"It's my business."

"And it's my business to keep them in sight until Tony comes. If you don't believe me, ask the Governor. Go on, call him."

Burnside hit the desk with his fist. "But you don't have to do it from my office! I've told you I don't want you around here. I don't like your line of work. I run a legitimate business for the Governor, and you're a danger, a grave danger. Just one of your filthy little tricks here, we could be closed down like that!" He slammed his palm on the desk.

The big man in the neat dark suit moved to the desk and looked coldly down at the glistening round face of the Virgin Islander. "I can't say that I'm in love with you either, Burnsie," he said. "You're a guy in a dirty business who doesn't want to look at the dirt. If we don't get those records back from the Wilder woman, we're all in the soup, you included. Ten to twenty in Attica easily, if not the chair."

"The chair! I have nothing to do with your tortures and murders! I know nothing about your work, and I don't want to know. I just want you out of here."

Whitehead shook his head. "You're pitiful, do you know that?" He pulled a chair close to the one-way window, where he could observe the lonely dining party below. He sat and rested his heels on the window ledge. "I told Tony to meet me here. I'll leave as soon as he shows. I'm not being paid to follow three blind mice around the city or to sit and listen to the bullshit of a black hypocrite."

Burnside said quietly, "What are you paid to do, Whitehead?"

The big man laughed. "You don't want to know, you just said so, remember? But just keep bugging me, Burnsie, and you may find out the hard way . . . Well, I'll be damned! Hey, do you know what they're having to eat in this great dining room of yours? Hot dogs! They're eating hot dogs! How about that!"

Burnside sighed, rose from his desk, and moved to the other side of his office as far from Whitehead as possible. There, a second one-way window overlooked the labyrinthian gaming room. He saw the women there gambling away their children's food money, and he knew he was in a dirty business.

He wished to God that he had stayed in Jamaica, where the dangers were known and uncomplicated, and he was prepared to meet them. Here, though he was wealthier than he had ever dreamed, he was caught in a hidden whirl of corruption, violence, and now murder.

53

He wasn't in on the planning, but he had eyes to see and a nose to smell.

He glanced at Whitehead and inwardly shuddered. No one called him "Whitey" to his face, for he made it plain that he didn't like the nickname. But to the black man from the Caribbean he was the epitome of the evil white man—on the surface a genial gentleman, inwardly a vicious enforcer for hire. Why the Governor, a man whom Burnside respected, let himself be talked into utilizing such a deadly animal Burnside would never know. Surely the Empress could have come into being without the help of Whitey. The devil was on the prowl, and people were dying. Where the Wilder woman fit in Burnside had no idea. And he didn't want to know.

Keep them away from here, dear God, he prayed. Just one more year, dear Lord, and this faithful, God-loving black man will have enough to buy a hilltop in St. Croix overlooking the capital and live graciously the rest of his life. Just one more year, dear Lord, don't let nothin' happen.

Whitehead was silent. He was watching three blind mice nibbling on hot dogs.

Toby Ferris was slumped in his chair, his eyes brimming with emotion. "I feel like I'm on the run with her," he said. "When she looks behind her, I do too. I feel that close. I never should have gone away. I didn't realize that two misfits together could make one fit. I guess I had to be away from her to learn that. Aw, nuts!"

Lillian said, "That's the way it always is in romances."

Toby suddenly smiled, and when he did his whole face lit up. "Holy cow," he said. "That's what it is, isn't it? The red-nosed buffoon is caught up in, hot diggity dog, a *romance!* The trouble is, it hurts. What do we do now, Ralph?"

Ralph said, "I can't get that poor woman out of my

mind. Blossom McNeely. She must have looked like a flower when she was an infant. It's a lovely name. Now she's wilted and decomposed."

Lillian said, "You don't have to be so graphic."

Ralph said, "What we do now is go home and regroup. I can think of two tacks to take. One is Opal's parents. As I recall, they live in Teaneck. Do you know their address, Toby?"

"God, no. I wish I did."

"Well, there can't be too many Wilders in Teaneck. I'm sure we can find them. The other is Opal's literary agent, the one who sold her book for her. I happen to know who he is, because I once wrote a book too, believe it or not, and I used him. Strange man, name of Renard Sanders." He looked at his watch. "Too late to get him now. We'll do it in the morning. Where's the check? I hate to think what these hot dogs are going to cost us."

The waiter approached. "No check, sir," he said. "Compliments of Mr. Alex Burnside."

"Is he back?"

"Yes, sir, but he's a busy man, sir. He expresses his apologies for not greeting you in person."

"Tell him thanks very much," Ralph said. He left a five-dollar tip on the table.

Lillian was incensed. "We should have ordered filet mignon, for Pete's sake. He should have told us beforehand, and we'd have known. He probably knew we ordered hot dogs, and that's why he picked up the check. They were pretty poor hot dogs, if you ask me."

Toby said, "The mustard was exquisite."

The gray Datsun was parked in a No Standing zone on Surf Avenue. Lawrence Whitehead leaned in the window and said to the driver, "You saw them inside, Tony, and there they are. The red Rabbit. Hang on to their tail."

The man in the car looked uncomfortable. His suit was

55

too tight, and he bulged. "This damn car is too small, Mr. Whitehead," he said. "Why can't I use the Caddy?"

"Because every second car in the city looks like the one you're in. Even if these dumb bunnies looked for a tail, they wouldn't see you. So I don't want to hear any more bellyaching."

"I just think we oughta buy Detroit," the man grumbled. "It's patriotic."

Lawrence Whitehead strolled away. Out of the corner of his eye he saw the gray Datsun ease off in the wake of the Rabbit. He shook his head and laughed. Patriotic! Tony Lukats didn't give a rap for his country. He just liked to tool along in a shining blue Cadillac.

Whitehead retrieved his Volvo from the parking lot and headed the car toward Manhattan. His muscles needed a little tightening. He parked in a garage near the New York Athletic Club. He would whomp whoever was on the squash court, then do sprints in the pool. He loved whipping the old school-tie set. They tried to be such good losers, it was laughable. When they asked, he told them he was a corporate expediter, which was true as far as it went. Most of his clients were corporate executives. Working for a politician was a new experience, and he liked it. The Governor was much more sensitive to bad publicity than the bastards who ran corporations.

Lawrence Whitehead swaggered just a little bit as he entered the sacrosanct confines of the club.

The next morning's *Times* and *Daily News* had short accounts of Blossom McNeely's death, including the names of the people who discovered her body.

7

The man in the gray Toyota looked at his watch and muttered a curse. He reached for the phone.

Lawrence Whitehead picked up the phone on the first ring.

"I'm down the street from the Simmons place," the man said. "This is a screwy operation. There's a man with a dog staring at me as if it was a private street or something and I didn't belong here. It's weird."

Whitehead sighed. "Aside from the man with the dog, what's up, Joe?"

"Our party is splitting up, Mr. Whitehead. Here it is only seven in the morning and the tall guy, the one with the red nose—"

"Toby Ferris."

"Well, he come out of the house a minute ago and got in his beat-up old Chevy that's parked in the street, and he's got the motor running. He's just sitting in there with the motor running."

Whitehead said patiently, "Old cars need some warming up, Joe. No sign of the others?"

"No, it looked like he was trying to sneak out without making any noise. Oh-oh, the motor died on him. The thing is, Mr. Whitehead, if he gets that heap going, should I follow him or should I stick it out here?"

"Is the red car still there?"

"Yeah, in the driveway."

After a moment, Whitehead said, "Follow him. If it looks like he's just going to a local store for a loaf of bread or something, let me know. I'll give you ten minutes. If I don't hear from you by then, I'll get someone else to cover the house."

The man said, "I'm due to go off at ten."

"Stay with him, you hear?"

"Sure, but after ten it's time and a half, right?"

Whitehead said quietly, "Stay with him, Joe," and hung up.

Toby Ferris coaxed the car away from the curb, drove to the end of Ralph's dead-end street, turned and drove back up the street to the corner of Savage Point Road. He felt exhilarated at being in action, and when he saw the man in the gray Toyota, he waved and yelled, "Howdy, neighbor." The man looked at him in sick surprise.

Toby was heading for Teaneck. Ever since he had discovered—down on the Mississippi Gulf Coast—that he was in love with Opal Wilder, he knew it was inevitable that he would meet her parents, and he looked forward to seeing them. His landlady had said philosophically, "I guess you can't avoid it, Tobe. But seeing your gal's mother can be a shock. You'll say to yourself, So that's what my pretty sweetheart's gonna look like twenty years from now. You can't help yourself. Just remember that when the time comes you'll be looking at her with *eyes* that are twenty years older. And she'll still look pretty as a picture to you." Toby decided he was going to kiss Opal's mother even if she was as ugly as a toad.

He knew that Teaneck was somewhere on the other side of the George Washington Bridge. All he had to do was take Route 4, and there it was. He got lost. He missed the Route 4 turnoff, got on a highway with two numbers, and when they divided he chose the lower number, which was 80. Some time later he was in the heart of Hackensack. He asked kind pedestrians and kind policemen to head him toward Teaneck. He entered the fair town at nine-fifteen.

At the bus station he found a phone booth with a local directory. There were four Wilders listed. The smart thing would have been to phone, but Toby disliked phones. As he had once explained to Opal, "It's either someone wanting me to do something I don't want to do or someone hollering about something I should have done and didn't." On top of this long-held aversion, he wished to meet Opal's parents face to face, and a phone call might be so utterly negative—"No, we don't know where she is"—and he might become so incoherent that he would lose the chance.

He bought a map at a stationer's store and sat in the chitty-chitty-bang-bang while he located the four streets on which the various Wilders lived. The first house was a large Tudor set in an expanse of lawn and budding trees. A maid told him that neither Wilder was home but that they had no child over eleven and certainly no child named Opal.

The second Wilder on his list was a Reverend Waldemar Wilder. Since ministers made Toby nervous, he was inclined to put him off to the last, but since the address was the closest to where he was, Toby grimaced and decided to brave it. The church was reassuring. It was a small, brown wooden structure set on a knoll, with a modest steeple and a humble air. The name on the glass-enclosed, outdoor message board was Church of the Almighty. The message was a disquieting one: "Lust in the heart is Satan's seed; the harvest is eternal fire."

Toby shivered. I don't lust for Opal, your reverence, he

59

said in his mind; I just want to sleep with her for the rest of my life.

The minister's residence next door was a white-painted frame with clean, stark lines unsoftened by any bordering foliage. The clergyman himself opened the door. He was a tall, gaunt man dressed in a white shirt, black vest and trousers. The angular face was lined and leathery, the gray hair and eyebrows wild and unkempt. Toby recognized the signs of a zealot.

"Excuse me, your reverence," he said, bowing and mentally clutching his forelock. "I'm looking for the parents of a Miss Opal Wilder. I was hoping—no, I can't say I was hoping—would you by any chance be her father?" He laughed fatuously, as if the thought that this crusty, hollow-eyed man could be the father of such a lovable creature as Opal was quite simply ridiculous.

The man's voice was deep and resonant. "We have no daughter named Opal," he said. "Who are you?"

"I'm nobody," Toby said. "Just someone who's looking for Opal."

The little eyes in the hollows glared at him. "I've told your friends that there's no Opal here. Now I'm telling you. Good day." He started to close the door.

A woman's voice behind him said, "Let the gentleman in, Father."

The thickets above the eyes lowered, and the man thrust open the door with a bang. He strode back into the house, saying, "If you want to entertain drunken bums, it's your misguided choice, Mother. I'll have nothing to do with it."

The woman was now revealed to be a rather tall person dressed in black with white lace at the neck and wrists. Toby's first impression was that she had Orphan Annie's face and hair, the horn-rimmed glasses giving her eyes that blank look. She studied Toby a moment, then

60

she said, "If you come in peace, let us talk in the kitchen." She beckoned him to follow her through the center hall toward the rear of the house.

"Yes, ma'am, I come in peace," he said.

In the kitchen she once again searched his face.

He said, "The good father's impression of me is quite wrong. I got my nose and eyes from—"

She held up a hand to stop him. "Is your name Tommy?"

"No, ma'am, it's Toby."

"Toby, of course," she said. "Toby Ferris!"

It was a small kitchen, with a table and two chairs squeezed into a corner. She gestured for him to sit. "Would you like some orange juice?" she said. "It's my one indulgence. I'm addicted to orange juice."

He gaped at her. "You know my name," he said weakly.

She smiled. "No, I'm not clairvoyant. Opal has mentioned you, and you do have a striking face. Now how about that orange juice?"

Toby said he would love some.

She took a half-gallon bottle from the refrigerator, saying, "It's only frozen concentrate, not the real thing, but it's so much cheaper this way." She poured a glass and handed it to him. She paused and said, "Where is she, Toby?"

He said, "Oh, Jesus, ma'am, I was hoping you knew."

She sat down in the other chair. "My daughter's in trouble, isn't she?"

Toby had a way of letting his shoulders slump when he was dejected. "I don't know, but it looks that way," he said. "When was the last time you saw her?"

"Oh, dear, I haven't seen her in ages," the woman said. "Not for two or three years, ever since that book came out. You're a good friend of hers, aren't you?"

61

Toby lowered his gaze. "I—I asked her to marry me."

"What did she say?"

"I don't know for sure." His voice rose in anguish. "She never got my letters!"

The elderly woman put her hand on top of his. "I know this, Toby Ferris, she likes you very much. You're the only one she's ever mentioned."

"But you haven't seen her for years."

She smiled secretively. "We talk on the phone," she said, glancing around to make sure she wasn't being overheard, "when he's not around. Oh, he's a good man, Toby, don't mistake that, and he was always a good father to Opal. I think he idolized her even when she started rebelling, perhaps especially when she started rebelling. He said, 'She's going to set her own course,' and he approved of that.

"The first break came when she got married in the park. He thought she should get married in the church and not by some strange-looking hippie who received his ordination by mail from San Francisco. But he got over that when she divorced that young man, and she was once again his little girl.

"But the book—oh, my, did you read it?"

"Yes, ma'am."

"You keep calling me ma'am. You never knew your mother, did you? You see, I know more about you than you think. Well, ma'am sounds like Mom, and if it doesn't make you uncomfortable I'd just as soon have you call me Mom instead of ma'am. It's what Opal called me. Just think about it, Toby, don't force it. How does it sound?"

Toby nodded.

"Waldemar and I still call each other Father and Mother even though she's long since grown up and gone away. We like it, no matter what anybody says. But when that book came out— By the way, what did you think of it?"

"I liked it."

"I didn't," she said. "It was filth. If she was going to write a book like that, she should have thought of her father and written it under a different name. I blame Opal for that. Father had the idea that everyone in the congregation read it and was looking at him in shock that he could have raised such a daughter. Actually, I don't know of anyone who read it, but that's beside the point. Father was horrified by it, and he disowned her as a daughter. He read her right out of the family. The trouble was, she *was* the family. You see, Father is rigid. That's one of his faults. He identified Opal with her book, and he rejected them both. I believe one should separate the two. If your daughter has a festering sore and pus comes out, you don't reject the daughter along with the pus, do you? She's still the same Opal, isn't she?

"Of course she is! So we've continued to talk on the phone at least once a week ever since the break. I don't like to do it behind Father's back, but there's no other way, is there? Would you like some more orange juice?"

Toby held out his glass, and she filled it.

"What kind of trouble is she in?" she asked softly.

Feeling more at ease, Toby was able to tell of tracking Opal as far as the mean apartment in Brooklyn. "She seems to be traveling light, like a kid running away from home," he said. "I don't know what she did with her furniture."

"It's in the garage," the mother said. "When she moved in with the McNeely woman, Opal asked if she could store it there. I said yes. Father raised a storm, but I told him it was better than storing it in a warehouse, which would cost a fortune. He saw the sense in that. He's a frugal man."

Toby said, "Did Opal work her way through college?"

"No, she didn't have to."

"I mean, clergymen aren't paid much, I've heard that.

It's none of my business, but how could he afford to put her through Stuyvesant?"

Her face turned blank. "I have a little of my own," she said.

"Oh."

They drank orange juice for a minute.

"She told me about your letters," the mother said. "She thinks you're the most wonderfully gifted man and you should write another book."

"I wrote one."

"Yes, you let her read the manuscript. She said you were trying too hard. If you would just let the writing flow, she said, it would be the funniest book in the world, like your first one."

His various reactions collided and left him mute. Finally he said, "When did you last talk to her?"

"It was four weeks ago, four and a half. She sounded her cheerful self. More than that, she sounded excited about something."

"What?"

"She didn't say exactly. Let me see, it was something she was working on, and guess who was involved! That man who's running for governor over in New York, the one they say is sure to win, what's his name? You know, the district attorney of Staten Island who broke up that gang of thieves two years ago. It was in all the papers."

"Not in Mississippi. We have our own thieves down there."

"Well, anyway, she said he was a bigger crook than those he sent to jail. Imagine that, the great gangbuster they call him, and he's more corrupt than Al Capone."

"But you can't remember his name."

"It'll come to me. I think of him as Buster because of that silly word, gangbuster. It's even ungrammatical. Gangbreaker might be more correct, but not gangbuster."

Toby studied her face and thought, So this is what Opal will look like. Not bad. Orphan Annie at sixty. He said, "I'm curious about Opal's name. It's not a saint's name, is it? I would think that a minister would give his child a saint's name."

"Oh, he did," the mother said. "He named her Wilhelmina, after his mother. I gave her the middle name, Opal. She was a precious jewel to me. When she started to grow up, the only thing she liked about her first name was the initials it gave her. W-o-w. Wow!"

Toby laughed. "I like that. It fits her too. Wow!"

A minute later he recalled something the minister had said. "Did other people come around here looking for Opal?" he asked. "I mean, in the last month."

"Yes, a big blond man, and there was another in the car. He seemed like a pleasant sort, the blond man, I mean, but somehow I couldn't think of him as a friend of Opal's. So when Father turned him away, I let him go. He wasn't someone you know, was he?"

"No," Toby said. "But I'd like to find out what he wanted. I have the idea that Opal is running, and someone is chasing her. Maybe this fellow is the one."

"Oh, my. He seemed such a likable man."

Shortly after that, Toby stood up and started to take his leave. "I enjoyed meeting you very much . . . ma'am," he said. "And if you don't mind, I'd like to kiss you."

"I don't mind at all," she said. "I think I'd like it."

He took her head gently in his hands and kissed her lightly on the forehead. "I hope Opal will be like you," he said.

As he was going through the hall toward the front door, the father appeared in the doorway of a side room. "If you find Opal," he said. "If you find Opal . . . tell her she's had . . . her mother worried."

Toby said, "I'll tell her, sir."

He stumbled over the sill going out the door.

* * *

As he drove off, he noticed a gray Toyota parked just around the corner of the next street. The man in it looked very much like Ralph Simmons's neighbor. It's a small world, he thought.

Where to now?

He had left a note on Ralph's kitchen table: "I figured you needed your beauty sleep, so I let you slumber on. I'm checking out Opal's parents. That leaves the agent to you. See you tonight."

So presumably Ralph was following up that lead.

Toby had the whole afternoon to himself. He was fascinated by the Empress of Coney Island. Opal had stayed there. Why?

Good question.

His geography was vague. He hoped he could find, first, New York City, then Coney Island. He was going to pay another visit to the Empress.

8

Ralph Simmons was a young sixty-three in mind and spirit and an old one in body. He was lying in bed at eight-thirty trying to tell his body to get cracking when Lillian came up from the kitchen with Toby's note. He groaned and got cracking.

Lillian said, "You don't have to go into the city, for crying out loud. Just call him on the phone. He probably doesn't know anything, and you'll be saved a trip."

Ralph said, "You don't know Renard Sanders. He's a secretive bastard who thinks every piece of information he has is worth a king's ransom. You have to squeeze it out of him."

She said, "You don't look so good."

"I feel fine," he snarled.

By phone he made an appointment to see the agent at eleven-thirty. He decided to go by train. "Parking is murder," he said.

He gave Lillian a perfunctory hug and set off for the station on foot. She watched him from the front porch, thinking he really should take off ten pounds. She scarcely noticed the gray Subaru parked near the corner or the short, slender man who got out of the car, stood a moment in indecision, then strolled around the corner after Ralph.

The man with the dog said, "He's following your husband, you know."

"Oh, hello," Lillian said, fumbling for a name and not getting it. "What do you mean, following my husband?"

"He's been parked there for two hours," the man said. "First there was a Datsun, but he followed your guest . . . I assumed he was your guest, the tall fellow with a red nose."

"Yes, Toby Ferris."

"Then this fellow showed up about three-quarters of an hour later. You can't help but notice these things. He just sat there for two hours. I thought he might be a burglar; there's a lot of that going around. Sometimes they phone to see if anybody answers, or they wait until the people go out, and then they very coolly break into the house and clean it out."

"I've heard of that," Lillian said.

"I thought I better keep an eye on him," the man said. "I thought sure he was planning to rob some house along here. But then when I saw him follow your husband, it was plain that he wasn't a burglar, he was just watching your husband. You're the new Mrs. Simmons, aren't you? May I offer my best wishes to the two of you."

Lillian stammered her thanks and returned inside. She must catch up to Ralph. First she had to get dressed. The next train was an hour away. She couldn't imagine Ralph conferring with the agent that long. She would lose him. There was a train from Little Neck in half an hour. Little Neck was a mile away. She had to get that train.

She grunted into clothes, hardly knowing what she was putting on. She got the address from Ralph's address book. Renard Sanders, 5 Rockefeller Plaza. She started walking the back road to Little Neck, thinking, They were after Opal and now they're following us, maybe they'll hurt Ralph, he's not as strong as he used to be, oh, he's no pushover, but if they hit him on the head, if they hit *anybody* on the head, he'll be hurt, right? Then she told herself to come off it, nobody was going to attack Ralph, it was all a coincidence, maybe the man with the dog was a nut and he just made it up—she didn't even know his name, he was just the man with the dog.

She barely made the train, perspiring profusely, moaning to catch her breath. Talk about Ralph losing ten pounds, she could lose twenty and be much better off. She sat in the train and oozed. It never occurred to her to take the advice she had given Ralph—to simply phone the agent and tell him to have Ralph call home. The fact is, she wanted to be there with Ralph to protect him from whatever was threatening him. She had the heavy pocketbook with her. She could do it.

Renard Sanders looked like a butcher impersonating a funeral director. He was round-faced and round-bodied, balding and sweaty-looking. The image he tried to project was something entirely different. Three-inch heels made him higher rather than taller. His expensive blue blazer was too tight. His manner, aspiring to courtliness, was obsequious. His office decor, intended to give the impression of establishment dignity, was schizophrenic. He bowed Ralph Simmons into his office, which had an Oriental rug on the floor and a dartboard on the wall. His desk was glass and chrome.

Following a pro forma exchange of views on the weather and the book Ralph had ghosted for a retired baseball player, which had been an infield pop-up, one swing and out, Ralph brought up the subject of his visit.

"Opal Wilder," he said. "I haven't got time to play games with you, Ren—"

The agent looked hurt. "Games?"

"I know you put a high value on the confidentiality of

69

your relationship with your authors. Just remember that she's a friend of mine and that I was the one who recommended her to you, Lord knows why. Just tell me what I want to know without futzing around."

Sanders said with dignity, "I do not futz around, Ralph."

"Good. Here's the situation. Opal has disappeared, I think she's in trouble, and I'm trying to find her. I'm hoping you can help me."

"Certainly," Sanders said. "I'll help every way I can. I'm sorry to hear she's in trouble. Nothing serious, I hope." He pressed his intercom button and said, "Felicia, bring me Opal Wilder's address."

Ralph shook his head. "We've been to her addresses, several of them. She's not there. She's running away." He held up his hand to stop Sanders's questions. "I don't know why. That's all I know. I want you tell me what she was working on. You've set up some writing and editing jobs for her. That was very kind of you, Ren. She needed the money."

The agent took the flattery at face value. "It was nothing," he said. "She's good at it. Besides, now that she's gotten that primal scream out of her system, I want her next book. She can be one of the good ones."

"I agree," Ralph said. "What was the last job you threw her way?"

Sanders frowned. "I am not sure I remember. You have to realize this is a very busy office—"

Ralph wagged his head in disappointment. "I'm not asking you for America's defense secrets," he said. "I'm asking you about a routine business deal for a lady who's running away from something. It could be the job you gave her. What was it, Ren?"

Sanders lowered his eyes. "I'm a little ashamed," he said. "I shouldn't have brought Opal into it. It was a project that had no chance of success. But I had this woman in my office, and I couldn't get rid of her. She kept saying that she had sensational information and all she needed was a writer to pull it together. As far as I could make out, she had nothing. Do you know what she was? She was an accountant. An *accountant!* Who ever heard of an accountant with a story to tell? So I introduced her to Opal." He squirmed in his chair.

Ralph said, "Tell me about it." He saw the shutters closing in the agent's eyes, and he said, "Don't hold back on me, Ren. You want to help Opal Wilder, don't you? So tell me."

Sanders relaxed. "You're a tough man, Ralph. Very well. Sarah Goode is an accountant, as I said, a C.P.A. She did my books for me early on, until I had to hire a full-time bookkeeper. I still use her to make out my returns. She's good, damn good, but she's the mousiest person you'd ever want to meet. Dull and reliable. A walking sedative.

"So I was surprised when she came to me claiming she had a sensational story. She talked and talked, and after a while I turned her off. She talked in spurts, disjointed, and I lost her. I honestly don't remember much of what she said."

"Try."

"Well, one of her clients is a man named Vito. Vito Sammartino, though many people don't know his last name. You've heard of Vito's on Fifty-third Street? It's a discotheque, Ralph, where the smart set and bigwig politicians dance with wild young women and think that, *man, that's living.* There's been talk of cocaine in a back room, but nobody's proved it, and I'm inclined to doubt that it's a regular thing. As far as I know, Vito Sammartino is a respectable businessman who has a good thing going. He wouldn't risk getting closed down by dealing in coke. I'll tell you who probably has sensational things to say. Vito. But he probably wouldn't risk that either. Too bad, it'd be a hell of a book."

When he stopped talking, Ralph said, "All you've told me is that Sarah Goode has a client named Sammartino who runs a disco."

"Well, there's more to it than that, but it's all jumbled up. As near as I can make out, Sarah was closer to him than an accountant usually is. He was forever making deals, and she was there to see that he had no problem with the law, I don't know. All I know is, her sensational information was about him and a series of deals he was involved in. And that's all I know."

"What sort of deals?"

"How would I know? She just rambled on. She had some papers with her—oh, and some cassette tapes. We put them on my player here, but they were fuzzy. There were some men talking, that was all. I couldn't understand what they were saying."

"Did she say who the men were?"

"I think she did, but they were nobody I recognized. One was a labor leader and one was the president of a corporation. Big deal. And she claimed one was this guy running for governor, Sylvan Brunner. That's when I decided she didn't have anything worth getting excited about. Brunner is just about the squarest man in the state. He wouldn't be involved in anything that would keep him out of the governor's chair."

"And that's when you sloughed her off on Opal."

Sanders looked hurt. "I look on it as the mating of two talents who will join their forces, so to speak, and nine months later produce a bouncing baby book." He beamed with enjoyment of his own joke. He had probably told it many times before to more appreciative audiences.

Ralph said, "And how many months ago did you sanctify this marriage of two talents?"

"Hey, that's not bad," Sanders said. "I sanctify their marriage. I like that."

"How long ago?"

"Maybe six or seven weeks."

Ralph asked for Sarah Goode's address, and while they waited for the invisible Felicia to produce it he commented on how healthy the agent looked.

Sanders smiled modestly. "We have this little place down Delray Beach, and we like to go down there between seasons. We just got back last week."

Fortunately for Ralph, Felicia interrupted Sanders's monologue on the problems of owning beachfront property. Ralph snatched the slip of paper and made a hasty departure, with hatred in his heart for the pompous little man who had an oceanfront cottage in Florida.

He bumped into Lillian at the outer door. She looked like she had just competed in the New York Marathon. Her oval face was red and running with perspiration, her great chest was heaving, and there was something wrong with her clothes. She couldn't speak. Ralph sat her down in Sanders's outer office, and the receptionist brought her a paper cup of water. Lillian's distress didn't prevent Ralph from noticing that the receptionist was a beautiful, dark-haired young woman with a figure like Loni Anderson's. The receptionist returned to her desk and resumed pounding a typewriter.

Ralph asked Lillian what the hell she was doing there, but she glanced at the receptionist and said, "Not here."

They went down in the elevator, Ralph supporting Lillian, who seemed a bit wobbly on her feet. They found an unoccupied bench on the mall not far from the skating rink, surrounded by a sea of tulips of all colors.

Lillian said, "Did you see that?"

"What?"

"She was beautiful and sexy, and she could *type!*"

"Maybe she makes a lot of errors," Ralph said. "What are you doing here?"

Lillian was finally able to tell him about the man with the dog, the man in the Datsun, and the man in the Subaru.

Ralph said, "The interesting thing is that they followed Toby too. He's been here only one day. So if we're actually being followed— What did this man with the dog look like?"

Lillian described him, and Ralph said, "I know him. He's an old woman, if you'll pardon the expression. He's the neighborhood snoop, but his information is generally correct. Lord knows what stories he's told about you."

"He wished us good luck."

"He didn't mean it. Good luck doesn't make good gossip. How about the man who followed me? Did you get a good look at him?"

"Sort of. Not really. I was looking at you, not him."

"Okay, look around, without being obvious about it, and see if you see him."

"Here?"

"He followed me, didn't he?"

The Rockefeller Center mall on a nice day in spring was always a mob scene, jammed with suburbanites, international tourists, and office workers goofing off. Lillian gazed at the stream of strollers, including many Orientals with cameras. She said, "He could be anywhere, Ralph. He wasn't someone who would stand out in a crowd. He was sort of ordinary looking."

"Great," he said. "I assume you'll be with me for the rest of the day."

"Someone has to look after you."

"Are you hungry?"

74

"Always."

"How about a hot dog before we tackle Sarah Goode?"

"We had hot dogs yesterday."

"How about a chili dog?"

They made their way to the Chihuahua.

Toby ran out of gas at the intersection of Cropsey and Neptune Avenues, just a few blocks short of the Empress of Coney Island. He sat and fumed for several minutes.

A policeman peered in at him and said, "You can't park here, buddy."

Toby cringed. Here comes another salvo in New York's war against him. He explained his predicament, and, lo and behold, the cop didn't give him a ticket. The cop pointed to a service station. "Go get some gas. I'll give you five minutes."

When Toby returned with a two-gallon can, he said to the cop, "You're not a native of New York, are you?"

"I was born in Coney Island Hospital. Why?"

Toby spread his arms and said, "I love New York!"

Still, he thought the policeman must be pulling his leg. He must be an outsider who hadn't caught on to city ways.

The gas transfusion revitalized the ancient Chevy. It chugged into the service station and refueled, then purred like a Mercedes as it rolled into the driveway of the Empress. The uniformed car jockey said, "You gotta be kidding," but he drove it off to the parking area.

Toby peered up the purple passage and thought, What now?

He didn't know.

9

The "ordinary looking" man said into the phone, "They went into an apartment building. I'm around the corner on York, out of sight of the building, so I gotta hurry." He gave the address of the building.

Whitehead said, "I didn't think they'd get this far. Get back there, Mac, and be careful."

"What's it all about, Mr. Whitehead?"

"It's about your neck, if you lose them."

The man mumbled, "You don't have to get sore," and hung up. He was aware that he was sweating.

Ralph had gotten the apartment number from Renard Sanders, so he and Lillian breezed past the doorman and continued to the bank of elevators. Sarah Goode worked out of her home, Sanders had said; consequently, the chances were good that she was there.

Lillian said, "How much do you suppose it costs to live here?"

Ralph said, "If you have to ask, you can't afford it."

The door to 10C was opened by a good-looking blond woman whose facial features somehow reminded Ralph of a shark or maybe Barry Manilow.

He said, "Miss Goode?"

"Who?"

"Sarah Goode. This is her apartment."

The woman said, "You're wrong, brother. There's no Goode, bad, or indifferent here. Now, please, I'm busy. The place is a mess." She started to close the door.

Ralph glimpsed a roll of carpeting in the hall behind her. "You just moved in," he said.

"How'd you guess?" the woman said.

"What happened to Miss Goode?"

"I haven't the faintest. Ask the renting agent. It's been grand talking to you," she said, and closed the door.

They located the renting agent in a real-estate office a block away.

He said, "If she was a friend of yours, I'm sorry. To me, she was bad news. Nobody likes a thing like that to happen in his building."

"Like what?"

"A double suicide. It makes the other tenants nervous, like it was something they could catch. I mean, it's depressing."

"Are you saying Sarah Goode committed suicide?"

"Don't you read the papers? It was all over the *News* and the *Post* for a couple of days."

"I'm afraid I missed it. What happened?"

"She and her lover killed themselves. I'm only glad they didn't use gas. They could've blown up the whole building."

"What did they use?"

"Plastic bags. I suppose it's as good a way as any, if that's what you want to do. Personally, I don't understand people like that. They're inconsiderate, that's what they are, thinking just of themselves, never mind about the other guy. I had to repaint the whole place even though it didn't need it. And do you know what else, I paid extra to fumigate it! Now you and I know that suicide isn't a disease, but I fumigated anyway and made sure everybody knew it. It's the psychology of the thing, do you know what I mean? You've got to remember the psychological factors if you're gonna get ahead. So I fumigated."

"How long ago did it happen?"

"Exactly a month ago, thirty days. Not bad, doing all that and getting in a new tenant in less than thirty days."

"Fast work. We're sorry to hear about Sarah Goode. Who did you say the lover was?"

"I didn't. It was some guy named Sammartino, owned a discotheque. A middle-aged man. Married. Can't get a divorce. Tough. My heart bleeds for the poor sap. Half the people on earth are women, and he goes and kills himself over one of them. Does that make any sense?"

"Not the way you put it," Ralph said.

A minute later, he and Lillian left the real-estate office.

He said to her, "We've come to what is known as a dead end. Dead and buried. I hope Toby is having better luck."

The coffee shop at the Empress of Coney Island made no pretensions to grandeur beyond the purple walls bedecked with gold coronets. Most of the tables were occupied, some by mothers and children, others by blank-faced gamblers grimly fueling the body for another go at Lady Luck. Pretty black waitresses flitted about, serving them. Toby Ferris sat at the counter and ordered a cheeseburger and a glass of milk. He didn't know why he had come to the Empress. He had no plan of action, just an intuitive sense that Opal was close by.

He had liked Opal's mother, and having seen the father, he understood what Opal was rebelling against. And yet there was something of her father in her, a staunchness that brought her through the storms of her life unbroken. It was a trait Toby lacked. He was the weak one who came to her and was comforted when his soul was battered. Sometimes she would simply hold his hand— one of his foster mothers did that for a period in his young life, and it had never failed to make him feel loved and wanted and a person of merit—and Opal's gaze would tell him that he was really quite admirable, although the words she spoke were frequently impatient: "If you want to blow your nose, do it yourself. I don't blow anyone's nose but my own." And as often as not, Toby would laugh.

He said to the waitress behind the counter, "Would you do something for me? Just hold my hand for a few seconds, please."

She cocked her head to one side. "Mine are wet," she said.

He said, "That's all right."

She shrugged and held his hand.

He said, "Thank you, that was very kind of you." He waited until she left to serve others before he dried his hand on a paper napkin.

When she returned, he said, "I'm just a dumb redneck from Mississippi, and I'm curious about this place. Do you mind?"

The black girl frowned. "I've known rednecks," she said, "and you're not one. Your hand says so."

Toby grinned. "You're goldarn right. I've never worked a farm in my life. You're pretty smart, do you know that? How long have you worked here?"

"Since it opened."

"The Empress of Coney Island. It sounds like a Mississippi riverboat, only one better. They were just queens, this one here's an *empress*. Did you ever think of that?"

"Makes no difference in my mind," the girl said. "It's a place to work."

She went off to attend other customers, and came back.

He didn't know whether it was because he fascinated her or because there was a stool on which she could rest at his end of the counter.

He said, "I'm looking for a lady who was here about five weeks ago. Name of Opal Wilder." Why not? She must have come here to poke around.

"That don't ring no bells."

"If I know Opal, she was asking questions."

"A lot of people do that."

"I don't know what questions she asked, but I'm sure she was curious about—"

The girl said, "Excuse me," and left once again. Five minutes later she returned to perch on the stool.

Toby said, "The lady was probably asking about how quickly the Empress was built. The way I hear it, it seems that they passed the law one month and the Empress was here the next. Like magic."

"I wouldn't know anything about that."

"Don't you wonder what happened to the people who lived here? This thing covers the whole goldarn block. There must have been hundreds of people living or working here. What happened to them?"

The girl said, "Is it you asking me, or is it the lady?"

"Both."

The girl said, "I don't know nothing. I'll give you the same answer I gave her. Go see the Goldmans."

"The Goldmans?"

"I shouldn't have said anything, 'cause I don't know nothing. It's just that an old lady came in here the day after we opened, and she sat down there at the end of the counter, and I asked her what she wanted, and she just looked at me and said, 'This is where our back room was.' I went like, so what else is new? You want to know who used to live here? She's one of them."

"And you told this to Opal Wilder?"

"I don't know who."

"And the old lady was Mrs. Goldman?"

"That's what she said. She looked so sad I felt sorry for her. She said she's now living at the Adamson Senior Citizen Conservatory. That's an old folks' home." She paused. "Maybe it would be a good idea if you don't tell anybody I opened my big mouth. I need this job, mister."

"Mum's my middle name," Toby said.

"Is it?"

"I won't tell anybody," he said.

The man called Joe said into the telephone, "This joker don't seem to know what he's doing. First he has lunch in the coffee shop and gabs with the countergirl, then he walks all the way here. It's called the Adamson Senior Citizen Conservatory. He's in there now. I don't know what he's doing."

"I have an idea," Whitehead said. "What did Mr. Ferris have to eat?"

"Looked like a hamburger and a glass of milk."

"Who was the countergirl?"

"I don't know. One of the black kids. They all look alike to me."

"Describe her."

"Oh, God," Joe said. "You know this singer, Melba Moore? That's what she looks like."

"Tell me this, Joe. Do they all look like Melba Moore?"

"Some do, and some don't. You know how it is."

Whitehead hung up the phone, then picked it up again and punched a number. "Raymond, I have a little job for you," he said. "Find out who's on the counter in the coffee shop. Yeah, I know. This one looks like Melba Moore. Never mind that, find out when she goes off duty and follow her home. She talks too much. Teach her a lesson, Raymond."

"How bad a lesson, Mr. Whitehead?"

"I leave that up to you," Whitehead said. "I don't want her talking to anyone else."

"Gotcha," Raymond said.

Whitehead hung up. There was a frown on his face. He hated to delegate authority in a situation like this, but a white man couldn't very well stroll into Bed-Stuy or wherever and do the job without being noticed. This Ferris character was getting to be a pain. It was time they had a little chat. The heap Ferris was driving was still parked at the Empress.

Whitehead checked the schedule, saw that an express bus was leaving from the Waldorf in ten minutes. The helicopter to the roof of the Empress would be faster, but it left from the East River heliport a mile away. The bus was his better bet. He glanced around his penthouse apartment, liked what he saw, and left. If Alex Burnside raised a fuss, that was too damned bad. Whitehead had a job to do, and he was going to do it.

Toby waited in the activities room for the Goldmans to be brought to him. The glass wall beside his chair would be open in the summertime, but it was closed now. It was still too early to let chill drafts stiffen ancient bodies. There were about fifteen people in the room, some at card tables, some at the pool table, some in the library corner at the end of the room. A few hardy ones were outside on the bowling green and shuffleboard courts.

Opal had come to this place. She had spoken to the coffee shop waitress and then come here. His hunch was right. The project she was working on involved not only the crooked gentleman from Staten Island whom her mother mentioned, but it also had something to do with this new gambling casino, the Empress of Coney Island. There was no other explanation for her visit to the Goldmans.

The woman stood in front of him.

"Do we know you?" she asked. She wore a knitted shawl over a pale-blue print dress. Her face held a tentative smile, hopeful that someone had actually come to visit them, suspecting, however, that there had been a mistake.

Toby jumped to his feet and bowed in a courtly manner. "Mrs. Goldman," he said. "And this must be Mr. Goldman."

The man in the wheelchair was grossly fat. His head was round as a bowling ball, quite bald and glistening; the ears and nose were small protuberances, the eyes were large and vacant. The unseeing stare was disquieting.

Toby grabbed the limp hand from the lap and shook it. "I'm Toby Ferris. It's a pleasure to know you."

The woman said, "It's not one of his better days, Mr. Ferris. He's been like this since the robbery."

Toby withdrew his hand. "I'm so sorry," he said. He pulled an empty chair closer. "Would you care to sit down?"

The woman said, "That's all I do is sit. But, okay, I'll sit."

Uneasily aware of the staring vegetable, Toby told her of the reason for his visit.

Mrs. Goldman said, "Yes, I remember your lady friend. We don't get many visitors. I don't remember her name, but I remember her. She seemed very angry."

"Opal. Opal Wilder."

"I knew a woman named Jewel once. It's a lovely name, but not as nice as flowers. Rose, Lily . . . you can almost smell the fragrance. I never knew anyone named Carnation, however."

Toby said, "I was told you lived on the site where the Empress of Coney Island now is."

The woman put a finger to her lips. "Shh, we weren't

83

supposed to be living there. It was only a store, a souvenir store. But we lived in the back room even though we weren't supposed to. There was just the two of us, and we were nice and snug. We were saving up to buy a little place in Florida. But that's all gone now."

The momentary glimpse of desolation in the old eyes chilled Toby. "What happened?" he asked.

"Well, someone was buying us out, all of us," she said. "The man came to us and offered us money. It wasn't enough, Mr. Ferris, so we said, not now, maybe in a year, come around next year. That would have done it, just one more year. The man was nice about it, and when he saw that we weren't selling he warned us that gangs of hoodlums were roaming the neighborhood, robbing and smashing and hurting and scaring customers away. Well, it was true, the arcade down the street burned down, and people stayed away.

"Then one night these two men broke in and started smashing the place. They took the money from the register—they were welcome to it, there wasn't much. They didn't take any of the souvenirs because they were cheap, you see, and they couldn't get a dime for them, but to us they were our living. To tell you the truth, I loved every one of them; they were really nice souvenirs.

"Harry was always a heavy man, not as heavy as he is now, and he was strong. I told him, Harry, don't do anything, these two men have baseball bats and you have nothing. But he wasn't made that way, God help us. He tried to stop them."

She turned her gaze to the lump of a man in the wheelchair, drawing Toby's eyes in the same direction. He noticed another imperfection in the roundness of the head—a depressed area over the left ear. She reached out a hand and gently traced the concavity.

"This is what the baseball bat did," she said. She

clasped her hands in her lap and sighed. "It's all gone. Harry. Florida. Our souvenir store. Our money. We gave what was left of it to the home when we came here. It's a sad thing, Mr. Ferris. If we had accepted the man's money, maybe we wouldn't get to Florida, but Harry wouldn't be sitting there like a—like a . . ." She stopped talking.

Toby found that he was clenching his fists. "It makes you want to kill, doesn't it?" he said softly.

"Yes, it does," she said.

He said, "The man who offered you money, was he one of the hoodlums who broke in?"

"Oh, no, he was white, seemed like a nice man. No, these were blacks. They couldn't have had anything against us, and yet they were breaking everything in sight. Ai, it was horrible." She waved her hands in a helpless gesture.

"And the police never found out who it was?"

"My fault," she said. "I thought Harry was dead, and I didn't make much sense, I guess. I felt like I was about to pass out, for the longest while I felt that—like I was looking through cheesecloth, do you know what I mean? I couldn't describe them. All I could say was that they were big, bulky bullies, and that one of them was named Raymond. I heard the other man call him that. And that was all. Isn't that pitiful? They smashed my husband's head in, and I couldn't describe them to the police! *Me-shuggah*, that's what I am, crazy in the head."

"I wouldn't say that," Toby murmured, feeling totally inadequate. "So you finally sold out to the same man who offered you money?"

"Not the same man, Mr. Ferris. The first man was blond like a Swede, a big feller. The second man who came was much older; he had dark hair combed over the bald spots. But they were from the same company."

85

"Do you remember the name of the company?"

"Checkers. No, dominoes. The Domino Something Company. Have you heard of it?"

"No," Toby said. "But wouldn't your husband have had to sign the papers? Whose name was your property in?"

"Joint, both Harry and me. This was in the hospital. The Coney Island Hospital. Do you know it?"

"I know a man who was born there," Toby said.

"Harry was in a coma, and to tell you the truth I needed the money to pay the hospital. Do you know what the man did? He asked if it was okay by me, and I said yes, so he put the pen in Harry's hand—you see the hand there in his lap, that's what it was like—and he guided Harry's hand, and that's how Harry signed the papers. Anyone could tell it wasn't Harry's signature, but the man had this woman with him who witnessed the signature and put a seal on it. Smart, eh?"

"Dumb," Toby said. "You could hold them up for a million dollars."

"You're kidding!"

"I'm no lawyer, Mrs. Goldman, so I don't know for sure. But I think you'd be smart to talk to a lawyer and see what he says."

Her eyes were wide open with wonder, and Toby fancied he caught a glimpse of the Sunshine State there.

He stayed and chatted with her for another fifteen minutes before he made his departure. Her parting words were ones of motherly advice.

She put a hand on his arm and peered into his eyes. "You're a good man, Mr. Ferris," she said. "You have a kind heart. But stay away from the schnapps; it's really not good for you. A little wine, that's okay, that's good, but some people can't take liquor, did you know that?"

Toby backed away, smiling painfully.

On the way back to the Empress, he stopped in a store and bought a pair of sunglasses, hoping they would hide the telltale eyes and place the blame for the nose on the sun. He felt better, but not much.

He was sunk in black thoughts when he entered the driveway to the Empress. People who used baseball bats to get the land would surely use bats to protect their secret. Opal was in great danger—

Thus preoccupied in thought, he bumped into a large man and momentarily lost his balance. The man gripped him and kept him from falling. Toby mumbled apologies.

The man said, "Nonsense, it was my fault. I was standing here blocking the path. Are you all right?"

Toby laughed. "No, I'm not. But it has nothing to do with you. No harm done."

The man turned his gaze to the ornate facade of the Empress of Coney Island. "I was just looking at this monstrosity and wondering how I could ever have had a hand in getting it built. It looks like a tombstone in Voodoo Land, doesn't it?"

"Someone said it looked like a Carvel ice cream cake."

"That's a good one," the man said, laughing. "Let me buy you a drink."

Toby focused on the man's face. He was a big one, all right, real pleasant looking, and he had blond hair, like a Swede's, and he was somehow connected to the construction of the casino. Toby's curiosity was aroused.

He said, "I don't drink, but I'll join you in a ginger ale, if that's all right."

"Great! Come on." As they walked toward the purple passage, the man said, "By the way, my name is Whitehead. Lawrence Whitehead."

Toby said, "I wouldn't have guessed," and they both laughed.

10

Vito's wasn't much to look at in the light of midafternoon. It was on a street of expensive restaurants, which weren't much to look at either, a few old town houses that had somehow avoided the wrecker's ball, and a few expensive apartment buildings. The string of colored lights that formed a gigantic V on the building's facade was unlit, giving the structure a desolate, skeletal look.

Lillian said, "It's closed, Ralph."

Ralph said, "Closed but hopefully not unoccupied. This is our last lead. We'll follow it to the end and then go home."

"What do you expect to find out?"

"Nothing."

"So let's go home. My legs are killing me."

"In a minute," he said. He knocked on the front door, which was so solid that his rap scarcely made a sound. He pounded on it with the meat part of his fist.

A voice behind him said, "Excuse me." It was a uniformed delivery man with a two-wheeled lift containing cases of Perrier water. "Would you mind holding the door open?" he said. Ralph dumbly turned the knob and pulled the door open. "Thanks," the man said.

Ralph made a face at Lillian, and they followed the

Perrier man. The dimly lit foyer was smaller than a theater lobby, though it had a caged ticket window and a narrow passageway to the disco proper. The Perrier man went through the passage and turned right. Ralph and Lillian followed him into the main arena.

In the empty dusk of the interior they saw the open dance area with a glass floor ringed by small, round tables and chairs. High above the dance floor were the speakers and the light-show paraphernalia. The Perrier man wheeled his cargo behind the long bar at the right.

"So this is a discotheque," Lillian said, looking around and nodding, unimpressed.

A door opened in the darkness at the far end and a voice called out, "How many times do I have to tell you not to come in that way? It ruins the carpet."

The Perrier man said, "Sorry, Mr. Sammartino," not sounding sorry at all. "The side door was locked."

A slender but powerfully built young man strode toward the bar. He wore black pants and a pale-blue formal shirt with ruffles, unbuttoned at the neck, no tie.

Lillian said, "Ooh, Rudolph Valentino." She slowly sat down on a chair at the nearest table.

Young Sammartino said to the delivery man, "Like hell it was locked. All you had to do was push it open."

He turned to Ralph and Lillian. "Sorry, folks, we're not open." He spent the next two minutes verbally raking the man for ruining the carpeting. The man calmly finished his delivery and departed.

Sammartino noticed that Ralph and Lillian were still there. "I told you folks we were closed. Come back at nine. . . . Better call for a reservation first."

Ralph said, "If you can spare a minute, we'd like to talk to you."

The young man grimaced. "I'm pretty busy, man."

"We're looking for someone named Opal Wilder."

89

Sammartino walked impatiently toward them. "Never heard of her."

"She was working on a project with Sarah Goode," Ralph said.

The impatience turned to anger. "Are you from the newspapers?" he said, sizing Ralph up with the eyes of a bouncer.

"No, just friends looking for a friend."

"Go look somewhere else. She's not here."

The muscular young man was crowding Ralph, and Ralph backed away. He sat down on a chair next to Lillian and pointed to a third chair. "Sit down, Mr. Sammartino. We apologize for intruding, but it'll only take a minute."

The man raised his eyes in exasperation to the darkness above.

Ralph introduced himself and Lillian. "We mean you no harm," he said.

The man said, "There's been a death in the family, you know."

"We heard about that," Ralph said. "Was he your father?"

The young man nodded, tight-lipped.

"All we want to do is find our friend, and it's possible you can help us. We think she's in danger because she received something from this Sarah Goode; we don't know what. But whatever it is, there are other people who want it—pretty badly, it seems, because they're trying to track her down. We started looking for her yesterday, and now, all of a sudden, *we're* being followed. To tell you the truth, I'm frightened."

"Me too," Lillian said.

Young Sammartino sighed. "I'm sorry for your troubles, folks," he said. "But I don't see how I can help you."

Ralph said, "It looks like whatever it is that Opal has and these people want involves your father."

"How do you figure that?"

"Well, Miss Goode and your father seem to have been close friends, and—"

The young man leaped at Ralph, grabbed his clothing at the chest, and raised him to his feet so that their noses were an inch apart. "You're not buying that bullshit, are you? It's an insult to my father's memory, God rest his soul, to say that he and that woman were lovers!"

"I didn't say that!" The young man was shaking him.

"And it's an insult to a man, a *real* man, to say that he committed suicide," the son said, quivering with rage. "That's bullshit! A real man, if he ever decided he didn't want to live any longer, which he wouldn't, but if he did he'd blow his brains out! None of this plastic-bag shit!" He abruptly released Ralph. "Now get out! You too, blondie."

"Here, now," Lillian burst out. She rose and thrust her great bosom against the man's ruffled shirt. "What kind of a bullyboy are you, picking on a man old enough to be your grandfather! You ought to be ashamed of yourself! Now, you just hold your temper like a good boy and sit down here until you're ready to act like a civilized person."

"Jesus!" the young man exclaimed.

Ralph said, "Grandfather? Father maybe, but not grandfather."

Lillian said, "What's your name, young man?"

"Sonny."

"Okay, Sonny," she said. "Sit down and tell us what this is all about."

Sonny Sammartino kicked a chair into position and sat down hard. He was breathing heavily.

"If you'll call off this blond wildcat, I'll tell you what it's about," he said. "That was a crappy, put-up job in that woman's apartment, and why the police fell for it I'll never know. Look, the suicide note. Written on her typewriter, supposedly by her. Strictly phony. The words are all screwy. *Totally happy together.* Baloney! My father wouldn't say that, and neither would she. She was a tough broad. *Together for all eternity.* I got news. My father didn't believe in God, and I don't think she did either. Would a man end his life to go into eternity when he didn't believe that there was one? My father was having a good time in this life, believe me, and he wasn't about to cut it short.

"Another thing about the note. It wasn't signed. If you were typing out a suicide note, wouldn't you sign it? This one wasn't signed. Okay? Okay? What do you make out of that?"

"You're saying it was murder," Ralph said.

"That's right!" Sonny said, slamming his hand on the table. "My father was *murdered!* And the dame was too. She could never have killed him and then killed herself. No way! No, someone killed the two of them and, in a half-assed way, tried to make it look like suicide. Ridiculous! In bed together? Horseshit!

"You know why? You know why it's horseshit? Let me tell you about my father. He was no angel. He did some fooling around with the broads, okay? He was a good-looking guy, and he liked good-looking women, and they were there with welcoming eyes, and so he did some fooling around.

"But with this Sarah Goode person? Do you know what she looked like? Blondie here is Marilyn Monroe compared to her."

"Thanks a lot," Lillian said.

"I'm not saying my father didn't like her. He did. She was damn smart, and she was useful to him. I think he felt sorry for her because she was such a homely dame, all skin and bones and white skin like the underside of a fish. My father was a kindhearted person, but even he would never think of taking her to bed as an act of charity. There are limits. Besides, I guess you can say at best he liked her like a sister, and you don't sleep with your sister, not when there are a lot of really good-looking chicks around tugging at your zipper. I told the police there was no way my father would get in bed with something like that, but the stupid bastards find him in bed with her, and they buy it!

"Okay, I don't know much about this Sarah person, but there's one thing I do know about her. She was a lesbian. Not a bull-dyke kind of lesbian, but the other kind, the kind that bull dykes go for, you know what I mean? My father told me about her, someone else told me, I forget who, and I could see for myself. Old Sarah would never be found dead in bed with a man! But the stupid bastards in the police department wouldn't believe me. They believe my father was in love with a homely lesbian with a clubfoot, and not only that, he was supposed to be so much in love with her that he killed himself because of it! How about that for stupidity?"

Ralph and Lillian shook their heads at the monumental stupidity of the police. Ralph said, "Do you have any idea who did it?"

Sonny shut down the anguish in his eyes by lowering them. "I think I've talked enough, Mr. Simmons," he said. "I have no idea where your friend is or how she fits into all this."

Ralph said, "That's what we're trying to find out. The same people who murdered the accountant and your father may be the ones who are after Opal Wilder. So it's important to know what Sarah and your father were working on."

A rough female voice came from the darkness behind Ralph. "Who are these people, Sonny?"

Sonny said in a tired voice, "Don't worry, Momma,

they're not from the papers. They're looking for a friend."

"How can it be?" the rough voice said. "They look for a friend by asking you what Vito and that woman were working on? It's none of their business. Come, Sonny, I need you."

As she came nearer, Ralph saw that the widow Sammartino was a slender woman with red-dyed hair piled high, heavily outlined eyes, glittering necklaces and bracelets, a flapper's dress that ended six inches above her knees, and the legs of a hosiery model. Befitting a widow, the dress was black.

Lillian rose and went to her. There were genuine tears in her eyes. "Oh, Mrs. Sammartino, we're so sorry to hear of your terrible loss," she said, embracing her. "You're being very brave." Ralph was astonished to hear a sob come from her.

Mrs. Sammartino appeared to be flustered. "Who are you?" she asked in the raspy voice that Ralph concluded to be the residue of several decades of booze, cigarettes, and loud laughter.

Lillian said, "Just call me Lillian. What's your name?"

"Gina," the woman said, then she frowned. "Thanks for your sympathy, sister, but you're barking up the wrong tree. I knew there was nothing between Vito and that dried-up prune. If there was, I'd have taken care of *her!*" The laugh was one explosive *"Hah"* which made Ralph shudder.

Lillian took her hand and said, "Come sit down here, Gina. Sonny was just saying how your husband loved no one but you."

"You're damn right," the widow said, sitting down.

Lillian said, "We were asking Sonny about your dear husband and the woman accountant only because we're afraid the same terrible thing is going to happen to my

94

niece. She's hiding from them, and we're afraid they'll find her before we do."

"Your niece? You're looking for your niece?"

Lillian sobbed again, and Ralph clamped a hand over his mouth. "Opal, that's my niece, Opal," Lillian continued. "She was working with the accountant, and now they want to kill her. We think it was the same business that killed your dear husband, and we want to stop them from killing Opal too. That's why you and Sonny have to help us, don't you see?"

The woman glanced at her son, who shrugged. She said in a softer voice, "Of course. Vito was a very successful businessman. Very successful, I'm proud to say. He had a way about him that made people trust him. He was very charming, of course, but it was more than that. He was honest, strictly honest, and he knew how to keep his mouth shut; you'd be surprised how important that is. People would come to him with their business problems, they would go up there to his private room"—she pointed upward toward the front of the building—"and they would ask him for help. They knew that none of their secrets would go out of that room. He was like a godfather." She paused, then said, "No, that's the wrong word to use, after that movie. He was a Mr. Fix-It, that's what he was. He would bring these important people together, and he would help them come to agreement. Isn't that a marvelous talent to have?"

"Golly, yes," Ralph said. "It's like a calling, a vocation. But where did this accountant woman come in?"

The widow peered at Ralph suspiciously, then, apparently satisfied, she said, "Well, yes, things got complicated. He was mixed up in so many deals with so many different people, and lots of money was changing hands, and Vito was wearing so many different hats, that it would have been easy to make a terrible mistake without knowing it. He could easily violate some tax law or some corporation law, I don't know. So he started having this woman accountant listen to the tape recordings—he always had his business conversations taped—and she would look over whatever papers and accounts he had, all strictly aboveboard, you understand, but they had to be straightened out in a strictly legal way. And I'll say this, that mousy little broad knew her business. Vito depended on her to keep him on the straight and narrow and to make sure he got his proper share. So that's where the accountant woman came in, Mr. What's-Your-Name."

"Simmons. And thank you for telling us all this. The question now is, what deals were they working on recently that might have caused someone to want to kill them?"

Ralph saw her face close up like a crocus at dusk.

"I wish I knew, Mr. Simmons," she said. "I truly do. But Vito said it was a confidential matter that he couldn't tell even his own wife and son. Isn't that right, Sonny?"

"Whatever you say, Momma," he replied.

Ralph said, "Do you suppose he had to keep it confidential because he was dealing with the next governor of the State of New York, Sylvan Brunner? Men in the public spotlight have to be pretty careful in their private business dealings, I suppose."

Mrs. Sammartino said, "Brunner? What makes you mention him? I'm sure if Vito were dealing with him, he would have told me. He knows I like to meet celebrities. What makes you think it was Brunner?"

"That's what Sarah Goode told her agent," Ralph said. "That the deals involved a labor leader, a corporation president, and Brunner."

The widow shrugged. "Well, if she said that, it's more

than I know." She stood up. "We have lots of work to do, Sonny and I. We're trying to carry on the business, and it's terribly hard. Are you coming, Sonny?"

"In a minute, Momma," he said.

She frowned, hesitated, then went off into the darkness at the rear.

Sonny said in a low voice, "My mother's being cautious because she thinks we still have some money coming from those deals. Myself, I think they killed my father. You have to understand that my father was a wheeler-dealer, he was a middleman, and a damn good one. People could come here to the disco, disappear for a few minutes upstairs, and no one would ever be the wiser."

He peered red-eyed at Lillian. "Is this Opal Wilder really your niece?"

Lillian said, "No, she isn't, Sonny. I said that just to calm your mother down. This whole thing must be very hard on her."

"It is," Sonny said. "She paints herself like that so no one will see. It's like a clown's mask. She's a nice person, and she really wanted to help you, but, well, that's the way she is."

Ralph said, "Tell us about the deals."

"I don't know the details," Sonny said. "I was busy running the disco, if you want to know the truth, but I knew something of what was going on. It started maybe two years ago, and it all circled around one thing—getting that casino built in Coney Island."

"The Empress."

"Right. There was some talk of our opening a disco there, but that's still up in the air. Frankly, I didn't think it was such a hot idea, and as far as I'm concerned, it's dead.

"Anyway, there was Sylvan Brunner, he didn't come here very often, but he was the big wheel as far as I could make out. Then there was the labor leader, that was Terry Shields, he's an old bastard, supposedly retired, but he still owns the C.W.W. lock, stock, and barrel. That's the Construction Workers of the World. And the third one is another old bastard, a guy named Everett Dolin. He's head of something called the Domino Construction Company. The union and the company are supposed to be enemies, but they're not, they're in this together."

"I take it that Domino built the casino."

"Right. And that's about all I know. I saw other people going up those stairs, but the only one I recognized was the black guy who operates the casino."

"Burnside."

Sonny nodded. "The other guys I didn't know. I think some of them were government officials, but that's only a guess."

Ralph said, "What went wrong, Sonny?"

The young man shook his head miserably. "It's a mystery to me. Poppa started acting funny, and so did Miss Goode. Nothing you could put your finger on, but Poppa always walked around like he was king of the world, not in an arrogant way but full of self-confidence, you know? And he was always happy and laughing and slapping people on the back. But then he became quiet, and suddenly he and Miss Goode were thick as thieves. What I think went wrong is, they found out about the tape recorder."

"Your mother mentioned that."

"Poppa was a very ethical man. A lot of his transactions were strictly words and a handshake, nothing in writing. He used the recorder only to protect himself in case somebody tried to turn things around. It didn't happen very often, but when it did he had the tape to cover his rear end. I think they found out about the tape, and I don't know what they thought. There were things on those tapes that could be very embarrassing.

"It was about that time that someone broke into the place. They took the money, and the only other things they took were the tapes in Poppa's desk. He told me they didn't get what they wanted, but he was worried that other people might be blackmailed because of what was on the tapes they took. The only conclusion I could come to was that he had given the Empress tapes to Miss Goode for safekeeping."

"So that's what Opal has!" Ralph said. "No wonder they want them back so badly. They'll kill her, won't they?"

Sonny ran a hand through his glossy black hair. "I don't know about that, Mr. Simmons. But if she has Poppa's tapes, she better stay away from Terry Shields's goons."

Lillian said, "Is that who's following us?"

"Could be."

"Holy mackerel!"

Ralph cleared his throat. "Don't get mad, I'm only asking the obvious question. Could your father have used the tapes to try to blackmail them?"

Sonny looked incredulous. "To hold up the district attorney who sent the Irish Mafia to jail? You gotta be kidding! That'd be suicide!"

"That's what they made it look like," Ralph said quietly. "How about Miss Goode? Could she have had a little extortion in mind?"

Sonny said, "I wouldn't put anything past her. I doubt it, but it's possible."

The mother called him from the far end of the arena.

"Coming, Momma," he said. He looked inquiringly at Ralph.

Ralph wrote his address and phone number on a piece of paper. "I think we're both interested in the same thing—tracking down the killers. If you come up with anything, let me know, damn it."

Sonny said that he would.

A minute later, Ralph and Lillian were out on the sidewalk. "Feeling better?" he asked.

"I need a drink," she announced.

He looked at her in concern. "Are you sure you're all right?"

They found a dimly lit cocktail lounge on the next corner. She settled into her padded booth with a sigh, and when her Bloody Mary was served, she drank deeply and said, "Ahh."

Then she said, "There's one further question about blackmail you didn't ask, Ralph. The question is, why is Opal Wilder hanging on to this stuff that can get her killed? Why doesn't she just turn it over to the police and be done with it?"

Ralph consulted his extra-dry martini and mumbled, "Good question."

A while later, she said, "My shoes are off, and I don't feel like cooking dinner. Why don't we eat here?"

"Toby said he would see us tonight. Maybe we better be there."

"He didn't say for supper," she growled. But she dutifully finished her drink, and they left.

They took a cab to Penn Station.

Another cab followed them.

11

Toby Ferris looked down into the red mist of his second Virgin Mary and smiled. It was the best Virgin Mary he had ever had, largely because it was a true Bloody Mary—with vodka. The man hadn't fooled him. From the first swallow Toby knew the vodka was there. Alarm bells rang, but he muted them. He was acting out a role. He was James Bond playing cat-and-mouse with the blond man across from him. He would manipulate the man into telling all he knew about the birth of the Empress and perhaps get a new lead to Opal's whereabouts. He felt he was being fiendishly clever, but his cleverness stopped short of probing the motive of the man for slyly plying him with alcohol. It didn't matter. James Bond could drink any mortal under the table. Moreover, the alcohol had calmed his nervousness, permitting him to concentrate on eliciting answers to his questions.

"Tell me this, Larry old friend," he said. "How did you know I visited the Goldmans?"

Whitehead laughed. "That's an easy one, Toby. You told me."

"I did?" Toby had no recollection of mentioning his visit to the rest home.

"Not in so many words," Whitehead said. "You asked

101

me if I was the one who offered to buy out the Goldmans, and I said that I was. There was only one way you could have known of the offer—that was from the Goldmans themselves. Therefore, you must have visited them. Q.E.D."

Toby said, "Hey, that's smart. Goldarn smart. Too bad about the Goldmans."

"I felt very sorry for them when I heard. . . . You seem to have an empty glass. How about another?"

Toby realized he was drinking too much too fast, but somehow another drink seemed like a good idea. The alcohol would break down the other man's defenses, he reasoned. He said, "Only if you join me."

Whitehead said, "Of course," and ordered the drinks.

Toby said, "Did any of the other owners have their headbones reshaped by a baseball bat? I mean, that sounds like strong-arm tactics."

"I heard it was a robbery."

"You're right," Toby said. "Were any of the other owners *robbed* the way the Goldmans were?"

"Not that I know of. Did Mrs. Goldman say that they were?"

"She mentioned a fire."

"Come on, drink up, Toby. This conversation's getting morbid."

"It is morbid, isn't it?"

"Why did you go out of your way to see the Goldmans?"

"Oh, I was just passing by and thought I'd drop in, do the neighborly thing and all that. Who were you working for, Larry?"

"I don't mind telling you. We used a few dummy names, but the real buyer was the casino corporation. Empress Enterprises Limited."

"It doesn't look very limited," Toby said, looking around the large cocktail lounge.

"It's a Caribbean company. The same people had gambling casinos down there, each with the name Empress in the title. Why are you so interested?"

"Since you didn't mind telling me, I don't mind telling you. I'm looking for a friend." The water in Toby's eyes caused his vision to blur. "A close friend," he said.

"Who is it? Maybe I know him."

"It's a her." Toby stopped himself from speaking further. It seemed to him that he was giving away more information than he was receiving. "Not to change the subject, Larry, but who are the real owners of this here gambling saloon?"

"I told you. They're Caribbeans."

"Is that a fact? I was told that some gangbusting D.A. had a good-sized piece of the action."

Whitehead was silent for a moment. Then he said, "Who?"

"That feller who's running for governor. You know his name."

"Sylvan Brunner?"

"That's the one."

"Who told you that?"

"A nice old lady."

"Mrs. Goldman?"

"No. Mrs. Goldman's the one who said you were a very nice feller. I hope she gets her million dollars."

"What million, Toby?"

"From the owners of this dump. They never got a good deed to the Goldmans' land, did you know that?"

"No, I didn't."

"I'm wondering about the other owners who sold out. Did you deal with any of them?"

"No. Why are you interested in them?"

"Not innerested in them," Toby said. "Innerested in owners of Empress. If I find out about the old ones, maybe I'll find out about the new ones."

"You mean the Caribbeans?"

"Yeah, them."

"How about one more for the road?"

"Good idea."

A half hour later, Toby was saying, "I love her, Larry. There I was a thousand miles away, and all I could do was talk about her to my landlady. Know why I love her? 'Cause she laughs at my jokes. No, thas not the reason, but it's important, don't mis-misunnerstand. You find a lady who laughs at your jokes, grab 'er and keep 'er, old friend, 'cause, 'cause tha's a good trait in a lady."

"I'm afraid I don't make many jokes," Whitehead said.

"Opal—did I tell you tha's her name? Opal Wilder. Do you know what her initials are? W-o-w—wow! And tha's what I feel when I think of her. I don't deserve her, don't tell me I do when I don't. She was too good for me, and now—" Tears were streaming from Toby's eyes. "And now somebody's trying to kill her! Tha's why I gotta find her. I couldn't go on living without her. Did—did you ever love anyone like that, Larry?"

"Haven't been that lucky, chum." Whitehead pushed back his chair. "What do you say we go for a walk? Clear the cobwebs."

Toby said, "How about another drink?"

"When we get back. A walk will do us good."

"Okay."

Toby stood up and teetered. Whitehead grabbed his arm.

"Need some air, need another drink," Toby said.

Whitehead guided him out of the building, down the side street, and up the wooden ramp to the boardwalk. Toby tripped on an uneven board and said, "Oops."

Toby walked without assistance on the boardwalk, although the boards going by underfoot made him dizzy.

"Watch your step, Larry," he cautioned the other man.

Despite the nippy breeze off the ocean, there was a surprising number of people on the beach. Since there were no lifeguards on duty, the people weren't permitted in the roiling water. Some sunned themselves behind canvas shelters, others tossed Frisbees, an activity that was forbidden on the densely packed beach in summer.

"Never got the hang of that," Toby said.

"It's all in the wrist," Whitehead said.

Many of the concessions fronting on the boardwalk were still closed. A lone hot-dog stand wafted its odors toward them. Also open were a clangorous video-game parlor and, surprisingly, a nearly deserted merry-go-round.

Toby tugged at Whitehead's sleeve. "Le's ride the horses," he said.

Whitehead said, "That's kid stuff. I have a real ride in mind."

"Whassat?"

"You'll see."

Looking up at the Cyclone's mammoth Erector set, Toby said, "I dunno, Larry. This fresh air is gettin' to me."

"Come on, it'll be fun," Whitehead said. "What you need is a little fun."

"I do?"

Whitehead bought two tickets and herded Toby onto the platform and into the rear tandem seat of the jointed twelve-seat car. "Buckle up for safety," Whitehead said jovially, and he clicked the safety bar in place before the attendant came to do it.

They sat there for five minutes while Toby nodded. Only two of the other seats forward of them were occupied. When it was apparent that no other thrill-seekers were going to come along, the bored attendant at the controls started them on the trip.

Alarm bells were clanging in Toby, but he said to himself, What the hell, he was with his good friend Larry Whitehead and he might have fun after all; besides, he was pressed against the back of the seat and couldn't have gotten out even if he willed it.

The car clacked slowly up the steep incline. When no other structures could be seen on either side and there was only sky around them, Toby said, "I wanna get off."

Whitehead chuckled. "Not yet," he said.

At the summit, Toby looked over the side, saw the ground and the squat buildings far below, and got vertigo.

Suddenly the bar wasn't there anymore. Nothing to hang on to. The car tilted downward and seemed to be catapulted into the open air. Whitehead said, "The bar's for sissies. This is the real fun."

Toby was pressed against the back of the seat and yet felt that he was being propelled out and down into empty space. He clung to the side of the car with both hands and wailed. . . .

They were at the bottom and shooting upward on an incline almost as high as the first. At the top the car whipped ninety degrees to the left, and Toby was being thrust centrifugally to the right over the side he was clinging to.

Whitehead shouted, "Now!" and Toby was over the side. The car was wrenched from his grasp. He bounced once on the narrow plank walkway, spun under the railing and down.

Whitehead glanced back as Toby disappeared; then he faced forward.

Toby's first thought was, Oh, Lord, I've goofed up again. His second thought was, Christ, I'm going to hurt.

The plunge downward seemed to take an eternity. *Now I lay me down to sleep, I pray the Lord my soul to keep.* Opal will grieve. I wanted to make her happy, and look what I'm doing to her. Oh, shit. Shit, shit, shit. What's going on? What's happening? My coat's over my eyes. I can't see. A dumb thing happened to me on my way to—

His whole body was jarred. There were no sharp pains, but he was twirling in a very frightening way, rolling down a hillside like a child on an outing. He did that once on an outing because the other kids were doing it. A disappointing experience. All he got was dizzy. He was dizzy now. And son of a goldarn bitch, he was falling again. How many times does he have to fall before it's over? There was no father or mother to catch him. Only Opal. She was going to try to catch him. "Get out of the way, Opal," he called. "Get out of the way!"

He landed more heavily this time. An all-points landing on his back, knocking the wind out of him. He was looking at the sky and at the latticework of the roller coaster as high above him as the Eiffel Tower. He couldn't breathe. He was going to be sick. He rolled on his side in a fetal position, and he concentrated on his paralyzed diaphragm. Get working, old buddy, you're supposed to help me breathe, remember? What a way to go! What a truly dignified way to go, falling off a roller coaster! Tobias Ferris, age forty-five, lifelong clown and goof-up, writer of "The Ferris Wheel," died falling off a roller coaster. No next of kin.

He started to breathe. Then he threw up. After a while he stopped retching. The smell of the vomit so close to his nose was exceedingly unpleasant. He wormed away from it. He became aware the he was on a pile of folded tarpaulins. They smelled almost as disgusting as the vomit. He patted them. Not exactly Sealy Posturepedic, but they did the job.

Finally, it was time for him to take stock of his situation. He moved his arms, his legs, touched his rib cage. No bones broken. He sat up. He had a headache and a residue of dizziness. He studied his surroundings. He seemed to be in a narrow enclosure alongside a large tent. There wasn't a soul in sight. He felt like the drunk in the joke who has fallen asleep in a cemetery and, on awakening in the morning and seeing nothing but tombstones, cries out: "Judgment Day, and I'm the first one up!"

Except he didn't feel like exulting. He felt awful. His mouth was an abomination and his nerves were jangling. He slid off the pile of tarps, and when the ground stopped undulating he moved away to peer up at the tent. Sure enough, the top of it was pitched at a forty-five-degree angle. "Dear God," he said. He looked far up at the crest of the Cyclone, then down at the tent, and pieced together what had happened. Some celestial hand had guided his free-falling body only inches away from a smashing impact on concrete to the gentle slope of the tent-top and down to a cushion of tarpaulins.

He had heard the old saying that God watches over children, drunkards, and fools. *Luckily I'm all three*, he thought.

He prayed, "I thank you, dear God, and I'll never touch another drop of liquor for the rest of my life!" Then he added, "After tonight. I need a drink badly, Lord. You'd feel the same way if you'd been through what I've just been through. But starting tomorrow, I promise."

As he looked for a way out of the enclosure, he thought blurrily of what had happened on the roller coaster. Then he said, "Yes, by God, I do believe that I was assisted out of that car as it hurtled 'round the bend. I do believe that my good friend Lawrence Whitehead put a hand and a foot on my ever-loving rear end and pushed. Well, the joke's on him. Here I am, little the worse for wear, looking for a way to get out of this goldarn place."

He found a rotten plank in the wooden gate, kicked it out, and made his exit.

At about the same time that Lawrence Whitehead strolled away from the Cyclone unnoticed, Toby Ferris trudged toward Surf Avenue in search of a bar where he could quench the conflagration that was raging through his system.

And at approximately the same time Raymond Johnson walked easily along Nostrand Avenue in the Bedford-Stuyvesant area of Brooklyn following the pert little figure of Marvell Short ten paces ahead of him. Nobody looked directly at Raymond; he was just too big to mess around with. Don't even notice him, man, and maybe you won't get him mad. She turned into Herkimer Street, and he did the same.

It was a block of row houses that had originally been middle-class residences of whites, then had sunk somewhat into disrepair with the influx of blacks, but was now making a comeback under the aegis of a block beautification committee. The unseasonable chill kept people off their stoops and away from their windows.

Raymond was vaguely disgruntled. If this were a white woman, Mr. Whitehead and his friends would think twice about teaching her a lesson in her own neighborhood. But since it was a black woman, it didn't matter. It was almost as if black people counted for less, and that bothered Raymond. But a job's a job, and he needed the bread.

Marvell swung into the areaway alongside the high stoop of her brownstone building. She stood before the grilled outer gate under the stoop and groped in her purse for her key. She opened the gate and stepped in.

Raymond stepped in behind her. He said, "You got a big mouth, sister," and smashed her skull with the sawed-off bat he had been hiding in his clothing. The pretty face

109

on the ground had the same look of surprise it had had when she half-turned around to look at her attacker. He knew she was dead. He had regretfully planned it that way. He didn't like to leave witnesses if he could help it.

He bent down, picked up the girl's purse, and put it in his pocket. He murmured, "Sorry, sister," turned and walked easily to the sidewalk. No one was nearby. Down on Nostrand he could see people walking briskly across the intersection. Here, however, it was as if everybody was dead.

He walked more quickly toward Nostrand. Marvell Short would go down as another push-in burglary that had ended fatally.

Ralph and Lillian arrived home at seven-fifteen. Toby wasn't there.

Lillian said, "What do you think, Ralph?"

"I think I'm going to check out the Wilders of Teaneck," he said.

Fifteen minutes later, he got through on the phone to the right Wilder.

A cold male voice said, "Talk to my wife."

Mrs. Wilder got on the phone and said that she was happy to talk to the Mr. Simmons who had been Opal's boss at the *Herald-Courier*. "She likes you, Mr. Simmons," she said. "Opal doesn't like many people. Sometimes I think she's overly critical, but she likes you."

She remarked on what a nice man Toby Ferris was. He had left about eleven o'clock in the morning, she said.

"Did he say where he was going?"

"No. He gave me a kiss, can you imagine that, and then he left. . . . Mr. Simmons?"

"Yes?"

"When you find her, let me know."

Ralph promised that he would.

After he hung up, Lillian said, "Where is he, Ralph?"

He sighed. "He could be anywhere, honey. He never drove a car during the time he lived here, so he doesn't know the area very well. He could be lost, or the car could have broken down."

"He was being followed."

"I know."

"You don't suppose—"

"No, I don't. Why don't you scramble some eggs?"

"I need a drink," she said.

"That's twice in one day."

"Just make me a drink, Ralph, and don't argue."

Ralph hugged her. "I'm sure he's all right," he said.

She said, "I'm not."

The phone rang at ten-thirty, and Ralph sprang to answer it. The voice at the other end was high-pitched and unintelligible, speaking a language that consisted of grunts and squeaks.

Ralph said, "You must have the wrong number," and was about to hang up when the voice said:

"No, smee!"

"Toby?"

"Rye."

"Where are you?"

The voice relapsed into the foreign tongue. Certain syllables were repeated: "coe" and "knee."

"Coney Island?"

"Rye." Weird noises in the background were intruding on the voice—sirens, whistles, animal roars, pings.

"Where in Coney Island, Toby?"

The voice spoke gibberish. Then it said a word that sounded like "Empress."

"At the Empress?"

The voice trailed off.

111

Ralph said, "Stay where you are. I'll find you." Then he heard a dial tone.

Lillian said, "I'm going with you."

He said, "Put on a jacket. It's cold."

While he was backing the Rabbit out of the driveway, Lillian spotted the gray Subaru parked near the corner. "There he is," she said.

Ralph stopped the car alongside the Subaru and lowered his window. The man sitting behind the wheel was looking the other way. Ralph said, "Pardon me, friend."

The man slowly turned his head toward Ralph. He had a sharp nose and deep-set eyes that glared.

Ralph said, "Thanks, I just wanted to see what you looked like." He drove on.

Lillian said, "He frightens me."

"Me too," Ralph said.

They made good time on the Belt Parkway and arrived at the Empress of Coney Island forty minutes after Toby's call. A lineup of gleaming cars waited for the attendants to park them. Ralph drove on by and parked on a side street. The wind off the black ocean was strong. The floodlit Empress was a great rectangle of warmth in the surrounding chill.

"First the parking lot," Ralph said. Lillian pulled her jacket tightly around her and shivered.

They found Toby's old heap in a far corner of the lot.

"If he's in there, he's at the slot machines," Ralph said.

They went up the purple passage into the warmth of the building.

Lillian said, "Ah, that's better."

Ralph growled, "I'm the only one here in sneakers." They plodded through the slot-machine area. The sounds weren't those he had heard on the phone behind Toby's voice. They roamed like peasants in a palace through the gaming room—"Notice the smell," Ralph said. "It's the smell of greed"—to the doors of the dining room, where a famous comedienne was frantically tugging laughs from the diners.

They checked at the registration desk. No Toby Ferris was listed. Ralph called Alex Burnside on the house phone and asked if he had any word on Toby.

Burnside said, "Wait there. I'll be right down."

Ralph grimaced. He didn't want to see Burnside; he only wanted to find Toby.

Burnside greeted them cordially, said he hadn't seen Toby. "What made you think he was here?"

"His car's in your parking lot."

"Strange, very strange," Burnside said. "I'll ask around."

Ralph sighed. "We've looked. He's not here."

"Let me see what I can do," Burnside said.

"We have to go," Ralph said, hustling Lillian off. "If you find him, hang on to him. We'll be back."

Outside, Lillian said, "He didn't look happy."

"Shoot," Ralph said, "we should have known Toby wasn't in there. He was pie-eyed. He'd have been thrown out hours ago. Come on."

Surf Avenue, even on a cold spring night when many of the stores were shuttered, still had something of a carnival air. There were clanging shooting galleries, hucksters shouting spiels, food stands, a fortune-teller. The people on the sidewalk were mostly young and deliberately weird, intermingled with a few subdued oldsters. Lillian was looking for Toby. Ralph was listening for the sounds he had heard.

He turned her into the face of the wind and said, "Let's try the boardwalk." He draped his arm around her shoulders to try to keep her warm. "Sorry," he said.

She said, "Who's complaining?"

113

The boardwalk was nearly deserted because of the wintry blasts. The merry-go-round man was pulling down his corrugated steel doors. As they looked, the hot-dog man switched off his lights. Only the video game arcade was still open. Ralph heard the screeches and cacophony of electronic caterwauling, and said, "That's it."

A wall of hot air, loosed from the ceiling, somewhat offset the wind coming off the ocean. Ralph gazed at the dozen young people standing in front of the flashing and flickering machines, and said, "It's a sickness."

One man stood motionless. His Brooks Brothers suit looked rumpled and soiled. He was leaning forward, his eyes fixed on Pac-Man as the animated circle voraciously consumed everything in its labyrinthian way. Ralph and Lillian stood beside him. Ralph peered into the glassy eyes and said, "He's mesmerized."

Lillian touched Toby's arm. "It's time to go home," she said.

Toby slowly turned to her, his face lighting. "Opal?" he said.

"No. Lillian. Come on, Toby, they're closing the place."

Toby put his arms around her, saying something that sounded like, "Good ole Lillyul. Where's Raff?"

Together they took him by the arms and led him from the place. Toby tried to tell them about the fascinating game he had been playing. He also suggested that they needed a drink. They sured and yopped and there-thered him until they got him to the car. The Subaru man loitered at the corner, but their whole attention was concentrated on Toby.

Lillian said, "How about his landlady's car?"

Ralph grunted, depositing Toby in the back seat. "We'll worry about that tomorrow," he said. "Right now we're getting the hell out of here, and fast."

"Do you think something's going to happen?" Lillian asked. She slid into the front seat beside Ralph.

"I'm spooked, honey," he said. "For some damned reason, I'm scared shitless." He never used words like that in front of women.

In the back Toby was trying to sing, "Another little drink wouldn't do us any harm."

Ralph concentrated on driving, and his trembling stopped.

12

The raging binge of a lapsed alcoholic generally goes on for days until it finally burns itself out along about the fifth day. Ralph didn't believe they could afford to wait that long. Toby Ferris was a snarling, slavering beast. One minute he was blubbering about Opal, the next demanding a drink. Ralph gave him a weak bourbon and water, and Toby sneered and called him a sanctimonious, hypocritical bastard and a few other things as well. Being stronger than Ralph, he wrested the bottle from him, but being falling-down drunk, he couldn't keep it. They tangled and fell to the floor of the kitchen.

Lillian finally broke it up by giving Toby another drink. She sweet-talked him up the stairs, promising to give him all the booze he wanted. He passed out on the guest-room bed. Ralph took off his shoes and put a blanket over him.

She said, "I hope I did right. I put a Seconal in it."

Ralph said through a swollen lip, "I hope he doesn't mess up the bed."

In the morning she gave Toby another drink of bourbon laced with Seconal. He fell into a fitful, mumbling sleep.

Ralph said, "Hold the fort, honey. I'm going to the

Courier morgue and check out a few things. Then I'll go get Toby's car. I'll be back as soon as I can."

He took the train into the city. A different thug followed him.

The head librarian at the *Herald-Courier* archives was a man only a year older than Ralph who looked to be a hundred and five. Ralph asked him when he was going to pick up his marbles, and the man said he should have done it when they installed the damned machines to replace the old clips. "You call this progress?" he asked.

Ralph got the microfilm on Sylvan Brunner and sat before the monitor. The information on Brunner was voluminous. He was forty-three years old and a lifelong resident of Staten Island, the smallest of New York's five boroughs. He graduated from Stuyvesant Law School and entered practice in St. George on Staten Island. He was too young for the Korean War and somehow managed to be too old for the Vietnam conflict. He wisely joined the Republican Party and joined every other organization in the borough except the American Civil Liberties Union and B'nai B'rith.

He was tall, broad-shouldered, well-groomed, and a rousing though humorless speaker. He rode the crest of local issues, whether they involved zoning laws, an addition to the zoo, the need for more police protection, pollution in the kills, or the numerous slights of the borough by the city and the state. He had a large face, a really large nose, green eyes that women seemed to find irresistible, and a jutting chin that turned blue in the late afternoon. He moved with vigor and assurance, and everyone knew he was a comer.

As an assistant district attorney, he managed to get some mention in the newspapers despite the restrictions put on him by the district attorney. He ran for the state assembly and won. After three terms in the assembly, he took on his old boss in a rare Republican primary and beat him for the nomination. In the general election he was elected district attorney by a comfortable margin.

Much of the material in the morgue file related to the various prosecutions he handled during his two terms as district attorney. He would have remained a big frog in a small pond, however, if it weren't for the series of trials that brought down the Benevolent Guardian Agency and the big-shot gangster who ran it, Michael McGovern. The B.G.A. had started as a small-time detective agency in Brooklyn, providing guards for various installations along the waterfront—baseball bats figured prominently in its acquisition of jobs—and had expanded rapidly to cover the whole Greater New York area wherever the opportunities for extortion presented themselves. Along the way many politicians were corrupted, including some high in City Hall and a select few in Albany.

Ralph skimmed through the stories. The D.A.'s of the other counties had clambered to get in on some of the action, but the main glory went to the man from from little Staten Island. He was the one who had labeled McGovern's B.G.A. the "Irish Mafia," though that criminal organization encompassed many nationalities. And it was he who became known as "The Gangbuster."

In the personal profiles of the man, he came across as the incorruptible crusader who had married a gorgeous and incorruptible Protestant American Princess, Lydia Long, and had sired two handsome, incorruptible children who were now in prep schools. He spoke lovingly of his old father, William Brunner, a former corporate executive now retired. The elder Brunner lived only a few miles away from Sylvan. The addresses of both homes were given.

None of the microfilmed clips mentioned an association with the labor leader Terry Shields or the construction executive Everett Dolin. And while Sylvan Brunner was quoted as favoring the Casino Control Law—"If it's an evil, it's a necessary evil," he reportedly said. "The millions of dollars it will earn for the state are needed to help educate our children"—there was no reference to either Alex Burnside or the Empress of Coney Island.

The file on Everett Dolin was practically nonexistent. He had served as an officer of several construction management groups and had been a fund-raiser for his temple. He became president of the Domino Construction Company in 1947 when his predecessor's drowned body was pulled from the harbor.

Terry Shields's file was also skimpy. In the thirties he was arrested several times and charged with assault on C.I.O. organizers, but was never convicted. It was a time when the upstart Congress of Industrial Organizations clashed with the entrenched American Federation of Labor. Young Terry was a bone-breaker for the A.F. of L. He became president of the Construction Workers of the World while he was still in his twenties and remained in that position for the next forty years. Several indictments were brought against him in the fifties and sixties, one for misuse of union funds and two for tax evasion, but he beat them all. A subsequent indictment for jury tampering came to naught. His record was unsullied.

Ralph sighed. Nothing sinister appeared. An accidental drowning and a few broken bones from long, long ago, that was all. He thanked the weary old librarian and took the subway on the long trip to Coney Island.

In the parking lot of the Empress, he had trouble starting Toby's old clunker. He spoke to it as to a horse. "Steady, girl, steady." As he drove out of the lot, he spied Alex Burnside in front of the building, greeting arrivals. Ralph waved, and Burnside started to return the wave, then stopped. The black man shook his head and grinned.

119

Ralph didn't know whether the grin was for him or for the tail who was frantically trying to flag down a taxicab.

When Ralph arrived home, Toby Ferris was just waking up. He was shaky, groggy, bleary, and sober. Lillian fed him chicken soup. He cried. He said he needed Opal. He groveled in self-detestation. He said he was lower than a snake's belly. He was the rear end of a worm. He apologized for his actions and told them to throw him out of the house, he was no good. Ralph told him he sure wasn't much, but they were stuck with him and to shut up. Then he took him for a walk. When they came to the shrubbery bordering Roger Meuwssen's property, Ralph said, "Not in daylight."

Toby said, "What do you know about this Meuwssen feller? Could he be mixed up with the black hats?"

Ralph shook his head. "Definitely white hat," he said.

Returning to the house, Ralph said, "Feel like a drink?"

Toby said, "Water. Tons of water."

They sat on Ralph's screened-in back porch with sweaters on, and Lillian joined them. Ralph said, "Okay, Tobe, tell us about it."

Toby drank lots of water while he talked. He broke into a feverish sweat, and Lillian put a blanket over his shoulders. He told of his visits to the Wilders in Teaneck and the Goldmans in Coney Island and of bumping into a nice fellow named Lawrence Whitehead. "I knew that goldarned waiter gave me real Bloody Marys, but I was trying to loosen this other feller up. Instead, I was the one who got loosened. Boy, did I get loosened!"

He didn't remember much after that. There were blank spots and other spots where the sequence of images was out of order. "I can't swear that he pushed me, Ralph. Once that handrail was gone, I was going over the

120

side sooner or later. Maybe he helped me, and maybe he didn't."

Ralph and Lillian related their own adventures. Then Ralph put in a call to the police detective in charge of the Blossom McNeely case.

Lieutenant Greenberg said, "Nothing conclusive, Simmons. The old lady died of a heart attack all right. Except for the torn finger, there's nothing to indicate that it wasn't an ordinary death from natural causes. Have you found the other woman yet?"

Ralph said they were still looking for her and hung up.

Lillian said, "Why didn't you tell him, Ralph? Why didn't you tell him?"

"Tell him what? They already know about Vito Sammartino and the accountant, and they called it a double suicide. What can I tell them about Toby? He fell off the wagon and then fell off a roller coaster. And we're being followed. Nobody's done anything to us; we're just being followed. It's annoying, but it's not a crime."

Lillian said, "What you should have told him was that they started out by following us, but it looks like they've changed their plan and are doing something else."

"What?"

"Pushing us off roller coasters."

"Would the cops believe Toby?" Ralph asked.

The offices of the Domino Construction Company were in a building on Forty-second Street east of Bryant Park. The lobby ran through to Forty-third Street, where there was another entrance.

At five-thirty all of the Domino employees had left for the day. Everett Dolin sat behind his desk. The other three men stood. Dolin was a short, small-boned man terribly conscious of his height and his pot. He was nattily groomed, with flowing gray locks and heavy upper eye-

121

lids that made his eyes look like those of a sinister Lauren Bacall.

Terry Shields said, "You don't have this place bugged like Sammy did, do you, Everett? If you do, I'd like to give you my rendition of 'Did Your Mother Come From Ireland'." He started to sing in a high tenor voice that was much appreciated at union dances and Irish wakes. He too was shorter than average but with a body that was wide and deep with concentrated muscle and fat. He had a round face, pushed-up nose, small eyes, and a bristly white crewcut. He looked ten years younger than his real age, sixty-nine.

Sylvan Brunner said, "Cut it out, Terry. This is no time for clowning." When he had gotten Shields and Whitehead to sit down, he said, "This thing is getting out of hand."

He turned to the tall blond man. "Who authorized you to throw that guy off the Cyclone?"

Whitehead said, "I authorized it, Governor. You built your Coney Island castle on sand, and this crazy guy was digging at it. He could bring the whole thing down."

Sylvan Brunner took out an inhaler and sprayed his nostrils. Everyone knew of his supposed sinus trouble—it was what gave a rumbling timbre to his platform voice—but his constant use of the spray was an irritating mannerism. "What I want to know is where we went wrong," he said. "And more importantly, what we can do about it. Terry, Ev, we've worked together for a long time, and we've used the services of Mr. Whitehead a number of times over the last few years, but we've never had anything like this. We're letting circumstances maneuver us, instead of us being in control. Damn it, I feel that I'm caught up in another Watergate, and I don't like it."

Shields squinted up at him. "Are you saying that we shouldn't have knocked off that double-dealing Sammartino and that blackmailing broad? Is that what you're saying?"

Brunner nodded. "That's where it started, isn't it? That was our first step in the cover-up. We handled it all wrong. We panicked. We tried to scare him, and we succeeded. But he didn't react the way we expected. Well, okay, that's water under the bridge. So we started the cover-up, we can't undo that."

He moved away from the desk and started pacing. "But don't you see what we've got ourselves into as a result? We still don't have the tapes, and things have gotten worse. Mr. Whitehead questioned the old lady the Wilder woman was living with, and gave her a heart attack."

Whitehead's fingers gripped the arms of his chair. "You can't blame me for that, Governor! You can't blame me for an act of God!"

Brunner sighed. "Okay, it was God who murdered her. The fact remains that because we thought there was a need to cover up, we've had three murders and an attempted murder. Who's going to be next? Are we going to murder the Wilder woman when we find her? And how about those friends of hers who are looking for her? Are we going to kill them too? Where will it end?"

Whitehead started to retort, but Shields help up his hand to stop him.

Shields said quietly, "We're only doing what's necessary, Sylvan. To answer your questions, yes, we'll probably have to silence the Wilder woman and possibly her friends. As I say, we'll do what's necessary, and that's all."

"My God, that's what I'm talking about," Brunner said. "We're the ones who are on a roller coaster. We go down one slope and have no choice but to go up the next. We're caught in a momentum that we're powerless to stop. Each murder becomes necessary."

After a while Whitehead said, "So where does that leave us?"

"Back in control, damn it," Brunner said. "We're in a strong position, so there's no need to get hysterical. The election campaign is a different matter. I can't let the slightest hint of this get around. That's the important thing. No more spur-of-the-moment actions." He sprayed his nostrils. "I understand there was another killing, Mr. Whitehead."

"An accident," Whitehead said. "Raymond used a little too much force in quieting the waitress."

"Okay, no more accidents, do you hear? Check every movement with one of us. What may seem necessary to you may not seem so to us."

Whitehead's curled lip was almost a snarl. "So what'll we do, Governor? You tell us, and we'll obey."

"I'm not criticizing you, damn it! You're a necessary part of our team. Continue your monitoring of these characters. They may still lead us to the Wilder woman. Is the telephone bug in place?"

"It is."

"Good. I have a feeling she'll call them. That's important. Just keep on top of them, but no accidents unless we say so, understand?"

Shields said, "I agree with the Governor, Whitey. But I don't think we should tie his hands completely, Sylvan. I think we should say this. If a situation comes up that calls for action on his part and he can't get in contact with one of us, then I think we should let Whitey use his own judgment. Is that fair enough?"

Whitehead looked inquiringly at Brunner.

Brunner frowned. "If it's really serious and can't wait."

Shields sat back. "Trust Whitey. He's a genius at creating accidents. You talked about murders, Sylvan. There were no murders. There was a double suicide, a

124

death from natural causes, a push-in mugging, and a drunk who fell off a roller coaster. And there aren't gonna *be* any murders. Trust Whitey."

Sylvan Brunner was the first to leave. He was late for a Knights of Columbus dinner.

Five minutes later, Terry Shields left by a different exit.

Lawrence Whitehead leaned on Everett Dolin's desk and peered down at him. "You're a quiet one, aren't you?" he said. "I can't figure out how you fit in. As far as I can see, you're a flunky."

Dolin returned the gaze with hooded eyes. "It's time for you to leave, Mr. Whitehead," he said.

Whitehead straightened up. "I don't trust you, feller. Whenever I've dealt with anyone like you, I've been sorry. Just remember my bag of tricks."

"I have a few tricks of my own, Mr. Whitehead," Dolin said.

"I believe it," Whitehead said.

After he left, Dolin sat at his desk until he heard the elevator close and whine on its descending journey. Then he opened a desk drawer, switched off the tape recorder that was hidden there, and removed the cassette. Like many small, slender men, his movements were graceful almost to the point of effeminacy.

He moved to his safe, opened it, and placed the tape inside. Then he closed the safe and twirled the dial to lock it.

He put out the lights and left.

13

Toby Ferris couldn't sleep. He commanded his brain to stop bugging him. Better yet, he said to his brain, start writing a "Ferris Wheel," that always puts them to sleep down in Miss.

THE FERRIS WHEEL, datelined New York. That's right, I'm up here in the Big Winesap, folks, and wishing I was down there piddling my life away on the beach, scooting around town on my ten-speed, and playing gin rummy with Mrs. Plotnik, my landlady. She cheats. I owe her two hundred and seventy thousand dollars, she says. Even so, I'd rather be playing with her than with some of the critters I've met up here.

You know the lake outside of town where the water is filled with cottonmouths and the shore is crawling with skunks? Well, that's New York City, folks. No place for a simpleminded country boy like me.

But I'm stuck here until I catch up with the lady I love. I let her go once, and now she's being pursued by a whole tangle of cottonmouths, or maybe they're copperheads, I haven't had a chance to examine their mouths closely. (Forgive me, this is one of my uncomical comical columns.) Anyhow, Opal, that's her name, Opal is my Siamese twin. I didn't know this until I was away from her. We have only one heart, you see, and I can't keep going for long less'n I get hitched up to her nice and proper, cause I'm like the Tin Man who ... where was I, yes, in love with Opal, and never mind saying I don't know what love is because I don't have a momma and a daddy like everybody else. On the contrary that gives me a great capacity ... capacity ... Capa City ...

He woke up in the morning saying "Capa City" and didn't know where it came from.

"I'm fine, Jim Dandy, couldn't be better," he said to Ralph. "Let's track down these cottonmouth bastards. You take this feller Everett Dolin, he sounds dull, and I'll take this union son of a bitch Terry Shields because I'm an old cesspool digger and I speak his language."

"What language is that?"

" 'Tote that barge, lift that bale.' "

"More like 'tote that bat, lift those funds.' But go ahead. I understand he has a great sense of humor."

They got the addresses from the phone book. Both the union and the construction company were on Forty-second Street, a block apart. From his friend at the newspaper morgue, Ralph learned that the Brunner-for-Governor Committee had just opened a headquarters on Fifth Avenue near Forty-fourth Street.

"Must be a good area for snakes," Toby said.

Toby was so hyperactive that Ralph decided to drive the Rabbit into the city rather than put up with him on the train. As usual, Lillian went along. "We're a team," she said.

Ralph abandoned the car to a garage on East Forty-third Street. He said to Toby, "If we're not in front of the Brunner headquarters, we'll meet here. Right here. If you get here first, wait for us."

Toby said, "Good plan," and strode away.

Lillian said, "Maybe we should have stuck together."

Ralph said, "Nothing can happen to him in midtown at midday."

She said, "You have more faith in Toby than I do."

Toby sat still for twenty minutes on a bare bench in the union's outer office, and when the fat receptionist finally said that Mr. Shields would see him, he leaped to his feet and charged down the hall to the far office, accidentally bumping into the receptionist. He blushed and apologized. She said, "I get off at four."

His entrance into Shields's office was an awkward plunge. Shields sat behind a bare desk like an Irish Buddha, a smile widening into a grin on his round face.

Toby said, "Begging your pardon for intruding and thanking you for seeing me, I'm looking for Opal Wilder."

Shields stood up and shook Toby's hand with what seemed like a catcher's mitt. "So you're Toby Ferris," he said. "I've been wanting to meet you."

Toby crumpled into a chair, stunned. "Then you've heard about our quest," he said.

"What quest?" Shields said. "I'm just proud to meet the author of *The Flood*. That was the name of it, wasn't it? *The Flood*? Some reviewers said you stole the idea from Bill Faulkner, or was it Mark Twain? But I think that's crap. You didn't do any stealing, did you?"

Toby said, "If I did, it wasn't on purpose."

Shields laughed. "I've done a fair share of stealing in my day, son, but, believe me, it was done on purpose. Now, what can I do for you?"

Toby's line of thought was hopelessly untracked. "I don't rightly know, sir. Your remembering my book after so many years has knocked me for a loop."

"You mentioned a name, Toby. May I call you Toby?"

"Yes, sir. Go right ahead."

"What's this 'sir' crap? Call me Terry. That's what everybody calls me when they're not calling me something else, like 'shithead.' I get a lot of that too."

Toby's mind was bustling about, heaving his thoughts back in line. "Not to take too much of your time, er, Terry, I'm looking for a lady named Opal Wilder."

"Am I supposed to know her?"

"Well, that's what I'm asking. Do you?"

"Sorry, not that I know of. Describe her."

Toby haltingly gave a description of the woman he loved.

Shields said, "Sorry." He said it sadly.

Toby said, "I think she has something you want back."

"Whatever can that be?"

"Something she got from a Sarah Goode who got it from someone named Vito Sammartino."

"Wait a minute. Weren't they the ones who committed suicide?"

"I've heard that."

Shields wagged his head. "Damn shame. Damn shame. I don't go out dancing very often, my old bones can't take it, but I've been to Vito's once or twice, and I thought it was a hell of a lot of fun. Had to rest up for weeks afterwards, ha-ha."

"Opal Wilder was investigating the Empress of Coney Island. You've heard of it?"

"Who hasn't?"

"She thought you were connected to it."

"Me? Now, how would an old hod carrier like me be connected to a gold mine like that?"

"It was just a thought, Terry. She believed the whole project gave off a certain aroma."

"A certain aroma?"

"I believe she smelled a snake. Forgive the expression, I wasn't referring to you. One of the things she was looking into was how these snakes got the land where the Empress was built."

Shields cleared his throat. "I can't say that I know what you're talking about, Toby, but, out of curiosity, how *did* they get the land?"

Toby said, "Do you know a man named Lawrence Whitehead?"

Shields tried to shrug humorously.

"Ask him about it," Toby said. "He was in on it."

"You don't say."

"Do you know a guy named Everett Dolin? He's president of—"

"Sure, I know Dolin." Shields laughed nastily. "Didn't I take him to the cleaners many times over the years! I loved picking that man's pockets!"

"He's in on it."

"In on what?"

"The casino deal."

"You think something crooked went on, is that it, Toby?"

"Yes, sir. I mean Terry. Are you sure you weren't lucky enough to get a piece of it too?"

"No such luck."

"Too bad," Toby said. "Do you know who's the head crook?"

"Tell me."

"The feller who's running for governor. Sylvan Brunner."

Shields whistled. "Well, I'll be a monkey's uncle! I thought he was so straight he was ready for sainthood. You never can tell, can you?"

"Do you know him?"

"I've bumped into him a couple of times at union functions. A hell of a speaker, but he's too right-wing for me."

130

Toby took a deep breath. "Were you ever in the up-stairs room at this discotheque we're talking about?"

"Good Lord, no. I didn't know there was one."

"It had a hidden tape recorder."

"Well, I'll be damned! You seem to know a lot about this, what did you call it, this casino deal. What are you after, Toby?"

"Just Opal Wilder, that's all."

"I sure hope you find her. What's your next step?"

Toby let his shoulders slump. "Well, I don't have much to go on. All I know is, she was asking questions about that casino on Coney Island. And the only thing I can do is follow on her trail and hope to come across her on the way."

"Poke into the casino deal, you mean."

"Yes."

"From what you say, it could be dangerous."

Toby nodded. "They plan to kill her, I know that, just as they killed Sammartino and the woman. They've already tried to kill me, but, goldarn it, I'll either find Opal or get killed, it's as simple as that."

Shields came around the desk and once again shook Toby's hand. "You're not only a hell of a writer, Toby," he said, "you're a brave man as well. I sure hope you find this lady friend of yours."

A minute later, Toby Ferris was out of the office, and Terry Shields was on the phone. "You were right, Whi-tey, this dingbat knows a bundle more than we thought. He needs a little discouraging. You're the expert on psychological warfare. Use a little of that. Incidentally, thanks for the rundown on the book. Now get the lead out, he's coming down."

In the elevator going down, Toby said to himself, Yep, that's a cottonmouth, all right. Or maybe with that bloated face of his, he's a puff adder. But, cripes, I didn't learn a blame thing except that he's in it up to his fat rear end, and I've seen face to face one of the bastards who's out to kill Opal.

Pausing in the lobby to get his bearings, he noticed a tall, broad-shouldered man walking away from him toward the exit. He had blond hair that was almost white. Appearing to be engrossed in his thoughts, the man veered into an alcove lined with telephone booths. Toby caught a glimpse of the man's profile and thought he recognized his murderous friend from Coney Island.

When Toby came abreast of the alcove, the man had disappeared in one of the booths. Toby felt a trembling in his knees. Was it really Lawrence Whitehead? Toby hesitated, suppressing a desire to take to his heels. What would Mike Hammer do? Travis McGee? The man was still in the booth.

Toby walked slowly into the alcove. There were many people going their way in the lobby behind him. Reassured, he edged farther in. He saw a hunched figure in the far booth. It didn't look like a human form. Closer, he saw that it was a topcoat draped over the telephone. He whirled to retreat. An arm gripped him around the shoulders, something acrid was under his nose, and a voice was saying, "Glad to see you again, old chum." Then the smell was gone.

His mind was alive, but the rest of him was dead. His limbs were those of a Scarecrow before Ray Bolger inhabited them. He willed himself to move, to get away from this friendly killer, but the circuits were out. Only the strong arm of Whitehead was holding him up.

A man entered the alcove and gaped in alarm. Whitehead said, "Nothing to worry about, pal. All he needs is a walk in the fresh air." To Toby he said, "Come on, Toby, we're going for a nice walk." Aside to the stranger: "He knows he can't handle alcohol, but what are you going to do."

Toby was gliding through the lobby. He tried to call to the passersby and couldn't. He felt like Topper being propelled by the crazy Kirbys. Whitehead continued to talk to him soothingly, as if jollying a drunken friend.

Gliding on the sidewalk was bumpier going. He was jostled several times by passing pedestrians. No one paid more than fleeting attention to the two men. At Fifth Avenue, the strong arm of Whitehead swept him across to the library corner and then into Bryant Park. Toby's mind recorded his sensations.

THE FERRIS WHEEL, datelined New York. I am in the process of being murdered, folks, not one of your everyday experiences. Please don't worry about me, because I'm completely anesthetized and I won't feel a thing when this fellow gets around to thrusting home with whatever he's going to use. I could say that hundreds of people are watching, but that wouldn't be true. They have looked at me but haven't seen me, if you know what I mean.

The sun is in my face, but I don't feel it. The toes of my shoes are scraping on the pavement, the only good pair I have. Two things keep me from enjoying the situation. In the first place, there's the indignity of the thing. I always thought I would go out raging against the enveloping darkness, fighting to the last. I'm being dragged like a side of beef to my destruction, unable to move a finger. It may be painless, but it's woefully inglorious.

The other thing: I have failed Opal. It's the story of my life. Ineffectuality, thy name is Toby. There's a great empty hole in me, and it's going to be filled with dirt instead of the woman I love. Maybe we'll meet, who knows. Maybe she's been killed and is already there, but how will she greet me after I've failed so ingloriously? There's that word again. It says something about my daydreams, doesn't it?

I am on a bench in a quiet corner of the park. I am lying there. Whitehead reaches into his pocket. Here it comes, folks. A knife? A gun? Aw, shit, it's a pint of whiskey! He's

133

spilling it on me. It's the weirdest thing. Now he's capped it and is putting the half-empty bottle in my jacket pocket. He has a cigarette lighter. It looks like he's going to set me on fire. Oh, well, that won't be so bad, after all—sort of a Viking's funeral, even though it's on dry land. There's some dignity in that.

Goldarn, he has lit a cigarette and is walking away. He smiles and says, "Have a nice day." I think I'm beginning to dislike him.

I am alone. I have no sense of smell, but I know what I smell like. I know what I look like. I lie here paralyzed . . .

The reception accorded Ralph and Lillian Simmons at the Domino Construction Company had less surface cordiality. Everett Dolin eyed them coldly with his hooded eyes from across his desk. "I have never heard of the young lady," he said. "Someone is playing a trick on you."

He denied ever having met Vito Sammartino or Sylvan Brunner. "I wish I had," he said. "He's going to be our next governor."

He acknowledged an acquaintanceship with Terry Shields from their labor dealings and with Alex Burnside. "I built his casino."

"How did you get the contract?" Ralph asked.

"What's that got to do with your missing lady friend?"

"Miss Wilder was investigating the construction of the Empress when she disappeared."

"She was wasting her time," Dolin said. "It's all a matter of public record. There were sealed bids, and ours was the lowest. Domino had been in business for sixty years. It's a respectable company. It got the contract. Your Miss Wilder can investigate all she wants; that's what she'll find out. Now, if there's nothing else, Mr. Simmons, I'm not retired like you, I have a lot of work to do."

Ralph, feeling dismissed, was about to get up out of his

chair when Lillian said, "You're a fascinating man, Mr. Dolin."

Dolin stopped fussing with the papers on his desk. "I happen to agree, Mrs. Simmons, but I'm afraid not many people feel that way. May I ask what you find fascinating?"

Lillian beamed at him. "Well, you're the strong, silent type. You're very decisive, I can tell that. And you're sexy. No, no, don't deny it, I bet you've broken many a heart."

Ralph cringed.

Dolin said, "Do you know how old I am, Mrs. Simmons?"

"That has nothing to do with it," she said. "Women go for the mature man who knows what he's doing, the successful man who's risen to the top of his company. I'm fascinated by men who take command. Would you mind telling me how you became president of this company? I'd really like to know."

Ralph relaxed.

Dolin's face was flushed. "There's not much to tell, dear lady. It's so long ago, thirty-five years, I scarcely remember. Nothing very glamorous, I assure you. I worked up through the ranks, as they say. I'm afraid that's not very fascinating."

"But to get to be president," she said, still beaming. "How did you manage that?"

"I didn't manage it at all," Dolin said with a dry laugh. "I was vice-president, and then the president died, and there I was. I hope I haven't disillusioned you."

"Oh, not at all! You were there to take advantage of the situation. Was the president an old man?"

"No, as a matter of fact, he was in his midforties. A young man really."

"Oh, dear, what was it, a heart attack? Cancer?"

"Will you believe this? He drowned!"

"You don't say!"

"It's an interesting story," Dolin said. "I was even almost heroic. I said *almost*. You see, we were doing a lot of construction work on the waterfront during the war years and for a number of years afterward. Do you know Brooklyn Heights? We were demolishing an old wooden pier there and were going to put up a new one. It was the heart of winter, and we really shouldn't have been working in that kind of weather, but Kolb, that was the president, Walter Kolb, he had signed a contract that had a penalty clause— But you're not interested in that. We had to get the work done or we'd lose our shirts.

"To tell you the truth, Kolb was not a well-liked man. He didn't trust anybody. He was always sneaking around, checking up after the men had left for the day. Well, this day, it was night really, he insisted that I go with him over to Brooklyn to see how far the day's work had progressed. Mrs. Simmons, it was *cold* out there, but he insisted on going out to the end of the dock, which was half demolished. I stayed back with a union man who was there and the night watchman. There was a fire in a drum, and we were trying to keep warm.

"Well, we heard this yell, and I looked out just in time to see Kolb go through a rotten timber and into the water. I was young and foolish. Without thinking, I shucked off my overcoat, and I ran out there, and I dived in after him. Does that sound heroic? It was the stupidest thing I ever did. I nearly killed myself. Within seconds I could feel myself freezing to death, and instead of looking for Kolb, I had to think of saving myself. Some hero! The men on the dock directed me to a ladder that was still in place, and I managed to climb out. Do you know what? I spent the night in the hospital, and I shivered all night long."

136

He peered sheepishly at Lillian. "Now why did I tell you that dumb, long-winded story? You asked me how I became president of Domino. That was how I became president—by jumping into the harbor and very nearly killing myself."

Lillian continued to regard him with adoring eyes, but her magic had run out, and Everett Dolin reverted to the hostile, closemouthed, busy executive he had been at the beginning of the interview.

They got no more from him, and they left.

Going down in the elevator, Ralph said, "One thing puzzles me. How did he know I was retired? I didn't tell him that, did I?"

"No."

"You really laid it on, honey."

"He loved it."

"There's something about that story of his."

"Didn't you believe it?"

"As far as it went. It sounded like an official version. I'd like to find out the unofficial version."

"Now?"

"If we have time. But first we have to collect Toby."

They walked around the corner and up to the Brunner-for-Governor campaign headquarters. The place was deserted except for two eager-faced young people who were unloading a carton of campaign leaflets and stacking them on an otherwise bare table. On the rear wall was a gigantic blowup of Brunner looking impossibly noble, flanked by American flags.

The young man said, "The campaign hasn't really started yet. The Governor has been in here exactly once that I know of, just to look around. So far, he's working out of his office in St. George."

The young woman said, "Vote for clean government," and handed them each a leaflet.

Ralph got the address of Brunner's office on Staten Island, and they left.

Toby wasn't at the garage.

They waited five minutes, then Ralph said, "Let's see if he's still at that union office."

The fat receptionist there said that Toby had left, maybe fifteen minutes ago.

Ralph said, "Back to the garage."

They went down in the elevator and out into the throng on Forty-second Street.

Something whacked the soles of his shoes hard. Toby felt it. It hurt. Well, that's progress, he thought. He tried to raise his arm. It moved a little bit. His lips felt dry, and he wet them with his tongue. He tasted alcohol. He became aware that his nose too was once again working. He smelled like a distillery.

He opened his eyes. The policeman who stood over him appeared to be nine feet tall. The policeman poked him in the ribs with his nightstick. Toby said, "Ow." He could talk!

The policeman said, "On your feet, Mac. Get moving." And he poked him again.

Toby tried to sit up. He couldn't make it. He peered around. Some people were looking at him. He saw pity, contempt, revulsion in their eyes. They were looking at a drunken bum. He tried to tell them that he wasn't intoxicated, that he had been assaulted by gas. Sounds came out of his mouth, but he knew they were unintelligible.

The policeman pulled him to a sitting position. "This is a respectable park," he said. "Go back to the Bowery."

Toby sat there like a lump, dying of humiliation. Old Larry Whitehead had fixed him good this time. He was being branded a public drunkard. A bystander came forward, crumpled a dollar bill into his hand. Toby started to cry.

"None of that," the policeman said. "You have one minute to get your smelly carcass out of here."

I'm going to be arrested, Toby thought. New York City was whomping my ass once again. They're on the lookout for me, goldarn it! *Bulletin to all points: Toby Ferris is back in town. He's asking for it, men. See that he gets it.*

The policeman pulled him to his feet. He wobbled and grabbed the policeman for support.

The policeman said, "That does it, Mac. Now you're gonna get it."

At the corner of Fifth Avenue, Lillian glanced across the intersection. She put a hand on Ralph's arm. "Over there," she said. There were at least fifty people within the purview of her pointing finger. "There. Up there," she said.

The middle landing of the staircase to the library, above the stone lions, extended the width of the building as a promenade bounded by foliage. At the far right of the landing stood a lone figure, a tall man with ash-blond hair. What was arresting about him was the rigid stillness of his body as he peered past the side of the library over intervening foliage, toward the park beyond.

Ralph said, "It can't be."

"You're right," Lillian said. "Let's take a look anyway."

They crossed at the red light against the flow of pedestrians. She checked once again the direction of the man's gaze and made for the entrance to the park.

As they entered, they saw Toby Ferris coming toward them, moving in rag-doll fashion. A large policeman was immediately behind Toby, and as they closed the distance they saw that the cop held Toby by the back of his jacket and the seat of his pants and was propelling him by what used to be called "the bum's rush." About a dozen people straggled behind.

Lillian cried, "Toby!"

The policeman said, "Out of the way, ma'am."

Lillian didn't get out of the way. She went to Toby and stood before him, thus stopping the procession. She said, "Toby, what's going on?"

The policeman said, "Do you know this character?"

"Certainly," Lillian said. "He's a famous writer, Toby Ferris."

"He's also a public drunk, ma'am. I'm taking him in where he'll be safe."

"Oh, no, you're not," Lillian said.

Ralph stepped forward, saying, "Now, now."

Lillian said, "This man isn't drunk. Someone's played a terrible joke on him. Can't you see? He's sopping wet! Is that the way a person drinks? By pouring it on his clothes? Here, feel!"

The officer felt, and Ralph felt.

She said, "It's all over him, right?"

The cop said, "But he's so drunk he can't stand up. Look."

He let go of Toby. Toby swayed but remained standing.

"And he can't talk straight," the cop said.

Toby, with great effort, said, "Dentist . . . anessesia."

Ralph piped in. "Good Lord, Toby, did you let him give you novocaine? You know you're allergic to novocaine! My God, it's a wonder you're not dead!"

The policeman said, "But—but—"

A bystander said, "Let him go."

Another said, "Yeah, let him go."

Ralph and Lillian convinced the cop there was no need to call an ambulance. "We'll take him to our own doctor," Ralph said. Lillian glanced toward the library promenade. The ash-blond man had disappeared.

Between the two of them, they managed to guide Toby

140

back to the parking garage, where they rescued the Rabbit and headed home. By the time they got there, Toby was able to locomote on his own and to speak freely.

He said, "It's lucky I couldn't talk. I'd have told the constable that the man who squirted me with nerve gas also pushed me off a roller coaster, and they'd have shipped me off to the funny farm for sure!"

He tried to laugh at his own debasement and couldn't. He was in a deep depression. "I'll never do Opal any good," he said. "She's going to hate me, I know that. I'm going back where I belong, the asshole end of Mississippi."

Ralph said, "Bull," and Lillian said, "You're really a lovely person, Toby."

That night Ralph dug out his copy of *The Flood* and read parts of it aloud. As it always happened when he tried to read a humorous piece aloud, he broke up and was unable to continue reading. Lillian finished the excerpt.

Toby said, "Hey, I guess that wasn't so bad, was it?"

"It's brilliant," Lillian said, and Toby grinned in embarrassment.

Later he said, "I'm not so sure I can face that Lawrence Whitehead again. To me, he's the Devil himself. He manipulates me like I was Charlie McCarthy. He seems to hypnotize me. I'm frightened, really frightened."

Lillian soothed him with hot chocolate.

14

Toby Ferris was still in sad shape in the morning. Part of his malaise was physical, the lingering effects of the nerve gas. A larger part was psychological, the painful wound of being labeled a worthless, ineffectual drunken bum. Ralph rousted him out of bed, and Lillian filled him with scrambled eggs and coffee. He lolled and drooped and lay down on the sofa.

"Don't you want to beard the lion in his den?" Ralph asked.

Toby moaned. "He'd only eat me up, and then spit me out."

Lillian spoke of Opal's plight. She likened Opal to Eliza and her baby leaping from ice floe to ice floe across the Ohio with vicious dogs snapping at her heels. Ralph said, "You may be worthless, as you say, Toby, but Opal doesn't believe that. She needs you. She's counting on the real you to save her from the killers who are only one step behind her."

The nonsense worked. Toby actually laughed. "The dogs I can handle," he said. "I'm murder on man-eating dogs. Lions too, goldarn it. Stop piddling around. Let's go!"

It was noon before they left home.

●　　●　　●

Sylvan Brunner's law office was on the second floor over a bank in St. George, a ten-minute walk from the ferry terminal. His view of the harbor and downtown Manhattan was partially blocked by a building across the street. The office looked more like the den of a landed gentleman than the workplace of an attorney. The desk was polished mahogany, and the leather chairs were deep and comfortable. It was a room for confidential conversations.

Brunner was in conference with some political aides when his secretary entered and whispered in his ear that a Mrs. Sammartino was in the outer office demanding to see him. He showed his aides out a side door, then took a moment to compose himself and zing his nostrils with spray.

Then he leaped to his feet to greet the widow of Vito Sammartino. He embraced her while murmuring words of condolence.

She said, "Thank you for sending flowers."

In place of the harlequinesque getup she affected at the disco, Gina Sammartino was dressed in black, her face clear of makeup except for a black border around the eyes; her red hair was pulled back severely into a bun. She let Brunner guide her to one of the chairs.

After a minute of conventional small talk, Brunner said, "I didn't know Vito well, only as the genial host at the disco the few times I've been there. What a shame!"

"I think you knew him better than that, Governor."

Brunner nodded. "I knew him well enough to like him and respect him. He was a fine man."

"You visited him in the upstairs room."

"Of course I did. He helped me out in a business deal. I'll never forget him for that."

"More than one deal."

"Perhaps."

"In fact, he put together the whole casino deal for you."

Brunner gazed at her coldly. "I think you've come here to make a point. What is it, Mrs. Sammartino?"

She said, "The discotheque business is funny. It's a high-roll gamble. When you put a million dollars in a disco, it's like betting your life savings on the roll of the dice at one of your casino tables. If you win, that's fine, but you have the dice and you have to keep shooting. Do you see what I mean?"

"It's risky, I don't doubt it." Brunner took out his inhaler and sniffed deeply.

"It's a fad business, Governor. You can be in one week and out the next. Sometimes it depends on the personality of one person. In our case, Vito was that person."

"Are you saying that business has dropped off?"

"Fifty percent," she said. "We reopened last week, and we're not covering expenses. It's not only that Vito isn't there, it's the way he died. It makes the customers uneasy; they don't want to be reminded of death. So they go somewhere else."

Brunner put on his noble look. "I understand what you're saying. You're in trouble financially. Tell me what I can do. Would it help any if my wife and I went there and we got our pictures in the papers? I'd be glad to do that."

"That's very kind of you," the widow said. "But I was thinking of something else."

"A loan? If you have a cash-flow problem, I'm sure I can advance you the money."

The small woman struggled out of the deep chair and stood erect in front of Brunner's desk. "As I said, my husband put together the casino deal. He was your agent in negotiating with state officials. Naked greed is a terrible thing to see, don't you agree? He passed money for you, Governor."

"Now, see here—"

"He worked out the details, and for a time he was your only contact with Mr. Burnside, your front man at the Empress of Coney Island. Funny name for a gambling joint, but who am I to say? What I *am* saying, Governor, is that my husband was your partner in that casino in everything but name. You paid him for his services, and that was all."

Brunner studied her. "Are you hinting that you have evidence of all this? Some tapes, for instance?"

"My husband and I were closer than you seem to think." Her voice, until now a monotone, quavered faintly. "He and I were on speaking terms. He told me many things. He told me about you and Mr. Dolin and Mr. Shields. I said to him, 'You're taking all the risks without any payoff.' But he was an honorable man, Governor, and he said he had an agreement with you and he would stick to it. He didn't know the kind of men he was dealing with, did he?"

"But you don't have any evidence of this strange story you're telling."

"Only myself and what I know. It's enough."

Brunner shook his head sadly. "I'm sorry to say, Mrs. Sammartino, that in your grief you've imagined a lot of things that aren't true. The shock of a loved one committing suicide can be more than one can bear. I sympathize with you." He put the inhaler to his nose.

"Thank you," she said. "Only he didn't commit suicide. He and that woman were murdered."

Brunner stood up. "I have a tight schedule," he said. "I'm glad that you came to me with your troubles. When you come to your senses and remember what you said here, please don't be embarrassed. I understand." He came around the desk to her.

She looked up at him. "You and your partners made a big mistake. How you could have believed that anyone would swallow that suicide story I'll never know. The poor woman was very homely and was about as sexy as a meatball. Did you know she was a lesbian?"

"I didn't know her at all!"

"Everyone knew she was a lesbian. No, Governor, they were murdered. I can prove that. And I think I can prove who did it."

"Is that why you came to see me?" Brunner asked. "To accuse me of murdering your husband?"

"No, I didn't," she said. "I came here to ask for my husband's share of the casino. There were three of you, and Vito makes a fourth. I, therefore, put in a claim for a twenty-five-percent share of the business. That's only fair, wouldn't you say?"

Brunner leaned back against the desk and shook his head. "Mrs. Sammartino, you leave me speechless. And what do you propose to do if we refuse to give you your share of this imagined business? Go to the police? Go to my opponent and see what he can make of it? What?"

Gina Sammartino smiled for the first time. "There'll be no need for any of that," she said sweetly. "I know that you'll see it my way. Good-bye for now."

She turned and left the office.

Brunner moved around his desk and slumped into his chair. After a minute, he rang for his secretary.

"Did anyone other than you see that woman come here?" he asked her when she entered.

She shook her head. "Lunch hour," she said. "I was the only one in the office."

"Good. She didn't come. We never saw her, remember that."

"Yes, Governor."

"You're a good woman, Florence. Now get me Dolin and Shields. Dolin first."

Dolin agreed with Brunner. "I don't see what else we

can do," he said. "This is worse than Watergate, isn't it? I mean, we're caught up in it and can't stop."

"This is the last one, Everett," Brunner said, and hung up.

Shields said, "The crazy little bitch! She can't prove a thing, but it would knock your campaign to hell and gone. Shall I talk to Whitey?"

"Do that, Terry, please. My head is killing me. I'm going home."

"Give my regards to your lovely wife," Shields said.

"I will, Terry, I will."

Brunner went home.

The ferry rose and fell on a gentle swell, and Lillian said, "Ooh, I'm going to be sick."

Ralph said, "Baloney."

She said, "Don't mention food."

The three of them stood at the iron gate at the front of the ferryboat, breasting the wind. The Rabbit was the fourth car in line behind them. It was a blustery spring day, warm rather than chill, and Toby Ferris stood tall, a Viking warrior peering ahead for a first glimpse of Wineland after many months on the wine-dark ocean. Ferris, the swashbuckling adventurer, took pleasure in mixing his historical metaphors. He saluted the Statue of Liberty, girded in scaffolding since it was discovered that the lady was a bit tipsy. He pondered solemnly the Island of Ellis and the dilapidated Jersey waterfront, the promise and shambles of America. "This is the best ride on the Eastern Seaboard," he said. Far ahead through the Narrows, he could see the majestic span of the Verrazano Bridge linking Brooklyn and Staten Island.

Lillian returned to the car to repair the wind damage to her hair.

Toby turned and looked up over the lip of the roof to the pilot's cabin, where he could discern a blurred figure.

147

He said to Ralph, "Wouldn't you give your eyeteeth and a couple of molars to be a ferryboat captain?"

Ralph shrugged. "For one day it would be fun. After that, it would be tedium, back and forth, never going anywhere but South Ferry and Staten Island, back and forth."

Toby said, "You have no imagination. I'd call it The Busted Flush, and Opal and I would live on it, and we'd run it down to Pascagoula in the winter—" Spray hit him in the face, and he said, "Goldarn it, you arranged that, Ralph! Cold water on my fevered dreams."

The boat slid, bumped pilings, glided into the slip, engines reversed, ramp lowered, and a moment later the red Rabbit was on Staten Island, a foreign land to the rest of the city.

Ralph parked in the bank's parking lot, and they trekked up to the law offices of Sylvan Brunner only to learn that he had left for the day. "Sinus headache," the secretary said with a pained look on her face.

Outside, Toby cried, "On to the lair of the beast!"

Lillian said, "I have to go."

Ralph said, "Why didn't you go on the boat?"

"I didn't have to go then."

"I'm sure the Brunners have a powder room," Ralph said.

In the parking lot, Ralph walked to the gray Datsun and said to the driver, "In case you lose us, we're going to Brunner's house."

The man stared straight ahead, grim-faced.

The ranch-style house stood on a grassy knoll, with flowering bushes huddled against it and glimpses of a pool and tennis court beyond. No other house was in sight. The driveway went through a copse of maples before ending in a circle before the front door.

Lillian said, "Money. Mon-*nee.*"

Toby said, "Probably inherited. D.A.'s don't make this kind of cabbage."

"His father's still living," Ralph said.

A uniformed maid led them to an informal playroom with a glass wall overlooking an empty pool and a tennis court, where a man and woman in whites were playing a slam-bang game, he trim and muscular, she his female counterpart.

The maid could be seen talking to the tennis couple. The man disappeared, and the woman strode with springy steps to the glass door in the glass wall and entered. She was handsome rather than pretty, with honey hair, angular face, and the small, close-set eyes that seemed to be the hallmark of the Seven Sisters.

She said, "My husband's not feeling well. May I help you?"

Toby said, "You sure play a mean game of tennis, Mrs. Brunner. It looked like you all were trying to knock the fuzz off the ball."

"We were," she said with a cold smile. "It's his way of relaxing. We don't play a game, we just wham it back and forth. Try it sometime, it's very therapeutic. What can I do for you, Mr. Simmons?"

Toby said, "I'm Ferris. He's Simmons. And that there is Mrs. Simmons. You were expecting us?"

"Not really," she said. "I'm sorry my husband's not able to see you."

Lillian said, "This is such a lovely place. I'll bet it has an exquisite powder room."

The woman glanced at her, then pointed. "It's just down there to your left," she said. "You've come a long way, then?" she said to the two men after Lillian departed.

"Probably a wild-goose chase," Ralph said. "We're

149

looking for a dear friend, and we hoped your husband might help us."

"Someone Sylvan knew in business?"

"Indirectly," Ralph said.

"Through Vito Sammartino," Toby added.

"I see," the woman said. "Tell me about this friend of yours while we're waiting for Mrs. Simmons."

"Have you been to Vito's?"

"A few times. It's not my kind of place."

"Well, you could say that Opal was working with Vito on the Empress of Coney Island matter," Ralph said. "That's Opal Wilder, our friend. She's missing."

"Sorry to hear that," the woman said. "Please sit down for a moment." She gestured toward the sofa, and she sat on the edge of a chair opposite them. "Now, how is the Governor involved?"

Ralph cleared his throat. "That's what we wanted to check out with him. I'll be honest with you, Mrs. Brunner. From what we know, it appears that Mr. Brunner has a secret interest in the gambling casino, and we wanted to talk to him before we went any further. Our information may be all wrong, and we want to nip the false story in the bud, so to speak."

"That's very intelligent of you, but—"

From the hallway, they heard Lillian say, "Oops," then, "You must be Sylvan Brunner! I'm very pleased to meet you. You're taller than I thought."

The two entered the room. Still dressed in his tennis shorts, he came forward with hand outstretched. "I was just coming to say hello when I barged into the dear lady here." He pumped their hands. "Lydia, I know there are things we must do, but I think we have time to offer our visitors a quick drink."

Ralph asked for a little anything on the rocks, Lillian a finger of sherry, and Toby some bubbling club soda. Sylvan Brunner had a double Alka-Seltzer, and his wife a sparkling empty glass.

Brunner heartily assured them that he had nothing to do with the Empress of Coney Island. "My gosh, that would be political suicide. Besides, I just couldn't envision myself doing a thing of that sort. It would go against everything I've dedicated my life to! Good golly!"

He told them with the same openness that if their friend was really in danger they shouldn't waste their time going down blind alleys. He gave it as his guess, however, that Miss Wilder was on some innocent mission and would reappear safe and sound from a visit to her parents in Teaneck. "Or wherever," he said.

Lillian was looking at him wide-eyed. "Where did you get your money?" she asked.

Ralph said, "Lillian!"

"I mean this place," she said. "It must be worth a million dollars. Is that too personal a question to ask, Mr. Brunner?"

Brunner laughed very, very heartily. "My goodness, no," he said. "We got this place years ago when things were much cheaper, and you ought to see the mortgage! My goodness, we can barely make the payments. We bought the place for the kids really, and the ironic thing is, they're both away at school. So Lydia and I are the only ones enjoying it." He laughed at the irony of it.

Lillian said, "How can you afford two at boarding school at the same time? That costs a small fortune."

Brunner put on a serious face. "You're right, Mrs. Simmons. But we've gotten some help from my father over the years. I don't mind saying I owe everything I am, everything I will be, to my father. He's a grand old man. If you want to know about me, go ask him, he'll tell you. I once stole a piece of candy from a candy store, and he made me go back and confess. Then he whaled the tar out of me!"

At some point during the discussion the austere Mrs. Brunner excused herself and left the room. And a short time later the visitors were shown to the door by a very gracious Sylvan Brunner. He even commented favorably on the red Rabbit. "It must make you feel young, Mr. Simmons."

On the street outside the Brunners' driveway, Ralph pulled over to the side and stopped. "What did we learn?" he asked.

"Not a goldarn thing," Toby said.

Lillian said, "We learned at least one goldarn thing. Both of these beautiful people are in it up to their necks, and she doesn't like it. She pulled a big goof. She called Toby Mr. Simmons. She not only was expecting us, she knew our names. She didn't know which was which, of course, but she knew one of us was Simmons. So how'd she know this? Why, from the gentleman in the gray Datsun! Ralph, you told him we were going there, and he phoned ahead. It's like one of those puzzles in a kid's book. All the dots connect."

"Brunner himself pulled a goof too," Ralph said. "He spoke of Opal's parents living in Teaneck. He never heard of Opal Wilder, and yet he knew that her parents lived in Teaneck. He tried to cover up by saying, 'Or wherever.' Does anyone vote that he hit on the name of the town by happenstance?"

Toby said, "I always wanted to use that word—happenstance! It's a lovely word. I'm going to use it in my next column, whether it fits or not."

Ralph said, "Where now?"

Lillian said, "Didn't the man invite us to talk to his father?"

Ralph said, "Since we're on Staten Island, why not?" He handed the road map to Lillian.

152

As Ralph drove on, Lillian said somberly, "We're caught up in something big, aren't we?"

After a long while, Ralph said, "We think we're traveling roads on that map, but I feel that they're threads of a spiderweb so huge that we can't see its outer dimensions, and there are man-eating spiders out there waiting for us. The question is, are we heading into the arms of another spider without knowing it? Or should we go home and lock the doors?"

No one answered, and Ralph drove on.

The man from the New York Fire Department flashed a badge and said to Sonny Sammartino, "Just a routine check."

Sonny made a face and said, "That's all we need."

The Fire Inspector was a small man with an ordinary grayish face. He wore a belt of tools around his waist.

Sonny showed him around to the fire exits; the man tested them and found them adequate. "We don't want one of those disasters here, do we?" he said. "Now show me the electrical system, and I'll take it from there."

Sonny led him to the fuse box in the storage area near the side door. The man took a long time testing one wire after another.

Sonny said, "Look, I have a lot of things to do."

The man said, "Go and do them. I won't be long."

Phones were ringing. Sonny said, "You can go out this door when you're finished." He went away to answer the phones.

Five minutes later, the man left by the side door.

153

15

Compared to Sylvan Brunner's estate, his father's home was a modest, typically middle-class one, a rambling two-story wooden structure set on a one-twenty- by two-hundred-foot lot. Seen from the quiet residential street on which it was located, there was nothing remarkable about it. Only when one was led to the rear of the house and out to the glass-enclosed gallery did one see that the house had a priceless panoramic view of New York Harbor and the glittering towers of Manhattan beyond.

An elderly housekeeper named Hilda, after having them wait on the front porch, returned to guide them through the darkened interior to the brilliance of the gallery. A large telescope, with legs that were permanently anchored to the flooring, commanded the place of honor facing the bay. A tall, heavyset man was perched on a cushioned stool behind it with his eye to the sight. He straightened and swiveled to greet them.

"You caught me indulging in my secret vice," he said in a voice that rumbled like distant thunder. "I'm a Peeping Tom, only there's nothing worth peeping at in those great big chicken coops over there—just businessmen heading toward apoplexy and women tied to electric machines. None as pretty as you, my dear," he said, sliding off the stool and clasping Lillian's hand.

"Now introduce yourselves, if you will. I don't get too many visitors now that I've outlived everybody except Methuselah."

His face was as wrinkled as a bloodhound's, with a long Silly Putty nose, pendant jowls, and an outthrust chin. He was dressed in a long, mustard-colored sweater-jacket with pockets that drooped. "If you're wondering, I'm eighty-four and still have all my own teeth. Here, sit over here where there's some sun. I hope you don't mind the heat. I keep it on all year round even when these glass walls are open. I live here on this porch, and I expect I'll die here, maybe thirty or forty years from now. I love the harbor. I regard it as my harbor. I once had an office in one of those chicken coops, and I was heading toward apoplexy too, but I got out in time.

"And I'm busier than ever, believe it or not. Do you know what keeps me busy? Pollution! That water is dying, and I'm doing my best to bring it back. I've been urging my son to hit pollution, but he says the people who are backing him wouldn't like it. I tell him to hit it anyway, they're not going to desert him to back that other nincompoop. But you know Sylvan. Pigheaded. Stubborn as a donkey. Ach, I guess he gets that from his old man.

"What would you folks like to drink? It's lucky I have a doctor who gives me the advice that I tell him to give me. In Latin, spirits are called *aqua vitae*, the water of life, and I believe it. I wouldn't be here if it weren't for a little schnapps now and then. So my doctor prescribes *aqua vitae*, and I follow his advice like a good boy. What will it be?" He bellowed into the house: "Henry!"

A middle-aged man, dressed like a butler, came from the house and made the drinks while old William Brunner seated the three around a coffee table. The old man remained standing. "I got that uniform for Henry a couple of years ago when an upstart family moved in down the street. I couldn't let them be the only family on the block with a butler, could I? No. So I got Henry a uniform. He's Hilda's son, a most capable chap."

The old man rambled on. His apparent compulsion to talk and the deep joy he seemed to take in doing it bore out the impresssion that he was indeed an old man who had few visitors.

Ralph managed to say, "We just came from seeing your son, Mr. Brunner."

A smile rearranged the wrinkles on the old man's face. "Ah, how is he? I don't see much of him these days, he's so busy running for governor. He'll make a great governor. Naturally, I'm his father, and you expect me to say that, but it's true nonetheless. The only times I see him is when I manufacture some legal business for him to do. But what legal business does a retired man have? A small change in my last will and testament, trouble with the Internal Revenue Service, insurance on the house. I could handle them myself, but they give me an excuse to see my son. How is he, Mr. Simmons?"

"I'd say fit as a fiddle," Ralph said.

"Splendid," the father rumbled. "He has a tendency to work too hard, and then his health suffers. If you're working with him, Mr. Simmons, keep an eye on him and see that he doesn't overdo. You can tell he's had it when he starts squirting that thing up his nose. He thinks he has sinus trouble, but he doesn't, it's just nerves. He's strong as a bull."

Ralph promised to keep an eye on him. "But we really came to ask about his investment in that casino on Coney Island," he said.

"Casino? Casino?"

"The Empress of Coney Island."

"Yes, I've heard of that. And you say Sylvan has an investment in it?"

"We have that impression. Maybe we're wrong."

"I'll have to ask him about it," the old man said vaguely. "For some reason we haven't been close since I turned my other house over to him and I was able to move back here. Handling the purchase was one of the first things he did after he was admitted to the bar. He knew I always loved this place, and when he heard that the owner had an accident he dragged me up here, and we were able to buy it back. I can't tell you how much pleasure that gave me."

Toby said, "Thomas Wolfe wrote that you can't go home again, but it sounds like you did it. You bought it *back*, you say."

"Oh, yes, didn't you know? It's a matter of public record. I first bought this house, let me see, in 1930, I think. It was the start of the Depression, and I had saved my money. Would you believe I paid only six thousand for it? And when I moved in, I sang. My young wife thought I had gone crazy. She was an American girl, and the only songs I knew were German." Suddenly he was singing a German lied in a booming bass voice.

The three visitors sat, stunned.

When he finished, he said, "That's what I sang to my bride, and she had the same look on her face that you have." His laughter rattled the glass panels.

Lillian said, "Do you know 'Bei Mir Bist du Schoen'?"

"The Andrews Sisters?" he said. "I'm afraid I don't."

Ralph said, "If you loved the place so much, why did you sell it? What happened?"

"Good question," the old man said. He went to the stool by the telescope and sat on it. "On December 7, 1941, the authorities found me out. Actually it was several months later. They came to me and said, 'We've uncovered your secret, Mr. Brunner. You're an enemy alien!' "

"An enemy alien!"

"Was it a mistake?" Lillian asked.

The old face crinkled with amusement. "No, it wasn't a mistake, Mrs. Simmons. I was exactly that. The country was at war with Germany, and I was still a German citizen. It was a case of monumental stupidity on my part. You see, I was born in Bavaria, in a small town that's not on your maps. In my teens I was a carpenter, a very good one actually. I turned seventeen in time to see some action on the Western Front before the Armistice put an end to that madness. I took an Allied bullet in the part where I sit down, which wasn't so nice. So I went back to my town, and there was no work. The country had come to a halt, the money was worthless.

"That's when I decided I was an able-bodied seaman. I walked all the way up to Hamburg and signed on a merchant ship, and in the words of your Mr. Dana, I spent two years before the mast. In 1920 we berthed in New York. I took shore leave, and instead of getting drunk and sleeping with a lady of the evening, I walked around the city and was amazed to see all the construction that was going on. I stopped at one site, asked for a job as carpenter, and I was hired on the spot!" He slapped his knee. "No questions asked."

Ralph said, "I think they call that jumping ship."

"Exactly! Well, I went on to other jobs and soon had a business of my own. I always intended to clear up my citizenship—it was just a matter of taking an overnight trip to Toronto, cut through a little red tape, and return as an immigrant—but this dummkopf was too busy to do that. It didn't seem important. I was a successful businessman, I was active in my community, fast becoming a pillar of

158

society, I got married to an American girl, and I bought the house of my dreams."

He peered at them, nodding his head ruefully.

"Sylvan was a long time in coming," he continued. "We wanted a large family. I don't know whose fault it was, my lovely wife's or mine, but for ten years we had no children until we were finally blessed with Sylvan. Then almost immediately the house was taken away from us.

"The authorities were very nice—some of them knew me—but they said, 'It may be only a technicality, Mr. Brunner, but we simply can't permit an enemy alien to reside in a house with such a commanding view of wartime shipping.' The chief of police was particularly saddened because he was a friend of mine, and I had to console *him!* It was a funny situation, if you think about it. So anyway, you asked why I sold it when I loved it so much. It was because a thickheaded German didn't take the time to go on a one-day trip to Canada."

Lillian said, "The publicity must have pained you and your wife very much."

"Not really," the old man said. "There was no publicity. It's all a matter of record, but my friend, the police chief, kept it out of the newspapers. But you're right, it would have been a terrible stigma for my wife and son to bear if it had become known by the neighbors. Ah well, it's ancient history now, isn't it? Sylvan's opponent is smart enough not to bring it up, it would only arouse sympathy for Sylvan, the infant dispossessed by war."

"But you waited more than twenty years to get the house back," Ralph said. "Wouldn't the new owner sell?"

"Ach, talk about pigheaded," the old man said. "I offered him twice what he paid for it, but he said he wouldn't sell for anything in the world. In the long run, the silly fellow outfoxed himself. He had a wooden deck and a wooden railing out here at the time."

159

He stood up and said, "Come here." He stood by the glass wall and pointed down.

They saw for the first time that the house was perched on a sloping cliff about sixty feet high.

"It seems that the gentleman had grown fat and heavy. He leaned on his wooden railing one night, and it broke. He was found down there the next morning with his head bashed in."

Brunner sighed. "A tragedy for him, of course, but an opportunity for me. I bought the house from his widow at a price that was more than it was worth. I felt sorry for the poor woman. It was the first bit of legal business that my son did for me. I was proud."

He moved away from the glass while the three guests continued to stare down into the rubble where once a man with a broken head had lain. When they turned away William Brunner was sitting on his stool, with a forearm resting on the telescope.

"Ships that pass in the night," he said, as if speaking to himself. "The old saying. I look out there at the water and see ships going silently by dark freighters and tankers, the gaily lit pleasure boats unaware that my eyes are spying, and I feel I am an outsider, an enemy alien all over again."

"Yes," Toby said. "That's right."

The man peered at him. "Are you an alien, Mr. Ferris?"

"A born alien, sir. An outsider from birth."

"Then you know what I mean. That man's widow, whose name I can't even think of at the moment—typical, typical—we passed each other, she was the dark freighter and I the pleasure boat because I was getting what I wanted, and then she was gone. I sometimes feel that Sylvan is passing me by in the same way, not intentionally . . . but because the currents are taking him to

Albany and beyond. But I'm beginning to sound maudlin. I see that you're ready for another drink. Henry!"

"Speaking of people who come in and out of one's life," Ralph said, "let me ask you about some of your son's associates. Have you ever come across a labor leader named Terry Shields?"

"Shields, Shields," the man said. "Yes. Yes, many years ago when I had my own construction business. Back in the late thirties. He would come to me every two years, put a gun to my head, and I would sign his contract. Good heavens, he must be in his seventies now. Have you seen him recently? How is he?"

Toby said, "He has a great sense of humor."

"Yes, he always had that. Telling me jokes while he was twisting my arm. I've been away so long."

Ralph said, "How about Everett Dolin?"

"Hah! I hired him!" the man exclaimed. "He was a terribly skinny little man—a boy really—but he had a great head for figures. He was a genius at making estimates. After I set him doing that, we never had a losing contract. Shrewd! A sort of natural shrewdness that few people have. Ah yes, Everett."

Ralph cleared his throat. "Was your company by any chance the Domino Construction Company?"

"It was, Mr. Simmons. But wherever did you come up with that name? I've been out of that company for many, many years. Did Sylvan mention it to you?"

"No, my wife and I had a little talk with Mr. Dolin. He mentioned a man named Kolb. Wasn't that it, honey? Kolb?"

"Walter Kolb," Lillian said.

The old man's face darkened. "I'd prefer not to talk about him. That man was my partner, and when the government forced me to get out of the business—"

"They forced you out of Domino?" Ralph said.

"Yes, didn't I tell you that? We were doing a lot of construction on the waterfront at the time. It was the same thing, Mr. Simmons, as with the house. 'We're sorry, Mr. Brunner, but we simply can't have an enemy alien working in full view of wartime shipping.' So I was forced to sell out to my partner. Didn't I tell you that?"

"I must have missed it," Ralph said.

The old man stood and pointed to an orange building at the tip of Manhattan behind Battery Park. "We had our office in that building, Kolb and I. I told you I had an office over there. Anyhow, the government gave me the heave-ho, and Kolb took over the business. And that was the end of that."

"Didn't you try to get it back after the war?"

"No, you can't put things like that back together again. I could never trust Kolb after that. Besides, I sold it to him, and he paid me money, a fraction of what it was worth. I couldn't very well claim that the sale was made under duress, not when it was Uncle Sam who was applying the pressure. In truth, I had no need to go back. I had tucked away money enough to last me the rest of my life, so I left Kolb in peace. Strange that Everett should mention him."

Ralph said, "Strange that your son would be associated today with people you were associated with generations ago."

"Not so strange. He knew them as a child, and when he became a lawyer, they helped him out by throwing a little business his way. Not that he needed their help. Sylvan was a go-getter long before he broke up the Irish Mafia. But you know all about that, I'm sure."

"Did they ever put the bite on you?"

"Who?"

"The McGovern Gang."

"No, not while I was with the company. Everett may

162

have had some trouble with them, but you'd have to ask Everett about that. It was after my time."

Toby said, "Did Opal Wilder come to see you?"

"Who?"

Ralph smoothly took over. "A friend of ours was doing research on your son—you know, gangbuster, governor and all that. Did a young woman come to see you in the last month or two asking about your son?"

"I don't think so. Henry, did we have a lady visitor?"

"No, sir."

"Then I guess she didn't. Was she good-looking?"

Toby said, "What's that got to do with it?"

The old man smiled sadly. "It's always a pleasure to look at a beautiful young woman, isn't that so?"

"Yes. Yes, of course."

The old man reminisced about his departed wife, after which the conversation flagged, and they rose to leave. He said, "If you see those old acquaintances of mine again, give them my regards, and tell them to come visit me sometime. Will you do that for me?"

They promised they would.

Though they were close to the ferry link to Manhattan, which was a more direct route home, Ralph chose to drive down to the Verrazano Bridge and take the circuitous route that brought them past Coney Island—past the Empress of Coney Island, which could be seen from the parkway—and on up to Savage Point on the North Shore of Long Island.

Lillian said, "I think it's a darn shame."

"What's a darn shame?"

"That that stinker doesn't visit his own father. He lied about how he got the house too, didn't he?"

"Who? The old man?"

"No, the son. And his father's so proud of him, too. What a rat!"

* * *

That night Opal Wilder called.

Toby was sprawled, spread-eagled, on the sofa, as if he had fallen there from a great height, gazing at the ceiling with wild eyes. Ralph was in his chair, last Sunday's crossword puzzle on his lap; he was trying to keep his eyes from closing. Lillian sat in her chair, untended mending in her lap, trying to watch a situation comedy on television, muttering comments which only Lillian Simmons could make. "I don't understand why she keeps falling in the pool. Anybody who's been knocked on the head would have sense enough to stay away from the pool. . . . Look at her blouse! Freshly ironed! Even drip-dry wouldn't dry that fast, for crying out loud!" She didn't expect anybody to listen to her, and nobody did.

They had talked themselves out. The frustrating reality was that they were no closer to finding Opal, and there was no next step for them to take. Toby had paced. Ralph had taken him for a walk, and Toby had pranced around him like a high-strung dog. Finally the distraught lover had sunk into a despairing lethargy, accompanied by sighs and moans.

The phone rang at twenty to nine. Ralph clambered to his feet and answered it.

"Hello, Ralph? This is Opal. Opal Wilder. I hope I'm not interrupting anything." Her voice seemed to fold in on itself as if it were coming through a tunnel.

"Opal, for God's sake! The only thing you're interrupting is your own wake. We've been looking for you. Are you all right?"

"Fine, Ralph," she said distractedly. "Listen, I don't have much time. I've been trying to get in touch with Toby Ferris. I called his number in Mississippi, but his landlady said he was up here looking for me. Listen, if you see him, tell him to stay—"

164

"Tell him yourself. He's climbing all over me trying to grab the phone—"

"He's there?"

Ralph was amazed at the many emotions he heard in those two words—astonishment, disbelief, delight, relief, among others too overlapping to sort out.

"Before I put him on," he said, "please understand that there may be a cockroach in the wire."

"A bug?"

"I don't know for sure, but I think it would be wise to assume there was. Now the next voice you hear will be that of your friend and mine, the eminent—"

Toby had the phone. He said, "Hey, Opal." The voice was small and muffled. He cleared his throat.

She said, "Oh, Toby, Toby, you darn fool! So you came up." There was a catch in her voice, and he pictured her shaking her head at his idiocy.

"Couldn't help it, had to, wanted to be with you, and all that."

"Listen, Toby. I want you to get on the next plane and go right on back to Mississippi." Her voice was firm. "Do you hear? I want you to get away from here. I'll write you when it's safe to come back."

"I can't do that, honey."

"Why not, damn it?"

"I drove up."

"Oh, for pity sake, so drive back! Just go back! I don't want anything happening to you."

"I don't want anything happening to you either, goldarn it. We're in this together."

"No, we're not! I'm the one in a jam, and you're out of it. I want to keep it that way, darling."

Toby said, "We have to get together. Where are you?"

Ralph shouted, "Don't answer that!"

Opal said, "Ralph's right. If we meet, we'll both be

165

caught. I couldn't stand it if you got hurt because of me."

Toby said, "Horsefeathers! We're going to meet, and that's that."

"Oh, Toby . . ."

He said, "I feel like a chili dog. How about you?"

"Oh, for heaven's sake, Toby! No, I don't feel like a chili dog. I'm calling from a pay phone—"

"Remember when you and Ralph and I used to have lunch together?"

"Oh, for God's sake, Toby—"

"There was a place we called the Chili Dog. Are you being followed?"

"God, I hope not!"

Toby looked at his watch. "I can be at the Chili Dog in three-quarters of an hour. How long would it take you?"

"You mean—"

"Why not? I'll shake my tail and see you at twenty to ten. I know a few sneaky tricks from my childhood."

"Oh, God, I'd love it! Are you sure?"

"Certainly. I'm the damned elusive Pimpernel, didn't you know that?"

"Make it ten," she said, and hung up.

After a minute, he turned to Ralph and said, "Do you have any thoughts on . . . how to shake a tail?"

16

Toby Ferris drove into the city in his landlady's Chevy. Ralph had wanted him to take the Rabbit, but Toby said it was too easy to follow: "It's a sore thumb on wheels." Yet he tried no evasive tactics on the Long Island Expressway, knowing that his vehicle was too ancient and so was his driver's license, which had expired some twenty years earlier. In Pascagoula he rode a bicycle, and he didn't need a license for that.

As he rattled toward the Midtown Tunnel, the anger rose in him like lava. He could see the gray Subaru in the rearview mirror. *That hyena expects me to lead him to Opal just like that, so they can kill her! He thinks I'm a dumb old country boy who rightly belongs in a home for the retarded!* Ralph hadn't been much help. One of his suggestions was broken-field running through the crowd at Times Square. But one doesn't run through Times Square unless one has just mugged a tourist.

Toby slammed the steering wheel with his fist, accidentally honking and getting a drop-dead glare from the driver ahead of him. Toby's lips formed a sneer. *Okay, no more Mr. Peaceable Rube! I'm the Wily Avenger leading the evil one to his own doom!* Then he thought: *I only hope it's the little shitepoke and not one of those burly bastards.*

167

Since Whitehead had branded him a drunkard, he decided to play the role for the sake of his pursuer. Making sure there were no cops' cars in sight, he swayed out of his lane several times. He slowed to fifteen, then jackrabbited ahead. On the Manhattan side of the tunnel, he turned uptown and found a parking garage on Thirty-eighth Street. He walked back toward the East River, not exactly staggering . . . but not walking in a straight line either. He remembered the area from his long sojourn in the city. Forty-second Street was the line of demarcation between the bustle of the neighborhood bordering the United Nations, above, and the section of warehouses and the Con Ed power station, below. At nine-thirty in the evening, the lower area was quite deserted.

He made it to Forty-second Street, turned right toward the river, passed the Ford Foundation building, which he considered the only civilized building in the city, walked under Tudor City Place past the Secretariat Building to the street bordering FDR Drive. He glanced back just once and said, Cripes, it's one of the big ones!

He rounded the corner and rested against the great wall that supported the Tudor City complex. No one was in sight. He moved farther along the wall deeper into the shadows. The big man strolled to the well-lit corner, glanced casually toward Toby. Toby slid to a sitting position, then fell sideways on the pavement. The man didn't appear to be interested. He studied the Secretariat Building for a while, then looked again toward Toby, who was now twitching. The man studied the U.N. building some more, then apparently decided to get a closer look at his stricken quarry. He sauntered toward Toby, who now with great effort was struggling to get to his feet with the help of the wall.

Having committed himself, the man continued his stroll

toward Forty-first Street, covertly watching the floundering drunk. A lurch took Toby closer. He spun and rammed his fist in the man's stomach. "Oof," the man said, and that exhausted the breath that was in him. Toby straightened him up and smashed a right to the jaw. The man, bent over, tried to scurry toward Forty-first Street. The pain in Toby's fist shot up his arm and exploded in his brain. The son-of-a-bitching gorilla had a concrete jaw! And when the said gorilla regained his breath, he was going to be more than Toby could handle.

Toby ran.

He flashed across Forty-second Street dodging cars, disappeared momentarily in the sliver of a park named after Ralph Bunche, then bounded up the stone staircase leading up to the dead end of Forty-third Street. At the top landing, he glanced back and saw the big man at the far corner of Forty-second Street, looking around frantically. Toby leaped up the remaining steps, walked swiftly west in a half-trot toward Grand Central Station, three blocks away.

He rushed across the great concourse of the terminal and went out the Vanderbilt Avenue exit. Panting, he rested against a pillar for a minute, and when his pursuer didn't appear, he proceeded north to his rendezvous at the Chihuahua, singing in his heart. He was going to see Opal!

He was early. Like many less-than-grand New York restaurants, the Mexican one was long and narrow with double booths on one side and single ones on the other. The plate-glass window facing the street was grimy. He jigged nervously, debating whether he should remain outside. The place was half-empty, too late for the dinner crowd, too early for the after-theater bunch.

He went in and sat in one of the single booths facing the entryway. Though his heart sang, his gut twitched

169

with anxiety. Downing food was an impossibility. He ordered a glass of ice water. He looked at his watch every thirty seconds. He tried to compose an appropriately lyrical greeting for his loved one. His mind was blank. He tried to compose a humorous one. His mind said it was no time for comedy.

The second hand inched past ten o'clock, took a week to cover the next minute—and then she was there. Standing uncertainly inside the door, taller than he remembered, hatless, hair much darker than her natural light-brown, long face, large eyes peering timidly about, large mouth without lipstick, dark-green jacket over green plaid skirt, legs heavier than he remembered, low-heeled brown shoes.

He stood up. She came and stood a pace away, facing him. She tilted her head in the quizzical way that he had always found endearing.

What he said was: "You've cut your hair."

She said, "I run my fingers through it, and it's combed. Convenient."

"It looks good that way."

"Do you feel like a chili dog?"

"No."

"Let's get out of here."

"Good idea." He put a five-dollar bill on the table.

"A one will do," she said.

He said, "That's all right. It was good water."

With shy courtesy, he let her precede him out the door. On the sidewalk, his hand found hers. They walked slowly toward Seventh Avenue. The wind from the northwest kicked up dust. They walked through the garbage smell from the refuse of other restaurants.

"Lovely night," he said.

"Superb."

"I've never been to a hotel in midtown," he said.

"Let's not. I wouldn't feel right."

"We don't seem to have many choices."

She said, "I still have the key to the apartment."

He stopped walking. "I saw her, you know."

"I didn't know that." She put her arm in his. "Okay, how about the Helmsley Palace?"

"I think I'd rather go to the apartment. Are you sure it hasn't been re-rented?"

"The rent's been paid for another month. And the subway's right over there."

He raised his hand. Taxi drivers had never stopped for him before. This time the cab stopped. "It's a magical night," he said.

Below Thirty-fourth Street the cab was able to make good time through sparser traffic. She said, "I went by the apartment to see if anyone was still watching. There didn't seem to be."

He said, "I'll kill them! I'll tear them apart with my bare hands!"

"Is that how you got rid of the one who was following you?"

"Yes." He held up his right hand. "I think I broke it."

She kissed it.

On the sidewalk in front of the apartment, Toby said, "How about the mean-tempered super? How do we get around him?"

"He won't be there. He's the laziest man on earth."

"I'll tear him limb from limb. I'll murder the bum."

"Who are you now?"

"Bert Lahr, the Cowardly Lion."

"Oh."

The lobby was deserted. The mail was gone from the table.

"I picked it up yesterday," she said.

Going up in the elevator, he said, "You read my letters."

"Yes."

171

After a pause, he said, "What did you think?"

She kissed him hard.

On the third floor, Opal opened the door to apartment 3H. She flicked on the light and sighed, "Oh, dear."

"What?"

"Blossom's furniture. I'm going to have to do something about it."

Toby entered fearfully. It looked blessedly homey. No sense of the presence of an outraged spirit or a grieving ghost. He relaxed. "Thank you, Miss McNeeley ma'am," he said.

Opal said, "She was a wonderful woman. I loved her. I know she would approve."

"Of what?"

"Us."

"Thank God for that."

She said, "The refrigerator is still on, but I'm afraid all I can offer you is some ice water."

"That's my beverage of choice in the finest restaurants. I've been terribly worried about you." He shyly embraced her.

"Me too," she said.

He said, "Isn't it warm in here?"

"Sweltering," she said.

She took him by the hand to the room that had been hers.

He said, "I've thought about undressing you. Is that all right?"

A minute later they stood facing each other, grinning self-consciously.

She said, "I never knew you were so strong. You have the long muscles of a swimmer."

"You have pretty good-looking muscles yourself."

She sat on the side of her bed. He sat beside her.

He said, "I now pronounce us man and wife. Who has the ring?"

She said, "Let's not get serious."

He said, "Of course not."

She suddenly tickled him in the ribs. He leaped on her in retaliation, and that was the start of that.

Quite a few minutes later, he toasted her with a glass of ice water. He lay back against the headboard and said, "Tell me about it."

She let out a long, shuddering sigh. "Get dressed," she said.

"I'm comfortable this way."

"I am too," she said, and kissed him on the stomach. Then she sat up. "It's the way I've been living, Toby. I've had to be dressed and ready to run."

When they were dressed, she said, "Don't look so sulky. It's the way it has to be."

He said, "I have Mrs. Plotnik's car. Let's head south."

She touched his cheek. "I'd love to, but I can't."

"Why not?"

She moved nervously about the room. "I just can't. I'd be running away from Blossom. The murderers are here, not in Mississippi."

"Was she murdered?"

"I'd call it that."

"Sit down, you're making me dizzy." He took her hands and sat her on her vanity chair. "Start at the beginning. You were introduced to the accountant lady by your agent."

"You've been busy," she said. "Yes, Sanders introduced me to Sarah. She was a strange little woman, all wound up and ready to snap. She told me she was working for the owner of a disco—"

"Sammartino."

"Yes, and that Sammartino, in addition to running his disco, was a fixer, a doctor of deals. He was a go-between, a real payoff artist. Smooth. You should hear some of the tapes.

"He secretly taped everything that went on; that's what started the trouble. He had been doing it for years, just to cover himself in case someone's recollection faltered. For instance, he might deliver five thousand dollars to a state assemblyman. Then if the assemblyman claimed he never received the money, Vito could play the tape as proof of delivery."

"Is that what happened?"

"Yes, this poor greedy assemblyman from upstate did just that. Sammartino played his tape, and not long after that the poor sap had a skiing accident, broke both his legs."

"But now Sammartino's principals knew about the tape."

"Who's telling this, you or me?"

"You are, sweetie. Who were his principals?"

"Suppose you tell me."

"No need to get huffy. Just trying to help out."

"Who?" she insisted.

"Well, the way I hear it, there was the contractor, Everett Something-or-other—"

"Dolin."

"There was the jolly labor leader, Terry Shields, and Mr. Integrity himself, Sylvan Brunner. Is that the lot?"

"Maybe," she said. "I have an idea there's a fourth person in on the deal, but I haven't been able to find out who. Anyway, they demanded that Sammartino hand over the tapes to them. Somehow he managed to put them off for a few days, but he wasn't about to let go of them. He was frightened, and he felt that as long as he hung on to the tapes they wouldn't dare kill him. They were his life insurance policy. He gave them to Sarah Goode for safekeeping, luckily just before the burglary at the disco."

"I follow you so far," Toby said. "But why did Sarah

need a writer? All she was supposed to do was sit on them, isn't that so? Why did she need you?"

Opal made a face. "One shouldn't speak ill of the dead, should one?" she said. "There were thirty-seven tapes, and all sorts of other documents and notes. If you've ever heard tapes of people talking, you know how fragmentary the information is, all out of sequence and covered over with inconsequential asides. Sarah Goode said she wanted me to transcribe the tapes and pull the story together in understandable order, so that if she ever had to take them to the police, for instance, she would have this forceful presentation of all the crimes committed, something like that."

"But you didn't believe her."

"We-ell, I don't know. I think she had in mind writing a book that would be one of the biggest exposés of corruption in the city's history. It would hit the bookstores at the same time that the principals were being prosecuted, and she'd make a million dollars."

"There's another possibility."

"What's that?"

"Blackmail."

Opal nodded. "I thought of that. But I don't think she was that greedily stupid. You don't blackmail people like that and live to a ripe old age."

"Okay, so she handed all this stuff over to you to make sense out of it."

"Yes, but the night she was murdered—"

"You're sure it was murder?"

"No doubt about it. I talked to her on the phone. She said a man named Whitehead was coming—"

"Good old Lawrence Whitehead."

"You know him?"

"Intimately," Toby said.

Opal frowned. "Anyway, she said she was sure he was

175

coming for the tapes and that he knew about me. She told me to get out of the apartment with them and to call her in the morning to see if it was safe to go back. When I called in the morning, a policeman answered."

Toby reached over and squeezed her hand. "God, that must have been awful."

"I'm okay," she assured him. "So I rented a room in the West Village, but I couldn't stay still, I couldn't think straight. I was frantic. I was worried about Blossom. If they came looking for me—she didn't know where I was, but if she told them that, they wouldn't believe her. So I called her at the bookstore, and she said, pish-tush, I was making a big deal out of nothing. I begged her not to go home, but she wouldn't hear of it. She said a woman's home was her castle, and she would pull up the drawbridge. I didn't know what to do."

"Why didn't you go to the police?"

She sighed deeply. "I knew by this time, from the afternoon paper, that it was called a double suicide. I couldn't go to the police and say that the same man who committed the double suicide was now after me and I was afraid for the safety of my roommate."

"You should have gone anyway."

"You say this?" she said in an incredulous tone. "You who believe the police are your enemies?"

"That goes for me, not you," he growled.

"The double standard strikes again," she said. "Anyway, I couldn't stay away. I left all my things at the rooming house and went back to Blossom's apartment. That was about ten o'clock at night." Opal shook her head, and there were tears in her eyes.

"The poor old dear believed in the innate goodness of men. 'Nobody will touch a hair on this old gray head,' she maintained. So we had some tea. And then came the knock on the door."

Toby went into the kitchen and returned with two glasses of ice water. "Here," he said. "It's a good year. You'll be amused by its special tang, not to mention the little crawly things swimming in it."

She grimaced and drank. Then she continued her story.

"Blossom and I sat looking at each other, not moving. After the second knock, we heard little metallic scratchings at the door. I went to the phone and said I was going to call 911. She said, 'No, you go out the window, I'll do that, it's you they're after, not me.' So I went out her bedroom window to the fire escape." With a snarl of self-contempt, she said, "I abandoned her."

"Hogwash," Toby said. "If you'd stayed, there'd have been two murders."

"That's what I keep telling myself, but if I hadn't come to live with her, she'd still be happily puttering around her bookshop and serving tea to her old friends. It's a—it's a terrible burden, Toby."

"You're blaming yourself instead of the murderer. It doesn't make sense."

Opal took a deep breath and let it out. "Anyway, it's done. I went up the fire escape to the roof with the idea of going across the roof and down the staircase. The stinking door to the stairs was locked! There were other fire escapes, but I chose to go back down this one. I wanted to make sure Blossom was all right. At the third floor, I looked in Blossom's window. There—there she was. Flat on the floor. The man was sitting on her. A two-hundred-pounder, and he was sitting on her stomach and smiling. I'll never forget it. If you've ever seen films of lions eating their prey with that happy, *intimate* concentration, that was this smiling beast."

"The white-haired one?"

"Yes. It took me a moment to see what he was doing. It was an ordinary pair of pliers clamped on one of her fin-

177

gers. He was saying, 'Just tell me where she is, Grandma.' His other hand was on her throat, ready to cut off any scream. 'It's your own fault, dear lady,' he said, and he gave the pliers a sudden twist. Blossom started to scream, his hand cut it off, and then she went limp.

"I banged on the window and screamed, 'Here I am, leave her alone!' "

"He saw me and sprang toward me. 'Wait,' he said. I clanged down those stairs, letting gravity do most of the work—I felt I was *floating* down—it's a wonder I didn't go sprawling and break my neck. Oh, God, he was fast, too. But he tripped and cracked his head on the railing. He must have stunned himself, because I hit the sidewalk and raced around the corner and ran until I collapsed and ran some more, and he never followed me. I thought I had saved Blossom, but she must have died when he twisted the pliers and she went limp. I hope that's when she died, because I couldn't bear—"

"She must have. You saw it. She went quickly and was out of pain. Then Whitehead went back and arranged things to make it look like a natural death. He's a clever bastard, and I thought no one could beat him. But you did it, Opal, you did it."

"Great," she said. "Did you hear that, Blossom? I beat the man who tortured you to death."

Toby said to the ceiling, "She acted heroically, ma'am. I'm so goldarn proud of her I'm about to explode. And I don't mind telling you I'm ridiculously in love with her, and I'm wondering, I'm hoping she can stand looking at this—this clown's face. . . ."

She came to him and touched his cheek. "It's a dear face," she said. "It looks lived in—"

"Sure, by hoboes who found the door open and wandered in."

"A caring face—"

178

"I'll get a nose transplant."

"Don't you dare! It's my welcome light. . . ."

He kissed her fiercely, and soon they were lying on the bed, fully clothed, embracing. "Must we stay clothed?" he said.

She said, "In Siberia, they do it with their clothes on."

"You're kidding."

"I don't know about the Siberians, but it can be done."

"Show me," he said.

And she did.

"Strange," he said. "Very strange."

They fell asleep, locked in an embrace.

A half hour later, the discomfort of the position woke him up. He stirred, and she sat upright. "It's only me," he said. "I think I better call Ralph."

She said, "It's one o'clock."

"He'll be awake," Toby assured her.

"How about the bug?"

"I won't say where we are. I'll just tell him we're okay. If I don't, he won't sleep a wink all night."

Lillian answered the phone.

Toby said, "Just tell him we're together, and we're safe."

Then he hung up.

"Son of a gun," he murmured to Opal, "he was asleep."

Opal was too.

So was Tony Lukats, curled uncomfortably on a canvas chair in the back of the gray van parked half a block away. He was not temperamentally suited to long, fruitless vigils. The tap had been on the phone in apartment 3H for more than a month, and except for the flurry of activity when the police found the body, there hadn't been a peep from the apartment. So Tony caught himself a little shut-eye. The telephone recorder murmured softly for about a half minute, not loud enough or long enough to awaken him, and went silent. But it had Toby's words in its memory bank.

At one o'clock, Vito's was going full blast. The disco beat pounded relentlessly on the hides of a near-capacity crowd of minor celebrities, almost beautiful people, and other nobodies, and the strobe lights slashed at their eyeballs, making them glint wickedly. They stomped, quivered, and jerked their spastic dances and felt that they were alluring; and to their partners, they were.

Gina Sammartino wore her mask of gaiety as she roamed through the dancers, dodging outflung elbows, greeting many customers by name. She wore her see-through blouse, knowing it was out of fashion, knowing too, however, that she had the best pair of knockers in the room and that they were good for business. Few men could keep their eyes away, particularly the older ones. "When you've got it, flaunt it" was somebody's motto from years ago, and Gina adopted it in an attempt to keep the business going.

A tall, dark-haired sport stood against the wall beyond the last table. He appeared to be a with-it character, garbed in a white silk shirt open at the neck and revealing a heavy gold medallion; he also had the required tinted eyeglasses and blow-dried hair—a handsome enough dude, yet apparently a loner.

Gina went to him, her handsome chest only an inch from his shirt. "Hello, big boy," she said. "Are you alone?"

He said in a low voice, "Sylvan Brunner sent me. Where can we talk?"

She grinned. "I knew he would see things my way. Let's go upstairs."

He mirrored her grin. "Good try, dear lady," he said.

"But the Governor wouldn't want this to go on tape. Let's go out here."

She shrugged. "Whatever you say."

They went out the side door behind a heavy drape to the delivery and storage area. He came to a halt near the fuse box, the door of which was unlatched.

She said, "I have a feeling we've met. Were you here with the Governor?"

"I'm afraid I haven't had the pleasure," he said. "He told me to give you what you deserve—within reason. He thinks twenty-five percent is too much. What's the figure you really had in mind?"

"I'm not bargaining," she said. "It was my husband's deal as much as anybody's."

"So you're sticking to your demand?"

"Only what's coming to me, no more," she said firmly.

He glanced at the fuse box. "Goodness gracious, this shouldn't be open." He reached up and opened it all the way.

She noticed idly that he was wearing gloves.

"Oh, my," he said. "That splicing doesn't appear to be insulated. Someone's been careless. Hold the door open, and I'll see what I can do."

She held the door open, even though it didn't seem necessary.

He pulled the raw coupling out of the box. He held the insulated part of the wire.

"Here, give me your other hand," he said.

She raised her hand uncertainly.

"Now hold this for a moment," he said.

His tone was so offhandedly commanding that she advanced her hand. Then she said, "No!"

He placed the open splicing in her palm and closed her fingers on it. Her body stiffened convulsively. There was a

181

sputtering, a curl of smoke, and the odor of burned flesh. And the lights went out.

The music stopped, and after a moment of dead silence the only sounds that came from the main dance area were human sounds and the scraping of chairs on the floor. There were some gasps, some startled laughs, a shout of "Right on!," frightened whimperings, then shouts for "Lights!"

In the delivery area, the only light was the weirdly shimmering glow that bathed the figure of Gina Sammartino.

Lawrence Whitehead murmured, "Only what's coming to you, dear lady." He went out the side door that led to the street. He pursed his lips and whistled soundlessly.

Sonny Sammartino handled the crisis well. The sudden blackout and the succeeding moment of crashing silence caught him in the corner of the room near a small vacant bandstand. He groped his way to it and stepped up. The dancers, trying to make their way back to their tables, were jostling and shoving other dancers amid some screams and curses of women being roughly molested by unseen hands and men giving way to panic. Sonny tried the microphone, knowing it was dead, hoping it wasn't.

He shouted, "Hold it!" But his voice was lost in the rising tide of hysteria. He shouted again, muffled by the blanket of blackness. From the sound he knew that a woman had fallen and was being trampled. He groped for the kettledrum, found it, grabbed the sticks, and beat out a fanfare such as one hears at a circus prior to the death-defying, three-and-a-half-turn leap on the flying trapeze. As a teenager he had played in a high-school rock band.

Gradually the turmoil quieted.

He laughed loudly, theatrically. "Where was Moses when the lights went out?" he cried. A few people tittered.

182

"He was at Vito's! Having a good time! Let's keep it that way! ... Now, we're going to have a torchlight parade! If Con Edison won't give us light, we'll make our own! You with matches, take them out of your pockets and light them. Scratch that match! You with lighters, get them out and flick them. Flick your Bic! Hold them high! Scratch your match, flick your Bic, that's the way! Great! Now move slowly—help that woman up . . ."

Within a minute, the bulk of the crowd was off the floor and at their tables.

"We seem to have lost our electricity, folks, but we're working to get it back on. Those who want to leave, feel free to do so. Forget the check, it's on us! God, what am I saying? The rest of you, just sit still. Do what you usually do in the dark. Whoa, not that, feller! Just flick your Bic, okay?"

He stepped off the stand and made his way to the side door, taking his elderly headwaiter with him. "Where's Mom?" he asked.

The waiter said he didn't know.

Holding a lighter in front of him, Sonny led the way into the delivery area and saw the strange transfiguration at the fuse box.

"Momma!" he cried. "Momma, what are you doing?"

He rushed to her, reached out his hands to grasp her, but the headwaiter pulled him back.

"Momma, let go!" Sonny cried.

The older man took off his belt, managed to get it around the woman, and pulled her away from the death grip of the fuse box.

The body slumped to the floor, and Sonny knelt by her.

His cry of "Momma!" was heard throughout the disco, and people felt an icy chill go through them. Most of them decided it was time to go home.

183

17

Toby Ferris woke up two more times that night. The first time, in the darkness, he stirred, and Opal Wilder was instantly awake beside him. He said, "Hey, Opal," and put his arms around her.

She said, "Hey, yourself," and snuggled against him.

Not fully awake, he realized what had been disturbing his sleep. He said, "In the morning we're going straight to the police. No more playing Run Rabbit Run."

Half-asleep herself, she said, "I did go to the police. Weeks ago. I walked into the police station and told the man behind the desk that I had evidence Sylvan Brunner was mixed up in a vast scheme of corruption. 'We know all about it,' he said. 'Him and Jimmy Hoffa and the Pope. We got our eye on them, ma'am, so don't worry.' I said a few demented things and got out of there. I realized the great District Attorney of Staten Island was like a god to the police."

"Former District Attorney."

"And next governor. They weren't going to believe a word I said. So I decided to do it Sarah's way. Then maybe they'd believe."

Toby wasn't satisfied, but he let it go.

The second time he woke up was at the first light of dawn. Ten to six. He was in bed and his loved one was beside him, but an almost painful restlessness forced him to slip out and go to the kitchen for more ice water. He splashed some on his face. He wandered into Blossom McNeely's room. His sense that something was wrong intensified. He went to the window and looked out. The sky was overcast. He looked down at the street through the open fire escape. Here was where Opal had crouched and witnessed a murder.

He peered down the street. A group of four men stood on the sidewalk alongside a gray van. They were the only people in sight. They started walking toward the apartment building. He recognized one of his pursuers, the skinny one. And he recognized the tall blond one.

He went back to Opal's room and touched her shoulder. "They're here," he said.

She leaped up, fully dressed. "How many?"

"Four. The fire escape's out."

"Oh, Toby," she wailed. "I'm sorry I got you into this."

"Time's awasting. Let's go."

"Oh, God, where? They'll block off all the exits."

"We can't stay here." He propelled her toward the door. "The stairs," he said.

"If we go to the roof, we'll be trapped."

"So we won't go to the roof."

They raced down the cement staircase, hand in hand, and stopped inside the exit to the lobby. "It's locked on the other side," she whispered.

They waited in the semidarkness.

Toby said, "It'll take them a minute to get through the outer door. They'll leave a man outside as backup. The others will go in the elevator to the third floor, and it'll take them a minute to get into the apartment and see that we're not there. Then what?"

"They'll go to the roof," Opal said. "They'll check all the fire escapes. Then they'll try these stairs."

"Maybe they'll head for the stairs first thing."

As if in confirmation of his speculation, the doorknob turned. They held their breaths. Toby gathered himself to spring. They heard scratching on the metal. Then a voice said, "Never mind that now. Let's go up. They won't get by Tony."

They heard the elevator open and then shut. "Thank God, it's slow," Toby said.

He edged the door open and peered out. The lobby was empty. The portion of the outer lobby he could see was also empty. "He's out on the sidewalk," he muttered. He took Opal's hand. It was cold and wet. They sidled along the wall to the superintendent's apartment. He put his thumb on the buzzer beside the door and held it there. They could hear it through the door, an irritating sound designed to pierce the ears of a sleeper. Toby's muscles twitched, his breath came in sobs.

"The son of a bitch is a sound sleeper," he muttered.

"His one talent," Opal said.

Finally the door opened a crack. Toby rammed it, and the two of them rushed past the sleep-sodden super.

"Immigration's after us," Toby said. "Close the door."

The man reflexively closed the door. Then he said, "*Wai-it!* No immigration after you!"

Toby flashed what he hoped was a winning smile at the short, powerfully built man in disarrayed pajamas. "Forgive me, Mr. Santiago, I just said that to make you close the door quickly. There are killers out there, four of them."

Anger won out over curiosity in the man. "Do you know what time it is?" he said.

"Yes. Yes, I do, Mr. Santiago. But the killers are the ones who set the time, not us. When they arrive, we run away, no matter what time—"

"So run away," the man said, putting his hand on the knob preparatory to opening the door. "You have my permission. Run away."

Opal put her hand on his arm. "You don't understand, Mr. Santiago," she said. "They're here to kill *me*. If I go out there, I'll be killed."

The man studied her for a moment, then dropped his hand. "No joke?"

"No joke."

He became aware of how he was dressed. He pulled up his pajama bottoms and led them into his sitting room. "Sit. I be right back." It was a cozy enough room, with a large, vividly colored picture of Christ—with flaming Sacred Heart exposed—hanging over a false fireplace, votive candles on the mantel beneath it.

Looking at the picture, Toby said softly, "What we need is a miracle."

Santiago was back, clothed in a bathrobe. His hair was combed. "Hokay, who these men, Miss Wilder?"

She thought for a moment. When Toby started to answer, she stopped him.

"They're Nazis," she said. "They don't call themselves that, but that's what they are. They're out to take over this country."

"Holy Virgin! Here? Land of liberty?"

Opal nodded. "I have proof of their plot, and they want to get it back. They plan to rape me and then kill me."

"Santa Maria!"

"I know who their leader is, but it's not safe to tell you. They might kill you too."

The man glared at her. "Who?" he demanded.

She said, "The man who's running for governor. Sylvan Brunner."

Santiago slapped his hands together. "I knew it!" he cried. "Any man that good has to be bad!"

He went to the phone. "We call the police."

"No," Opal said. "Some of the police are in on it."

Santiago nodded knowingly. "The police!" he said.

187

"They'll be coming here, Mr. Santiago," Toby said, standing up. "When they don't find us upstairs they'll want to ask you questions. Is there a place to hide?"

The man thought a moment, then beckoned them into his bedroom.

Lawrence Whitehead was bleary-eyed from lack of sleep and from the cocaine he had taken in celebration when he had arrived home. His questioning of Santiago was not as acute as it would have been ordinarily. Santiago insisted, "She not here." And Whitehead believed him, because the nosy neighbor in 3G had told him the same thing. No one had entered apartment 3H, she told him.

Still, Whitehead insisted on giving Santiago's apartment a cursory search, and Santiago retreated before him, demanding that he not disturb his pregnant wife. "Due next week," the super said. "She have bad night, finally go to sleep. No wake her, please."

Whitehead pushed into the bedroom, glanced contemptuously at the figure almost buried in blankets. Only the dark head of hair showed on the pillow above the blankets. It was obviously not the Wilder woman, who had light-brown hair. He poked in the closet and retreated. The bulk of the woman under the blanket was unbelievable.

"From the look of her," he said to Santiago, "she's ready to have quintuplets."

"Yes, she get very big," Santiago agreed. "And she like pillows under cover with her. You know how women are." He shook his head at the strangeness of females.

After Whitehead left, Santiago shook his fist at the closed door and said, "Nazi!"

Toby was red-faced and gasping when Santiago pulled down the covers. "I goldarn near suffocated," he said.

Opal was too limp from the release of tension to laugh.

They waited an hour before deciding it was safe to move. One man would be left in the van to keep watch, they surmised, and the others would have gone away. They still couldn't go out the front door or use the fire escape without being observed. Santiago urged them to remain with him until dark, but Toby and Opal thought they should get far away from the building while they had the chance. Finally the super led them through the basement and out an exit to the avenue around the corner.

Opal said, "Mr. Santiago, I've done you an injustice. I owe you my life." And she kissed him.

Santiago scowled in embarrassment. "My wife die in childbirth many years ago. I think of her now." He retreated into the building.

Toby and Opal walked hand-in-hand to the subway. There she insisted on going off alone in the direction of Brooklyn.

"I'm almost finished," she said. "It won't be long."

He said, "Call your mother. Tell her I'm in love with her."

She looked at him, her head to one side with the quizzical look, and he nearly melted into the sidewalk.

He watched her go down the subway steps, thoroughly rumpled and yet so goldarn beautiful.

Twenty minutes later he ransomed the Chevy from the parking garage on Thirty-eighth with the last money he had on him. He headed for the Queensboro Bridge because he didn't have enough coins to pay the tunnel toll. Looking back, he saw that he had reacquired his tail. He wondered if it was the man he had slugged the night before.

At the Queens end of the bridge, he found that he was lost in Long Island City. The Subaru followed.

The man in the Subaru said into the phone, "He just went down a dead-end street. I could pull him over if you want."

Whitehead lay in bed with his eyes closed. "Not now, Mac. We'll have our little chat with him later."

"Well, damn it, let me lead him out of here! We'll be here all day."

"Just hang in there. It'll be all over tonight, I promise you."

Whitehead hung up and tried to go to sleep. The smell of burning flesh was in his nostrils. Nothing like this had ever happened before. He slept fitfully.

Toby drove up Steinway Street. The Subaru, instead of hanging back, was right behind him. Toby saw an overpass ahead and the Subaru signaling a right turn. Toby made the turn and a few blocks later made a left—at a signal from the trailing car. He found himself on Grand Central Parkway near La Guardia Airport, and he knew where he was. He waved to the man in the Subaru, and the man waved back.

Sonny Sammartino was not handling his mother's death well. He had lost both parents within a space of five weeks. He screamed at the Emergency Medical Technician who came in the ambulance. "She was murdered!" He screamed at the policeman. "She was murdered, I tell you!" He screamed at the Medical Examiner.

The Medical Examiner released his lapels from Sonny's clutches. He said coldly, "She was electrocuted, that's all I know."

The policeman said patiently, "According to your own story, she was holding the exposed wire and the door to the fuse box. Do you have any idea why she would do that?"

"She didn't do it!" Sonny said. "She doesn't know electricity; she'd never go near that box!"

"It looks like that's what she did," the policeman said. "I'm sorry."

The second policeman said, "Were you having any trouble with the lights?"

"No, they were working perfectly!"

The second policeman sighed. "That's what comes from not knowing anything about electricity. It's a bad situation, feller."

The headwaiter took Sonny home in a cab. He reminded Sonny that he was an old friend of the family and he would take care of arrangements. He gave Sonny a sleeping pill and put him to bed. Sonny was almost catatonic in his posthysterical state, and he went immediately to sleep.

In Savage Point, Toby told Ralph and Lillian of his meeting with Opal. He yawned, stretched, and said, "I think I'll take a nap." And he did.

18

Sonny Sammartino woke up in a full-fledged rage. He staggered around his bedroom on sedated legs, throwing on his clothes, growling, snarling, cursing incoherently. His father had been murdered and dishonored, and Sonny had bided his time. His mother had said, "Not yet, Sonny, let me work something out." And he had waited like a castrated choirboy. She never told him what plan she had in mind. Now she was dead, cooked like a roast in a microwave, and she would never tell him. To hell with all that! His course of action was clear and immediate. *Revenge!* The lumpheaded police were doing nothing. To hell with the police! If he was to continue to call himself his father's son, if he was ever again to hold his head high, he had to do what a man had to do—kill the mortal enemies of his family, let the next sunrise fall on their life's blood.

He took a revolver and a photocopy of his permit from a bureau drawer and jammed them into his jacket pocket. He put a fistful of bullets in the other pocket. He had four men to blast—Brunner, Dolin, Shields, and the sneaking hit man, whoever he was. He would get the name from the other three, and he would track him down and splatter his conniving brains all over the floor, walls, and ceiling.

He forced himself to sit down and control his breathing. He needed help. He couldn't do it alone. The headwaiter, bless him, was an old man with legs that kept threatening to collapse. He would be worse than no help at all. It had to be someone who knew that his father's death was not suicide and who had his own motive for snuffing out this conspiracy of evil. There was only one—that guy who had come to see him, Ralph Simmons. He had a friend on the combine's hit list, and he wanted to save her.

Okay, okay, Sammartino, he told himself, you gotta tone it down. This Simmons didn't look like the kind of guy who would go out on a kill party. No talk of *omerte*. Just be the bereaved son and all that.

He took a deep breath and let it out. He picked up the phone and tapped out Ralph's number.

"Hello, Mr. Simmons. Sonny Sammartino. We have things to talk about. I'm coming out."

Toby Ferris awoke with a smile on his face. In his dream, Opal had caught a fish and didn't know what to do with the slippery-flappery thing. She had squealed, and Toby had laughed. But reality soon encroached on his euphoria, and a quivering anxiety set in. Opal was still in terrible danger. Somewhere. And with the anxiety came urgency. He never should have let her go off alone. At least he should have forced her to tell where she was holed up. Then he could have gone there secretly and taken her away.

When Toby arrived downstairs, Ralph said, "Better grab a bite to eat. Sonny Sammartino is coming."

Lawrence Whitehead woke up and felt invigorated, his little breakdown of the morning forgotten. He was doing push-ups when the phone rang.

"Junior Sammartino just phoned Simmons," the voice said. "He's coming to pay Simmons a visit."

"Good. Things are coming to a head."

Sonny's flashy blue Camaro screeched to a halt in front of Ralph Simmons's house at seven-thirty in the evening. He forced himself to walk at a normal pace up the path and—when Ralph opened the door—into the house.

He was introduced to Toby, and Lillian said, "We're just finishing up a snack. Would you like to join us?"

"God, no," Sonny said. Then realizing that he sounded ungracious, he said, "Ask me if I'd like a drink."

He downed the drink quickly while he talked.

"My mother's been murdered," he said.

Lillian said, "Oh, my God!"

"She was a good person, no threat to anybody, and they killed her," he said. "It looks like they're killing us off, one by one."

"And Opal is next," Toby said.

"Your friend, yes. They'll get her for sure, all because of that stinking casino, the damn Empress of Coney Island. We oughta bomb the place to hell and gone."

"Right," said Toby. "Right after we get Opal out of danger."

"Okay, there are four of them," Sonny said. "There are the three we know and the killer himself. We have to find out who he is."

Toby gave him the killer's name, Whitehead, and he described him. "A tall fellow built like a wide receiver. Blond hair that's almost white. Always neatly dressed in conservative clothes."

Sonny grimaced in disappointment. "No, that's not the guy. The last person I saw my mother talking to was a big, dark-haired guy in casual clothes. He was wearing tinted glasses."

"About six-four?"

"He was over in the shadows, but, yeah, about that."

"You can bet it was Whitehead. He arranges accidents."

"My mother was electrocuted."

Toby nodded. "That was Whitehead."

"How do we find him?"

"Don't worry. He'll find us."

Sonny said, "I think the first order of business is to get them to call him off."

Ralph said, "How do we do that? Appeal to their better instincts?"

"No," Sonny said. "Blackmail. The way I figure it, Brunner is the head man. He's also the most vulnerable. He's running for governor, for God's sake, and one word of this that gets out could knock him right out of the race."

"He knows that already," Ralph said. "That's why he's trying to shut us up."

"Suppose," Sonny said, with a sly smile, "suppose we show him that there are too many of us to shut up. There are the four of us here and your lady friend who has the tapes. If there's one more *accidental* death, we tell him, the rest of us go to the Manhattan D.A. with the story. After all, both my father and mother were killed in Manhattan. And we go to the newspapers. And we go to the other schmo who's running against him."

Ralph said, "What exactly are you proposing?"

Sonny's eyes gleamed. "All four of us go to Brunner's house—right now—tonight—and we tell the son of a bitch point-blank that unless he gets the killer off our tails we go public, and he's sunk! How about that?"

Ralph rubbed his chin. "I don't know—"

Toby stood up. "Sounds like a goldarn good idea! Let's go!"

"Wait, wait," Ralph said. "If we all go, he'll have us all together, and if Whitehead happens to be there—"

"Don't worry about that, Mr. Simmons," Sonny said. "I brought along a little protection." He showed the gun. "It's legit, I have a permit. But I don't think Brunner would have any of that, not in his own home."

Lillian said, "How do we know he's there?"

"We'll give him a ring."

Ralph said, "It still sounds dangerous. I think Lillian should stay here."

"I'm not staying anywhere," she said. "I go where you go, Ralph."

Ralph sighed. What's the sense of having mature judgment when you're outvoted? Besides, there was a chance that Sonny's gung-ho scheme might work and Opal could come out of hiding.

They discussed the idea further, and it was decided that Ralph should make the call. There was no need to worry about the telephone eavesdropper, since the call was going to the eavesdropper's employer.

Ralph dialed the number and got through the servant to Brunner himself. "There's something we have to discuss with you," Ralph said. "It concerns the matter we talked about. We'll be there in about an hour." He hung up before Brunner could respond.

The Camaro was a two-seater with scant room for extra passengers. The Rabbit was a bit snug for four. So they took off in Mrs. Plotnik's Chevy with Toby Ferris driving, since he knew the old car's crotchets and could guarantee to keep it moving.

The mood was one of high spirits, as if they were driving off to a college football game. If they had known that Toby's license was twenty years out of date, it wouldn't have mattered. They were quite unbalanced by their own exuberance.

"Here we come, Mr. Gangbuster!" Toby cried.

Ralph and Lillian sang, "Hail, hail, the gang's all here."

Even Sonny Sammartino, the only one who knew there was going to be a killing at the end of the ride, was caught up in the crazy sense of release. He joined in to sing, "What the hell do we care, what the hell do we care . . ."

Wiretapper to Whitehead: "These lunatics are heading to the Governor's house!"

Brunner to Whitehead: "I don't want them here. They could raise an unholy stink. Stop them."

"No matter how?"

"Just stop them. Don't let them get near this place. . . . No matter how."

Toby behind the wheel, musing:

THE FERRIS WHEEL, datelined New York City. I'm on a high, gentle reader, I'm higher than Timothy Leary. I'm Saint George charging off to Saint George to slay the dragon, and the poor old animule doesn't stand a chance. He's deader than King Kong at the foot of the World Trade Center. I'm about to rescue my damsel from the dungeon, and we're going to marry up for the rest of our days. Nights, too . . .

He had no chance to get lost in the streets of Manhattan, with three passengers to give directions. By eight forty-five they reached the Battery at the southern tip of the island, fifth in line to board the next ferry.

The high spirits oozed out of them, and they were silent. Ralph muttered, "This is the damnedest, stupidest thing I've ever done." But Toby Ferris and Sonny Sammartino were grimly determined to complete the mission.

Toby reported that their follower was two cars behind

them. "The gray Toyota," he said. "He must be the little feller. He looks like he's barely peeking over the dashboard."

Sonny said, "If he gives us any trouble, we throw him overboard, okay?"

Toby said, "It'll be my pleasure." He forced a laugh.

Ralph said, "We're all crazy."

The orange-colored ferryboat that eased into its berth with much churning of water at five to nine was a triple-decked monster. The lowest deck, open front and rear, was spacious enough to accommodate three lanes of cars, about ten to a lane. The two upper decks, with separate overhead entryways, offered molded plastic seats and benches, a snack bar, and rest rooms for foot passengers. Toby maneuvered the Chevy over the drawbridge through the left lane to the front of the boat, where he turned off the motor.

In the silence that ensued, Ralph said, "Okay, guys, here we are, all four of us confined on a boat that is going to be traveling over deep water for the next twenty minutes with a killer in a car somewhere behind us—"

Lillian said, "He's two lanes over, Ralph."

He went on, "The same waters that years ago received the body of one Walter Kolb and God knows how many other people who had become inconvenient to the purposes of the triumvirate who now find *us* inconvenient to their purposes. Nice going!"

Sonny Sammartino said, "What's he talking about? What's he talking about?"

"I think what he's saying is that we shouldn't have come this way," Toby said.

Lillian shook her head. "They wouldn't try any funny business here," she said firmly.

Toby got out of the car. "I'm going to roam," he told them. Ralph's gloomy description of their situation worried him. Maybe they *would* try some "funny business" on the boat. Cars were still entering from the rear. He went up the stairs to the second deck and was surprised to see that over a hundred passengers had boarded and were seeking seats in the large inner area and in the windblown side galleries. He walked the length of the boat on one side and back on the other. Beyond the outside gallery he could see metal steps and a gangway leading to the bridge.

He reentered the inner area, saw a black door in the forward bulkhead marked No Admittance. As he watched, a gray-haired man, dressed in a white sleeveless shirt and navy trousers, opened the door and entered. Before the door swung closed, he saw the man mount a half dozen steps to what was certainly the bridge. Obviously the commander of the vessel using an interior entryway, he noted idly. He trudged to the top deck, a more open area that on a beautiful day provided the best view of the great harbor. On a chill spring night, however, it was sparsely populated.

The passengers on the two upper decks were the usual New York mix of classes and nationalities, from Puerto Rican family groups to tired businessmen. Not a menacing one in the lot.

The boat was now moving. He returned to the bottom deck and slowly strolled along the rows of vehicles, studying the occupants. Many of the cars were vacant, their passengers having gotten out to stretch their legs and enjoy the view. The short man with the sharp nose and deep-set eyes sat in the Toyota with his face turned away from Toby. A telephone receiver rested in his lap. Toby wondered if it was an open line to Whitehead. He wondered where Whitehead was at the moment.

When he came back to the old Chevy, Lillian sat in lone nonsplendor in the back seat. He said, "Would madam care to dine at the captain's table? Dress informal. Come as you are."

Lillian made a face. "It's warmer in here," she said.

"It's warmer up in the lounge."

She said, "I'll stay here."

Ralph and Sonny Sammartino were in the small throng facing into the wind in the front of the boat. Toby said, "Our friend in the Toyota seems to be alone. I think he's more scared of us than we are of him."

Sonny said, "Which one is Ellis Island?"

Ralph pointed into the darkness where the shape of the old immigration building could scarcely be discerned.

Sonny said, "Poppa came through there when he was two years old."

Toby stared at the melancholy sight of the Statue of Liberty trussed from torch to toe in a network of steel girders. It reminded him of Gulliver immobilized by the Lilliputians. Miss Liberty captured by tiny men, greedy men. "Holy Virgin! Here? Land of liberty?" Santiago had said. Toby found the sadness intolerable. He had a sense of impending disaster.

He said, "You men stand here and point the way to Staten Island. I'll go check on the mood of the natives."

He went up to the passenger deck again and roamed disconsolately, not knowing what he was looking for. He noticed for the first time two young men wearing gunbelts. They were dressed as the captain was, in white shirts and dark-blue pants. He figured they were transit police, and his sense of fear was somewhat eased. Nothing was going to happen on the boat, he concluded.

Passing the snack bar, he decided to take some hot tea to Lillian. With the plastic cup in hand, he went down the stairs and found he had descended at the wrong end. He threaded his way along the center line of cars. There was little room to walk between the cars and the support columns that rose between the car lanes. At several spots the space was so narrow that he moved between the columns to the next lane.

He was nearly to his destination and he was moving from one lane to the other when the sound of voices stopped him. Though it crackled with electronic static, he recognized the awful voice. He peered around the pillar and saw that he was only three feet from the rear of the gray Toyota. The driver held a CB mike to his face. Apparently the phone wasn't working, because the voice he heard came not from the telephone but from the CB speaker installed under the dash.

"Stay in the rear, Lennie, and be ready to *squawk* when we make our *squawk,*" the voice of Lawrence Whitehead was saying. Other garbled words came though, and the driver said something Toby didn't catch.

Then the scratchy voice said, with gaps punched in it by static: ". . . good news . . . over soon . . . spotted Wild Woman of Borneo, Len . . . there next . . . them all!"

Then there were the sounds of signing off.

The tea in the cup was burning Toby's hand. He switched it to the other hand and backed away. He made his way to the rear and sat on a bench. He replayed the words over and over again in his mind, trying to make sense of them. Then he walked along the side passageway to the front and got in the Chevy. Ralph and Sonny, having had enough of the dank wind, were there with Lillian. He handed the tea to Lillian. He didn't hear what they said. He felt stunned.

He said, "Listen." He gaped through the windshield at the dark bluff ahead that was Staten Island. He said, "Whitehead is waiting for us. I heard him on the CB. I don't know how, but he's going to stop us. He said 'we.' Sounds like he has his army there, with our friend in the Toyota bringing up the rear. Ralph was right. 'Into the valley of death rode the six hundred.' We're heading into an ambush, and we're gonna be bushwhacked for sure. Who knows anything about Staten Island?"

The others acted as stunned as he felt. They made him repeat what he had heard several times.

Sonny said, "I get the picture. No matter what road we take, they'll get ahead of us. . . ."

Toby said morosely, "This here 1969 Plotnik shimmies when she goes over fifty-five."

"They'll get ahead of us," Sonny continued, "and at some quiet spot they cut us off, and then cut us up. I'll get a couple of them with this—" He slapped the pocket holding the gun. "But God knows what sort of cannons they'll have."

"Wait," Ralph said. "This Whitehead seems to be in the accident business. He probably has a car crash in mind. Force us off the road, over a cliff, into some trees, into an oncoming truck—"

Sammartino gripped the door handle. "The first thing we do is throw this monkey overboard."

Ralph said, "No need for that. Just throw his distributor cap. That'll fix him."

Toby said, "Not yet. Last resort. I'm trying to figure out this spotted Wild Woman of Borneo thing."

Lillian said, "They have side shows in Coney Island, don't they, like they do in the circus? Maybe that's what—"

Toby pounded the steering wheel. "That's it, Lillian!" he said loudly. Then in a lower voice, he said, "With all that static and distortion, I heard it wrong! Whitehead wasn't talking about a wild woman. What he said was 'the Wilder woman'! They *spotted* the Wilder woman, not in Borneo—that was just my imagination. What he said was they sighted the Wilder woman in Coney Island! And they're going there after they take care of us. And then it'll be over. That's what he said."

He peered at the others with wild eyes. "What lies ahead is trouble, folks, and trouble rhymes with bubble, and our bubble is burst. They're not going to let us get to Brunner's place, you know that. So what do we do? We can't turn the car around—but, by God, we can turn the boat around! Ralph and Lillian, you're innocent bystanders. You stay here."

He gazed at the glowering face of Sonny Sammartino. "Sonny, are you willing to hijack this goldarn ferryboat?"

19

Toby Ferris and Sonny Sammartino strolled toward the door marked No Admittance. The armed policemen were not in sight. Toby muttered, "It wasn't locked when the captain went in. He just turned the knob. Let's hope."

He glanced at Sonny. "Stop acting like George Raft," he said.

Sconny scowled and said nothing.

Toby halted with his back to the black door, reached behind him for the knob, and turned it. The door opened a crack. He exhaled and said, "Slide in. Act like you're going to the men's room."

Sonny sidled through the door. Toby scanned the passengers. No one appeared to be interested in the man with the red nose standing by the black door. He slid through the door, closed it, found the locking lever. The door locked with a *click.*

A voice from above said, "Is that my hot coffee?"

Sonny's voice from above: "No, old man, it's the cold muzzle of a gun against the back of your neck."

A disgusted voice: "Shit!"

Toby leaped up the steps. The curved bridge was wide and shallow, with barely enough room for Sonny to stand behind the seated captain. The gray-haired man half-turned his head to glance at Sonny, then frowned at Toby.

"No one's allowed up here, mister," he said. "Better get back. We're docking in a minute."

Toby peered through the glass at the drab-orange docking area and at the plank-lined slip toward which they were gliding over the black water. He said, "Sorry, Captain, there's a change of plan. We're not docking."

"Who says?"

"Killer," Toby said. Sonny shoved the gun harder against the man's neck. "Killer Furillo."

The captain put a pained look on his face. "You drunken bastards get the hell out of here," he said. "I've got work to do."

The boat was entering the slip, its motor quiet.

Toby said, "You're backing this boat, or you're a dead man."

Ordinarily no one would believe such a statement from the likes of Toby Ferris, but his fear and excitement produced a harshness in his voice that must have sounded authentic.

"So be it," the captain said. He turned the wheel to align the boat properly in the slip as it glided toward the drawbridge.

Toby glanced desperately at Sonny, saw the storm of murderous anger building there. "Don't do it, Sonny," he said.

He studied the moves the captain was making in maneuvering the boat away from the sides. He knew that the captain would shift into reverse at the last moment to bring the boat to a standstill.

Sonny's voice was laden with frenzy. "We have to make the bastard—"

Toby said soothingly, "He will. Don't worry."

205

When the boat was only a few yards from the draw-bridge, the captain shoved the control forward, and the water churned in front of the boat. The engine was in reverse.

"Keep it there, Captain," Toby said, and he clamped his hand on top of the captain's, shoving the control into full reverse. The boat stopped a yard from the drawbridge, then started to retreat. The captain tried to pull his hand back, but Toby used his other hand to prevent him from doing it.

"Let up, you fool!" the captain said. "We'll crash into something! You can't see from here."

"Just get us out of the slip," Toby said.

He felt the captain's hand relax under his, as he made an adjustment in the boat's line of retreat to avoid ramming into the plank siding. Toby studied the man's face: even-featured, strong lines, patches of red on the cheek-bones. He guessed the man was of Norwegian descent, a race of seafarers.

While the man concentrated on his work, Toby talked.

"We're not drunk, Captain. We're scared. Mafia gunmen were waiting for us. If you had docked there, my friend and I would have been dead within minutes. My friend here with the gun is not really a killer. I just said that to frighten you into doing what we told you. You don't scare easy, do you?"

"Just doing my job," the man said through clenched jaws. "Get out of the way so I can see, damn it."

"Sorry," Toby said, and shifted his position as much as he could without relinquishing his hold on the reverse lever. He said, "They've already killed this man's mother and father, and they're out to kill the rest of us. So you see—"

A buzzer sounded somewhere in the controls.

"What's that?" Sonny cried.

The captain grinned. "The crew. They wanna know what's up."

Toby looked out the curved window, saw that the boat was clear of the slip, fifty yards out into the bay, not enough room yet to turn the boat around. He heard someone trying to open the black door at the foot of the stairs.

The buzzer sounded again. The captain looked at him inquiringly.

Toby groaned. "I don't know what to tell them. Tell them the truth."

The man studied Toby for a moment, then flicked the intercom to the On position. "We're being hijacked by two armed men," he said quietly. "No danger so far. Let's keep it that way. Don't know if there are confederates on board. Are the guards there?"

"Right here, Captain," a voice answered.

"Listen," the captain said. "I repeat there's no danger yet. The only danger can come if you guys try to act like heroes. I don't want any gunfire. Our first duty is to protect the passengers. So keep those guns holstered. And tell that damn fool who's trying to get in the door to stay away. He'll only start a panic among the passengers. That's all we need now, a passenger stampede. So the order is, stay calm, act normal. Don't do anything till I tell you. Got that?"

"Yes, sir," the voice said. "Sure you're all right?"

"I'm fine. Just don't rock the boat."

He clicked off the machine and looked up at Toby. "What now?" he asked.

Toby relinquished his hold on the reverse lever. "Thank you, Captain," he said. "Turn the boat around before we ram something."

"Good idea," the captain said. He switched the motor to forward and started the turn. "What's our destination, if I may be so bold as to ask?"

The majestic span of the Verrazano Bridge was now dead ahead, three miles away. Toby slumped against the bulkhead. "Captain, I don't know my directions very well, but I think our first step is to go past that there bridge."

"No, sir," the captain snapped. "That way lies the open ocean. I'm not taking this boat into the ocean! You're crazier than I thought."

Sonny jabbed his gun into the man's neck. "Do what my friend says, old man!"

Toby sighed. "Ease up, Sonny. The man isn't afraid of your gun." He turned to the captain. "You have to take our word for it, we're not crazy. The gang that's after us are the crazy ones. They plan to kill my fiancée. She's in Coney Island. All we ask you to do is take us to Coney Island and drop us there. Then you can head on back to Staten Island. Please."

"Drop you off? Where?"

"Why—why—anywhere," Toby said.

Sonny said, "The old Steeplechase pier, Captain. No danger of running aground. The water's deep."

The gray-haired captain peered up at Toby. "Does your friend still have his gun to my head?"

"Yes."

The man sighed. "Then I guess I'll have to do it. I always wondered how she'd make out in the ocean."

He headed the boat down the Narrows. The night was clear, the wind chill, as they plowed past the dark shapes of merchant ships at anchor.

Ralph and Lillian were out of the car. She muttered, "Oh, my God," several times. Other drivers and passengers thronged the forward end of the boat to watch their destination recede into the night and an unknown new course pursued. The mood was one of puzzlement and excitement with here and there an angry comment on the quality of the ferry service.

"We're turning around."

"What's going on?"

"My wife'll never believe this."

"If we go back to Manhattan, I'll scream."

Ralph felt disoriented, unpleasantly confused. "I'm too old for this sort of thing," he said to Lillian.

She said, "They're doing it, Ralph! I think it's thrilling. But what are we supposed to do?"

"We're innocent bystanders. Remember?"

The hell with feeling old, he told himself. The fat's in the fire, and I'm supposed to sit back and watch. I'm starting to shake, and I don't know whether it's from the wind or from fear. That's great, simply great.

He said to Lillian, "You stay here. I'm gonna check on old ferret-face in the Toyota. I'll be right back."

She went with him.

They made their way out of the crowd to the lines of cars. They were all unoccupied except one. The man in the Toyota had a mike to his mouth.

Ralph said, "No, you don't." He went to the car, grabbed the CB antenna from the roof, and tugged the wires loose.

The man cried, "Hey!" and got out of the car.

Ralph threaded his way through passengers to the side of the boat and threw the rod into the water. He felt ten years younger.

Lillian said, "He has a gun, Ralph."

Ralph glanced at the enraged gunman. "He's crazy enough to use it. Let's go up here." He pulled her up the stairs to the main passenger deck.

Here the people were standing in groups, fidgeting. The air vibrated with their anxiety. They were not far from panic. He sensed that the only thing that kept them from going berserk was that there was nowhere for them to go. No exit. They were in the middle of the Narrows.

His eyes were caught by a dark-haired man who remained seated, peering around in bewilderment. On the seat beside him was a concertina.

Ralph went to him and said, "Is that yours?"

The man stared at the instrument. He said uncertainly, "*Si?*"

"Do you know the 'Beer Barrel Polka'?"

"Who doesn't? Old chestnut."

"Play it."

The man gaped at him.

Ralph made a circular gesture at the restive crowd of passengers to indicate dancing.

The man's eyes lit in comprehension. He grabbed the concertina and stood up. Ralph gave him a fast one, two, three beat with his hand and said, "Loud. Play it loud."

The man played an initial flourish and swung into the rousing melody. For a long moment the passengers were shocked into immobility. They glared in the direction from which the music was coming. Then they shrugged. Their bodies relaxed. Some started to move to the music's beat.

It was Lillian who started the dancing. "Come on, Ralph," she said, bouncing to the beat, her eyes sparkling.

"You know I can't do the polka," he grumbled.

"Who cares?" she said.

Pretty soon, others joined them. Still others started singing the words, and those who didn't were clapping to the rhythm.

Lillian said, "You're a genius, Ralph," and she hugged him.

Passengers from the top deck came down the stairs to see what was going on. A woman said, "I thought this was the ferry to Staten Island."

A man said, "I'll be damned! We're on a cruise."

His companion said, "Let's see if the bar is open."

Ralph stopped dancing, feeling more disoriented than ever. "God, what have we started?" he said.

The armed guards were now in sight. One was stationed outside the black door to the bridge. The other was confronting the slender concertina player. The man stopped playing.

Ralph touched the guard's arm. "Let him play," he said. "It keeps the passengers quiet."

The guard said, "But the regulations—"

"Do the regulations cover this situation?" Ralph asked.

The guard said, "Not exactly."

Ralph said to the bewildered musician, "Play. You're doing great."

The music recommenced. The guard peered closely at Ralph.

Lawrence Whitehead sat in the front passenger seat of the blue Cadillac. Tony Lukats was behind the wheel. Three armed associates were in the back. Whitehead said, "Follow the shore. Keep them in sight." Lukats drove slowly along Bay Street.

Whitehead picked up the phone and said, "Governor, there's something screwy going on. Looks like they've taken over the ferry and are heading down the Narrows."

He heard nostrils being sprayed, then Sylvan Brunner's voice. "What does your man on board say?"

"We've lost contact, Governor. The CB is out of commission, and the phone isn't working."

"You're to be congratulated, Mr. Whitehead," Brunner said. "Does it appear that they're heading for the Empress?"

"I can't think of where else."

Brunner said, "If they go past the bridge, head for the

Empress. I'll meet you there. Do you think you can do that?"

"Sure thing, Governor," Whitehead said. He looked at the receiver in his hand, then he spit viciously out the window. Murder was in his heart. He mentally signed warrants not only for the five people who were causing him so much grief but also for this sarcastic, snot-nosed bastard who was running for governor. Someday, somehow . . .

Toby sat in a chair alongside the captain and chatted. He told him about his love for Opal and the danger she was in. He told him about Lawrence Whitehead and his genius for faking accidents. And the captain responded with interest, while he guided his boat through the black waters down the middle of the Narrows.

"Over there," the captain said. "You can't see it very well. That's Bay Ridge. That's where I was born. My father came from Norway. He was a ship's captain, a real ship's captain, not like me chugging back and forth across a stinking bay. What did your father do?"

Toby said, "I don't rightly know. I was found in a garbage can behind a seafood restaurant. I always thought of him as a mackerel."

The captain said that his name was Rolf Anderssen. "But naturally nobody ever calls me that. I'm Andy Anderssen, and there's no getting away from it."

"So you're Captain Andy," Toby said. "Wasn't he the captain in *Showboat*?"

Sonny Sammartino, who had been puzzling over the music coming from the passenger section, said, "Son of a gun, that's what you have here, old man! It's a *showboat!*"

The captain said, "Tide's turning, taking us out. Not sure there'll be enough water at that pier you're talking about. One thing I'm not going to do is run this boat aground. . . . One of the crew's looking at us from the port gangway. Better raise that gun so he can see it."

Sonny raised the gun, scowled at the timid crewman, who retreated out of sight.

At a pause in the music, the captain said, "I think I better say something to the passengers."

Toby said, "You're the captain."

Anderssen flipped a switch and spoke. "This is your captain. We are about to sail under the Verrazano Bridge. Go on with your funmaking. There's been a slight detour on our trip to Staten Island. To tell you the truth, we've been hijacked. However, none of us are in danger. One of the hijackers just said this is a showboat. Okay, for the time being I want you to look on it as that. A fun boat. We'll get you to Staten Island as soon as we can. Meanwhile, enjoy the cruise." He switched off the speaker.

There's a would-be comedian in every crowd, and the crowd at the front of the car deck was no exception. He was a beefy salesman type with a flushed face and a loud voice. He declaimed to his audience: "We're being hijacked to Cuba, ladies and gentlemen. The island paradise of our dreams. Palm trees swaying, rum and Coca-Cola at poolside, native girls in bikinis—"

Another man said in alarm, "Hey, we're starting to hit waves!"

The comedian went on blithely, "Surfing in the Bay of Pigs." Spray hit him in the face, but no one laughed.

A male voice said, "Ten to one we don't make it to Atlantic City."

A piping voice: "I'll settle for Atlantic City."

As the ferry rode uneasily into Lower New York Bay under the high span of the Verrazano Bridge, a blue Cadillac was rolling smoothly over it en route to Coney Island.

20

Captain Andy Anderssen was bringing the bulky boat straight in from the sea, slowly, ever so slowly, toward the old pier. "The first grain of sand we hit, I'm backing up," he warned.

"Fair enough," Toby said.

"Say a prayer to Saint Elmo."

"He'd hear it better coming from you."

"I'm busy! Ask him to watch over us, goddammit!"

Toby said a silent prayer. He could see the purple backside of the Empress a short distance to the right. He added a postscript to his prayer: "Also, your sainthood sir, if you're not too busy, please help Opal Wilder too. That's W-i-l-d-e-r. Thank you."

The ferryboat was gently rising and falling with the undulating water. The passengers were now singing a slower tune. He recognized it. They were singing "Nearer My God to Thee," but with the addition of a calypso beat provided by the Latin music man, which took some of the solemnity from the hymn.

The pier crept closer. It appeared to be deserted. The captain said, "If we touch it, it'll fall down." By skillful maneuvering, he halted the boat a foot from the end of the pier, which was higher by about three feet than the car deck of the ferry.

Toby reached for the microphone. "May I?"

"Go right ahead."

Toby said over the loudspeaker: "Coney Island! All ashore who's going ashore! Ralph! Lillian! Our apologies to the rest of you folks. It was all in a good cause, believe me." He clicked off.

The comedian, down below, said, *"This* is a tropical island?"

Ralph and Lillian edged past him, got beyond the gate, and looked at the pier with trepidation. Not only was it chest-high and going up and down, but a two-tiered wooden railing blocked their way.

Lillian wailed, "Why can't they steady the boat, for crying out loud? I can't climb onto that, Ralph."

A crew member was reaching for them.

Ralph said, "Yes, you can."

He picked her up like an awkward bag of laundry and, aided by an upward thrust of the boat, cast her rolling— and squealing—under the lower railing onto the pier.

A crewman had hold of him. Ralph said, "There's a gun trained on your back. Better let go."

The man relaxed his grip, and Ralph leaped, clutched the railing, slammed his midsection against the end of the pier, finally kneed his way onto it. He sat up and looked back. The boat was receding. In the forefront of the small throng of passengers, still only a few yards away from him, the angry gunman from the Toyota was pointing a gun at him.

The comedian yelled, "Here's one of the hijackers! He has a gun!"

He backed away, but other men in the crowd swarmed over the unfortunate gunman, wrenched the weapon from him, threw him to the deck, and stomped on him as if on a poisonous insect.

Ralph had to grin as he and Lillian got stiffly to their

215

feet and made their way shoreward toward the great boardwalk.

Up on the bridge the captain shot an inquiring glance at Toby. "How are you two gonna get out of here?"

"Good question," Toby said. He knew they couldn't depart by the way they had entered: there were a hundred people outside that door, including two armed guards.

The captain said, "Sorry, can't hold it. We're backing off."

Toby said, "Thanks for everything, Andy. See you around."

The captain, concentrating on pulling his boat out of danger, said, "Hope you save your girl, Toby. Can you swim?"

Toby didn't hear the last question, because he was out the side door on the gangway, with Sonny right behind him. He saw that his idea of swinging down to the lower deck and leaping from there onto the pier wouldn't work.

He said, "Wait a minute," to Sonny, raced back to the bridge, and handed the car keys to Anderssen. "It's the old Chevy," he said. "I'll call for it when I'm ready."

He raced back down the steps and plunged over the side into the blackness of the ocean:

THE FERRIS WHEEL, datelined Coney Island. I think I just committed suicide, folks. You all know I can't swim worth a damn, but I just jumped out of the frying pan into the icy deep. Goldarn it, this water is cold! My bloodstream has icebergs in it. Now I know what cryogenics is all about. Wake me up in about a hundred years or so, and I'll tell you if I want to go on living. Hope Brother Elmo is watching. Oops, just swallowed a gallon, not one of your tastier treats. They say this water is polluted, and I do believe I'm chomping on a banana peel . . .

216

He came floundering to the surface, gasping and gagging.

A voice nearby said, "This way. Swim with the swells, and rest in the troughs. It's not far. You can do it."

His clothes were dragging him down.

Sonny Sammartino was beside him. "Just don't panic, Dad," he said. "I was a lifeguard in high school. That's it, you're doing the classic dog paddle. Great form! Come on, we're almost there."

Ralph and Lillian reached the boardwalk and mingled with the small crowd of observers who gathered to watch the two clothed swimmers come ashore.

"They're probably drunk," a gravel-voiced woman said.

One of the distant figures on the beach was staggering, and the other was helping him. By the time they reached the steps from the beach to the boardwalk, they were both staggering.

Ralph called to them, "Terrible, terrible! You'll never make the Olympics that way."

The woman said, "The Olympics? With their clothes on?"

Ralph said, "It's a new method of training."

The woman said, "With their clothes on?"

Toby's teeth were chattering. He was shaking all over. Young Sammartino was winded.

Ralph said to Lillian, "Gotta get these men into some dry clothes." He took Toby by the arm. Lillian walked alongside Sonny Sammartino. Ralph said to the crowd, "They'll be all right. The Olympics will be a breeze after this."

A few of the onlookers followed, but the last of them dropped off before the soaked party reached the back of the Empress.

Toby pulled away from Ralph. "They said they saw

Opal, dad-gum it," he said excitedly. "She must be close by."

"Yeah, but where?" Lillian said.

"Close enough to be watching," Toby said. "Let's just sort of mosey around the building. Maybe we'll see her."

Sonny said, "Nuts, I'm for going right in and getting that bastard Brunner."

Ralph said, "You two look like creatures from the slime pits. At least comb your hair." He handed them his pocket comb.

Lillian said, "Let me." She combed their hair, then stepped away and studied her work intently.

"That's good enough," Ralph said. "Let's go."

Toby said, "No charging in till we get the lay of the land. From here, we skulk."

"Skulk?"

"Skulk."

"How can you skulk when the grounds are all lit up?" Ralph wanted to know.

"Follow me," Toby said.

A bag-lady leaned against a building on the far side of Surf Avenue, her face hidden under a misshapen hat. She gave the appearance of being bone-weary. She wasn't acting. Opal Wilder had spent much of her recent days and nights at this lookout point observing the comings and goings of people in and out of the Empress of Coney Island. The rest of her time was spent in the room she had rented nearby, transcribing tapes and putting the story together one piece at a time.

She didn't know what she was looking for. She had seen Blossom's murderer several times, the white-haired psychopath Lawrence Whitehead, and she had even spotted the popular gubernatorial candidate Sylvan Brunner. But her sightings only tended to prove the connection of

218

those two to the casino. She hadn't set eyes on the other two, Everett Dolin and Terry Shields.

She gripped her torn shopping bag and was about to leave when she saw a most peculiar group of people saunter around the corner of the casino. What was strange about them was the furtiveness they displayed despite their efforts to appear casual. Moreover, two of the men were in extremely rumpled suits.

She gasped when she recognized Ralph and Lillian Simmons and then the beloved face of Toby Ferris under plastered-down hair. An unknown fourth person was with them. This one had his hand in his pocket, not in a natural way but rigidly, tensely.

She stood transfixed, at first disabled by surprise, then by indecision.

The four sauntered toward the main entrance, where the proprietor Alex Burnside stood facing a dark-blue Cadillac that was standing in the drive. As though watching a silent film, she saw the unlikely foursome stop and talk to Burnside, who appeared to be shooing them off. She saw everyone, including Burnside, stiffen into immobility, then slowly turn toward the Cadillac. The unknown man with his hand in his jacket pocket sank into a half-crouch, and the hand in the pocket moved. Both Ralph Simmons and Alex Burnside held out their hands to stop him, and Burnside spoke. Opal didn't hear his words, but from the movement of his head and body she felt sure he said, "Don't be a fool!"

When the young man froze in his posture, the rear door of the Cadillac on the side that Opal could see opened, and two men got out. They circled the car, approached the young man from his rear. One of them reached into the young man's pocket and relieved him of whatever he had been holding. It looked like a gun.

Then the fearful figure of Lawrence Whitehead

emerged on the far side of the Cadillac. He nodded politely to the foursome and gestured toward the entrance. Burnside apparently disagreed, because he tried to prevent the party from entering. Then he moved slowly aside and permitted the group to pass—Whitehead with Toby, chatting, then the other three captives, followed by the two gunmen from the car. The limousine moved forward into the parking area, after which a uniformed valet came out from behind a bush and stared at the group now going through the great castle doors to the interior of the casino.

Opal wailed, "Oh, my God!" and crossed the avenue, dodging cars. She straightened her ragged clothing as best she could, took off the shapeless old hat and stuffed it in the shopping bag, then discarded the bag under a shrub. If anyone had tried to stop her, he would have gotten a fist to the solar plexus and been left gasping on the pavement. Fortunately the valets were occupied by the arrival of several cars, and Opal went past them into the casino.

Instead of following the purple passage, she plunged into the slot-machine area and paused at a point near the reception desk and the elevator bank to the upper floors. The group wasn't in sight.

Muttering a short expletive, she hastened past the reception desk and peered at the floor indicators over the elevator doors. Two of the elevators were at rest at the lobby level, three were descending, and one was rising. The rising one continued without pause to the top floor and stopped.

She was aware that the reception clerk was watching her with a mixture of amusement and contempt. She went to him and said, "May I ask what's on the top floor?"

The man said, "The Princess Suite, dearie. Are you thinking of renting it?"

She said, "No, I'm not, buster. I'm thinking of smearing that nose of yours all over your face."

"Oh, my," the man said in mock fear.

She turned and disappeared into the maze of slot machines. She stood before a machine with her hand on the lever and tried to think. That damned Toby Ferris! She had told him to stay away! And now they had captured him! They couldn't let him go now. They had gone too far. They had to kill him. She was pretty sure they were holding him and the others in the Princess Suite. It had taken her no more than a minute and a half to cross the avenue and arrive at the elevator bank. They had to have been in the rising elevator! Had to! If not, Toby and his friends could be anywhere in the building, and she would never find them.

She groaned. That damned Toby Ferris, with the red nose and the endearing personality! Why did she have to fall in love with him! . . . Call the police, she decided. No matter how awkward it might be, at least Toby would be safe if—if the police got here in time! And if they believed the word of a ragged bag-lady! *Sure, sure, Jimmy Hoffa and the Pope, we're watching them.*

She kicked the machine in fury, then headed for the elevators. She was glad Toby and her mother had liked each other. That was one thing, anyway.

Ralph Simmons gazed down the main room of the Princess Suite and thought, *What an appropriate place to die in.* It looked to him like the inside of an expensive coffin, provided with all the comforts for a long trip, including a well-stocked bar and a fireplace. The far end of the room, carpeted in rich burgundy, was a raised area that gave the impression of being a separate room, a mezzanine. The whole was an opulent set for a Fred Astaire-Ginger Rogers movie, except that this time the dance was macabre, and he felt depressed, frightened, helpless, and angry with himself. Lillian's hand in his was moist. Impressions came to him as through a film of Vaseline on a camera lens. His brain, jolted by too many sensory perceptions too quickly, was tuning down sharpness and contrast to preserve the system from burn-out.

The two gunmen were the leaner ones called "Mac" and "Joe" by Whitehead. They stood on either side of the phony castle door to the suite, alert and poised to strike. Their guns were visible in shoulder holsters. Lawrence Whitehead was being unctuously polite, but it was apparent that his pose of urbanity was slipping badly. Alex Burnside was in a barely controlled rage.

Burnside said in a voice resonant with anger, "You just take these people out of here, Whitehead, and take your skullbusters with you. This is a law-abiding hotel."

Whitehead said, "Can't do that, Mr. Burnside . . . sir." Not pleasantly. Nastily. "The boss is coming, Mr. Burnside . . . sir," he said.

Toby Ferris and Sonny Sammartino were wet roosters, red-eyed from the salt water, pugnacious, yet helpless. They looked like protestors who had just been quelled by police hoses. Puddles formed under them on the burgundy rug. Burnside told them not to sit on the satin sofa, for God's sake, man, please.

Ralph wandered to the great glass window at the far end of the mezzanine, and gazed out into the blackness that was the Atlantic Ocean. He said in a dull voice, "This window opens."

Lillian said, "Don't try it, Ralph. It's a long way down, and you still haven't made out a new will."

He grinned a lopsided grin. "That's what I love about you, Lil. Always practical," he said, and their hands clasped.

She said, "Stay close. When the time comes, I want us to go together."

"We're not going anywhere," he growled.

His strange mood of detachment continued. He saw the others in the room as actors in a play. In the middle ground, the two soggy clowns spoke. Sammy said to Toby, "Is that the one?" And Toby said, "In person." Sonny wandered to the fireplace, where he selected a poker. Then he walked past the Othello-like character, Burnside, who stood brooding by the television console. He smiled at the black man—and lunged at the big blond man who had murdered his parents.

Sonny swung the poker, but Burnside suddenly had him in a bear hug from the rear, and the poker dropped to the floor. The gunmen at the door had their weapons out, but Whitehead stopped them with a motion, then picked up the poker. Sonny spit in his face, and the blond man, using the poker as a skewer, rammed it into the clown's stomach. But at the last fraction of a second Burnside pulled his captive back and threw him to the floor behind him, where he lay curled in agony, clasping his stomach.

Ralph and Lillian went to him. Over the reclining form, Ralph saw Toby Ferris at the fireplace tool stand, seeking a weapon. Ralph said quietly, "Not now, Tobe. They're watching."

Toby stared at him blankly for a moment, then moved to help him half-carry Sammartino to the mezzanine. Looking back, Ralph saw Whitehead and Burnside in a confrontation. For a moment it appeared that Burnside, like Sonny, was going to get the spear in his belly—then the white man relaxed and tossed the poker at the black man's feet. Contemptuously.

Sonny Sammartino lay on the floor of the mezzanine. He let Ralph and Lillian unbutton his shirt. They saw the puncture wound welling with blood. "Just stop the bleeding, and I'll be okay," Sonny said.

Lillian turned her head toward Lawrence Whitehead and cried, "Murderer!"

Burnside came to them, saw what was needed, and fetched a sheet from the bedroom. Ralph and Lillian wound the sheet tightly around Sonny's middle. "There," Ralph said. "What you always wanted—a red cummerbund."

"It's white," Sonny said.

Ralph said, "It won't be for long."

He stood up and said to Burnside, "We never did thank you for the free meal."

The big man didn't reply.

Ralph said, "It's lucky you have a red rug. They're going to kill us, you know."

Burnside shook his head. "Not here. Not in my hotel."

"I hope you're right, Mr. Burnside," Ralph said. "But no matter where they do it, they've tied you into it, haven't they?"

Burnside moved away and took up what appeared to be his chosen station in front of the TV set.

Whitehead sat alone on the satin sofa. Mac and Joe were once again playing palace guards at the door.

Lillian said, "What are they waiting for, for crying out loud?"

Toby Ferris, sitting on the step to the raised area, said, "The boss. Whitehead said the boss was coming."

Sonny Sammartino rolled to a sitting position on the step beside Toby. "We're not doing so good, are we?" he said.

Toby said, "I'm sorry I got you into this."

Sonny said, "Nuts, I got myself in." He raised his head. "You wanna know something? I wasn't going to Brunner's to talk to him. I was going there to kill him."

"Maybe you'll still get your chance."

"I'm sure gonna try."

Ralph Simmons, sitting behind them on a small sofa, listened to the conversation and felt unutterably sad.

21

Opal Wilder stood before the castle door to the Princess Suite, paralyzed. She had raced this far to rescue Toby Ferris from captivity and certain death. He was somewhere on the other side of this idiotic portal. She had no key to it. There was no way she could force it open. Therefore, in order to gain entrance she would have to push the buzzer. The door would then be opened by one of four people: Lawrence Whitehead, Alex Burnside, or one of the two gunmen she had seen enter the building. End of rescue mission.

She raged at her own impotence, her impulsive foolishness. She saw now that her only sane course was to go to the police. She had already wasted precious minutes. She turned—

The elevator doors opened silently. Of the five men who were on it, she knew three by sight. Terry Shields, built like a miniature tank, low and powerful, was first to emerge.

"Ho, ho, what have we here?" he said.

Sylvan Brunner was next, the poster man with quick nervous steps. He peered at the bag-woman coldly.

Everett Dolin stood in the elevator doorway, blocking her way.

Opal said, "Going down," and pushed roughly past the slender man. She bumped into the two other occupants of the elevator. They were the beefy driver of the dark limousine, Tony Lukats, and an even larger black man.

Shields said to the latter, "Bring her back, Raymond, so we can have a look."

Opal backed out into the hall, frantically thinking, *Who am I, what do I say?* Then it came to her.

"Going down?" she declaimed, pointing dramatically to the floor and then to the ceiling. "Or going up? That is your choice, brothers! Down to the torments of hell—or up to the everlasting joys of heaven. There's no time. The choice must be made now. The end of the world is just around the corner!"

Brunner growled, "Get her out of here."

Shields said, "Hold on, Sylvan. The lady intrigues me."

Opal pointed to him. "There's a sensible man. He chooses salvation, no matter what his sins. Who will join him? There is yet time to be saved!"

"What are you doing on this floor, sister?" Shields asked.

"Seeking sinners, brother. Seeking repenters."

"Did you find any?"

"I arrived up here, and I looked down at my hands, and what did I see? I saw that I had forgotten my holy tracts and receipt forms. I was just going to retrieve them when you arrived."

"Receipt forms?"

"For donations to the church," Opal said. "Many people choose to leave their material possessions to the church."

"What church is that, sister?"

"The Church of the Almighty." As soon as she said it, Opal knew it was a mistake to use the name of her father's church. She added, "Of the Almighty Angels." But it was too late.

Shields said, "Yes, I think I've heard of that church. Let's all go inside where we can talk."

Opal dashed for the elevator. "I'll be right back," she said.

Shields said, "Raymond, escort Miss Wilder into the suite."

Opal straightened her shabby clothes and stood tall. "You can all go to hell," she announced.

Ralph Simmons witnessed the reunion of Toby Ferris and Opal Wilder from his seat in the balcony. Lillian was clutching his arm, and there were tears in her eyes. He saw the bag-lady enter as if she were a princess entering her own chamber, the Princess Suite, glance around with royal disdain until her eyes lit on Toby Ferris, who was rising to his feet. Ralph felt the magnetic force that coursed between the two.

Others were speaking, but Ralph didn't hear them. He watched Toby being drawn to Opal, and her to him. They came together and joined hands, rapt in each other's gaze.

Toby said, "Hey, Opal," and she said, "Hey, yourself," and they were in each other's fierce embrace.

Ralph's vision blurred. The embrace was broken by Lawrence Whitehead. The stage was now crowded. There were now four gunmen acting as palace guards. They were invited by Shields to guard the portal from the outside. Their departure cleared the area somewhat. Whitehead held Opal by the arm and spoke boastingly of having "all five pigeons in one coop," but Sylvan Brunner spoke to him, and he relinquished his hold. Opal and Toby joined the watchers in the balcony.

Ralph looked down the room at centerstage, where Brunner, Shields, and Dolin were in somber discussion with Whitehead. Two of them had drinks in their hands, Shields and Whitehead. Ralph Simmons wondered what they were talking about. They seemed strangely indecisive, as if they were waiting for something or someone.

Sylvan Brunner was saying, "Here's the fix we're in, damn it! These crazy people were almost certainly seen entering the building. We have to assume that. Their stunt was all over the car radio while I was driving in. The TV people are probably heading this way. For all we know, we're in Macy's window. Okay, in a moment through the kind offices of Mr. Whitehead we'll have what we want from the Wilder woman, and we'll be in the clear. Great! Then what? We all know what has to be done. But then what? That's what I'm asking. Then what? God, this is insane!" He took out his inhaler, and breathed deeply.

He was seated on the satin sofa, along with Whitehead. Shields and Dolin sat facing them in easy chairs. The four of them agreed that getting rid of the bodies presented a problem. They couldn't be dumped, as they might normally be, in the wilds near JFK, not when their names are likely to have been connected with the Empress.

Whitehead suggested an accident: "Listen, they get off the boat here, and they're met by a confederate in a hot car—"

Brunner thought that a nice, clean cremation would be their best bet. "Who do we know in the business?" he asked.

Shields said he preferred cement.

Dolin didn't say anything.

Burnside, not party to the discussion, moved toward the captives at the far end of the room to offer them drinks, a ridiculous amenity under the circumstances.

Sonny Sammartino peered up at him. "A drink?" he said. "If you birds are gonna kill us, I demand a last meal and not just a drink! How cheap can you get, for God's sake?"

228

Ralph said to Burnside, "You'd better pour a stiff one for yourself. You're gonna need it."

"I just might do that, Mr. Simmons," Burnside said softly.

Ralph heard Sylvan Brunner say loudly, "Well, it's about time we found out, damnit!"

And Whitehead rose stiffly, came to Opal, and brought her back to centerstage. Burnside fetched a spare chair from the bedroom for her to sit on. Whitehead jovially called it the "witness chair."

Toby went with Opal and stood behind her chair. Terry Shields made a joke of it. "Looks like she has a defense lawyer, Sylvan," he said.

Brunner, the former D.A., did the questioning, brief as it was. The witness was surprisingly cooperative.

"Where are the tapes?"

"In my shopping bag."

"Where is the shopping bag?"

"Under a bush in front of the casino."

"Which bush?"

"The second one on the left as you come in," she said.

All the other actors seemed disconcerted that the questioning ended so abruptly. Brunner told Alex Burnside to find the bag and bring it back.

He said to the princess, "If you're wasting our time, lady, you'll regret it."

She said, "What'll you do? Kill me twice?"

Burnside went out the door and returned almost immediately. "He's here," he announced.

The great hulking figure of William Brunner entered. There was nothing cordial in the rumpled face. His eyes were but little glints in the dark caves that were his eye sockets, as he took in the scene. Behind him, Burnside completed his exit.

The old man spoke in the voice that was a rumble of distant thunder. "What's all this about, Sylvan?"

To Ralph Simmons in the balcony, the senior Brunner was the star of the show making a star's entrance, all the more impressive since Ralph hadn't known he was in the cast.

Everett Dolin tried to lead the old man to one of the chairs, but was shoved aside. The old man seated himself unaided, like a king placing his royal rump on a throne.

Sylvan Brunner leaned forward with his hands clenched. "We wouldn't have asked you to come, sir, but we have a big decision to make, and we wanted you to know all the ramifications. We also thought you'd be pleased to be in on the end of our hunt." He nodded toward Opal Wilder. "This is the woman who's been giving us fits."

He introduced Sonny Sammartino, and said, "You've met the other three," indicating Ralph, Lillian, and Toby.

Lillian, not quite grasping what was going on, said, "Hi, Mr. Brunner. How's the pollution fight going?"

Toby Ferris spoke up in an ordinary conversational tone. "Don't you see, Lillian, that you're talking to the king of pollution? The people we thought were the king-pins of this stinking outfit are only the Three Stooges. The real expert on corruption and pollution and extortion and all the rest of the slime is the kindly old enemy alien from Staten Island, William Brunner." He touched Opal's shoulder. "Did you know that, Opal? That the old faker was really—"

The old man's voice rumbled: "Sylvan, the red-nosed fellow is giving me a pain."

Sylvan Brunner nodded to Whitehead. "Deliver the message."

Whitehead moved toward Toby with a look of pleasure on his face that was almost sensual.

Toby held up his hands. "Whoa, man, I get the message."

Whitehead rammed his fist into Toby's stomach. Toby collapsed to the floor. Whitehead said, "The medium is the message, old buddy," and he kicked Toby in the face.

From his perch in the balcony, Ralph Simmons saw the kick. "Let's go, Lil," he said.

Lillian bent over Toby. There was blood on his face. She glared up at Lawrence Whitehead and said, "You ought to be ashamed of yourself!"

Opal slipped out of Whitehead's hands and went to Toby.

Ralph studied the four corrupters and their chief executioner. He said, "Point of order. While we're waiting for Mr. Burnside to return with Miss Wilder's shopping bag, will you satisfy my curiosity on a few points? They involve you, Mr. Brunner."

The old man nodded coldly.

Ralph eased into the seat Opal had been occupying. "You told us, sir, about how you lost your house and your business because of the enemy alien thing. You said you never tried to get your business back after the war, but I suspect that wasn't true. You did get your business back, didn't you?"

The old man barely nodded.

Terry Shields sighed noisily. "Ancient history," he said.

"Everett Dolin was your surrogate, wasn't he?" Ralph went on. "You hired him as a youngster when jobs were scarce, and he's always been faithful to you. He's still your surrogate in Domino, isn't he? And he was your surrogate when you got your company back from Walter Kolb. Mr. Dolin tells a wonderful story of diving into the water of the bay trying to save the man. How did it really happen, Mr. Dolin?"

The sleek little man shrugged.

Ralph turned to Terry Shields. "You were there, Mr. Shields. How did it happen?"

"Who says I was there?" Shields said belligerently.

"The *Herald-Courier* morgue, that's who. The story identified you as being with the watchman. Which was very strange, because the president of a union doesn't visit a lowly watchman on the waterfront on such a bitterly cold winter night. I imagine that your most difficult job was inducing Kolb to go to that rotten pier in that weather. Anyway, once you had him there, the rest was easy. One of you whopped him on the head with a piece of wood—I suspect it was the union man—and then the two of you lugged him out on the pier and rolled him into the water. But who was it who thought of dunking Dolin into the drink to make your claim of trying to rescue him seem more authentic? That was a smart touch."

"Thank you," Shields said.

Dolin said, "I like my version better."

"The accidental death, yes," Ralph said. He looked at Whitehead. "Mr. Brunner was concocting accidental deaths long before you entered the picture, Whitey. That's why he likes your technique so much—it's really much smoother than his. Forgive me for saying so, Mr. Brunner, but the accidental death of Robert Fullerton was a crude piece of business. I don't wonder that you couldn't remember his widow's name. Who was it who accidentally threw him down the cliff in back of your house on Staten Island? Was it Sylvan? Or the two of you together?"

Sylvan Brunner was glaring at Lawrence Whitehead. "What's so funny?" he snapped.

"Nothing," Whitehead said. "Nothing."

Ralph said, "It's just that one doesn't expect a clean-cut, red-blooded, newly sworn officer of the court to be pushing people over cliffs, especially, in retrospect, when that person is running for governor."

Sylvan Brunner said, "I don't know where you got all this garbage."

Opal Wilder had come back and was standing beside Ralph's chair.

"Tell him, Opal," he said.

"There was a police report on the accident," she said. "It stated that the young lawyer Sylvan Brunner had gone to Fullerton two days earlier in an attempt to buy the house for his father. It also stated that the railing on the back deck didn't just collapse. It was broken by a sledge hammer. The marks were on the wood. The question is, who did it?"

"There was no report," the old man said.

"There was a report, and you know it," Opal said. "It was suppressed by your old friend, the police chief, but it wasn't destroyed. I looked it up."

Sylvan Brunner said, "Where the hell's Burnside? If I listen to any more of this crap . . ."

Ralph said quickly, "No insult intended. We're only asking a few questions, that's all. For instance, when did you get into the extortion business, Mr. Brunner? It was long before your son broke up the Irish Mafia, wasn't it? The voting public doesn't know that when the great D.A. of Staten Island broke up McGovern's gang, he was destroying the only rival to your own extortion network. You have it all now, don't you?"

The massive bloodhound face of the old man showed no emotion. "Yes, I have it all, Mr. Simmons," he said.

Ralph stood up. "Thank you," he said. "Do you mind if I say you're still an enemy alien?"

He and Opal retreated to where Lillian and Sonny Sammartino were ministering to Toby Ferris. "How is he?"

"Groggy," Sonny said. "He's coming around."

Whitehead was calling Opal back to the "witness

233

chair." She said to Ralph, "Don't let him do anything reckless." Then she was once again the princess marching to the inquisition.

Ralph sat on the settee next to Lillian. She said, "The tapes aren't in that bag, are they?"

Ralph shook his head hopelessly. "I don't think they are."

Abruptly Alex Burnside was back in the room carrying the shabby shopping bag. In an obvious state of agitation and ignoring the questions thrown at him, he held the bag upside down and dumped the contents on the floor—rags, the remnants of a sandwich, an old floppy hat. "No tapes," Burnside said. "Nothing." The voice was the voice of doom, and Ralph Simmons shuddered.

Burnside moved to his post by the TV set.

Opal half rose, and Whitehead shoved her back onto the chair. From out of nowhere a thin, stiletto-style knife was at her throat, the point in the hollow over the trachea. Her back was turned to Ralph Simmons in the balcony. Whitehead faced him head-on.

"Where are the tapes, dear lady?"

"Go to hell, you sadistic bastard."

"Oh dear, my hand must have slipped. Where are the tapes?"

"You're a real lady-killer, aren't you? Why don't you crush my finger while you're at it? I know you enjoy doing that."

Sylvan Brunner said, "For God's sake, tell him!"

The rumbling voice of the old man said, "Hurry it up, Mr. Whitehead."

"Very well, we'll go directly to the heart of the matter." With a lightning-quick motion, the blade flicked in front of Opal, out of Ralph's sight. From her rigid back and from the look on the faces before her, he knew that the man had sliced her.

Whitehead paused only a moment to survey his handiwork, then his hand moved again, and Opal's sudden intake of breath was audible as a low, inside-out scream.

The sequence of events that ensued happened quickly, each succeeding moment bringing a new act of violence that rose out of the preceding one with a terrible inevitability, or so it seemed to the observer.

It started with Toby Ferris lunging toward the tormentor. Sonny Sammartino lunged a fraction of a second later, and knocked Toby far to one side, shouting, "He's mine!"

He threw himself on Whitehead, his hands clutching the man's throat. A second later his whole body was suddenly caught up in a spastic seizure, then it relaxed and slid twisting to the floor, the red fluid spurting from his chest above the red cummerbund. The spurting stopped, and the blood flowed into the carpet. Sonny Sammartino lay on his back staring at the ceiling, his hands still curled into claws as if he were finishing the job of strangling his parents' murderer in the afterlife.

Ralph yelled, "Burnside!"

The large black man, momentarily mesmerized, moved. He said loudly, "That does it, Whitey!"

Whitehead started toward him with the bloody stiletto in his hand.

Burnside had a gun pointed at the advancing killer. The black finger squeezed the trigger. The bullet entered the white forehead and blasted out the back of the skull, and Whitehead's body fell like a tree.

Terry Shields said, "What the bloody hell!" and tried to rise.

Burnside looked as if in surprise at the gun in his hand, then at the four corrupters—Everett Dolin, Terry Shields, Sylvan Brunner, and the old man whose face now seemed to be decomposing.

Opal remained slumped in her chair. Toby crawled to her on the floor and pulled her down. Her face was frozen in an expression of horror. He lay on top of her as if he were a bulletproof blanket.

"The Empress is dead," Burnside said in a tone of great sorrow. "You killed the Empress."

The great portals were flung open.

The first gunman leaped into the room. It was Tony Lukats. The moment it took him to take in the scene was his downfall.

The second bullet from Burnside's gun slammed into Lukats's chest.

Lukats looked down in disbelief before hitting the wall and sliding down.

The second and third gunmen were in the room before the fate of the first one had time to register in their brains.

Joe took Burnside's third bullet in the eye. He dropped his gun, put his hands to his face, and fell forward.

Mac got off two shots. The first hit Burnside in the shoulder. The other came in a reflexive action of the trigger finger after Burnside's fourth bullet had bored through his heart. Mac's shot was off target. It sliced through Toby Ferris's buttocks as he lay protectively atop Opal. He said, "Goldarn the goldarn!" Then he said, "Oh, shit."

Abruptly there was silence. All action ceased. Burnside faced the open door, but no one came through it. Everett Dolin had a glazed look on his face. Terry Shields was squinting at Burnside, his tough old body crouched for a lunge. Sylvan Brunner was frozen in the act of rising. The old man was eyeing Burnside balefully.

Burnside called, "Come on in, Raymond."

For a long moment there was no response. Then the remaining gunman in the hall said, "You play rough, brother. I'm leaving."

No sound could be heard from the hall.

Burnside's eyes were fixed on the doorway. Then he silently stepped sideways, one step, two steps, three steps, until he was against the wall on the same side of the room as the door.

Suddenly a large black body was hurtling through the doorway. It rolled acrobatically and halted in a prone position with a gun aimed at the spot where Burnside had been seconds before. When the gun tardily swung toward him, Burnside dispatched his fifth bullet and blasted the top of Raymond's skull. The body didn't fall. It was already prone.

Burnside leaned against the wall, breathing heavily. A glistening spot on his jacket was spreading. The nauseating smell of fresh blood filled the room. Lillian, who had risen to her feet, eased herself back onto the settee in a moment of dizziness. Burnside said in a voice of great wonder, "I'm still here!" His gun, with one bullet left, dangled in his hand.

Ralph Simmons was about to sink wearily back into his observer's perch when he saw old William Brunner rise from his chair and amble unhurriedly to the corpses of the dead gunmen. The old man bent down, then started to straighten. Ralph saw that there was a gun in each hand.

In the same second, Terry Shields sprang from his crouch, drove his hard body into Burnside's midsection, and wrenched the gun from his hand. He stepped back a step from the wounded black man and said, "You're dead, Burnsie."

Burnside said, "I know," calmly, in a lifeless voice.

Old William Brunner called, "Sylvan," and he tossed one of the guns to his son, who remained on the satin sofa. The gun landed in Sylvan's lap and fell to the floor. The candidate for governor made no move to pick it up. He was trembling.

The old man said, "There's work to do, son! You and I! Come on!"

Sylvan didn't move.

Ralph Simmons understood the old man's reasoning. They still had a chance to eliminate the witnesses and with luck get out of the building without being recognized.

Sylvan's strange inertia distracted the old man, so that Ralph was only two paces from him before the old man noticed him. Ralph's idea was to grapple with the old man and take the gun from him. He was too far away. He would lunge, but he knew he would receive a bullet before he touched the old man. He lunged. There was nothing else he could do.

Suddenly the bloodcurdling screech of ten thousand devils filled the air. The gun pointing at Ralph wavered, and the bullet hit him in the arm. Lillian rushed, screaming, at Shields and smashed his head with the fireplace poker. Shields's finger tightened on the trigger of Burnside's gun, and the last bullet from it slammed into Burnside's chest. Even while Shields and Burnside were falling, Toby Ferris snatched the gun from the floor near Sylvan Brunner's feet, rolled off Opal's body, aimed the gun at the old man, who was about to shoot Ralph a second time. He aimed for the man's chest and hit him in the knee, shattering it. The old man went down sideways, like a toppled statue. Ralph Simmons fell on top of him. After a while he became aware that the old man wasn't breathing.

He heard Everett Dolin say, "Come on, Sylvan. It's time to go."

Lillian tugged at him. "Sit up, Ralph," she said. "I can't help you if you don't sit up."

Then there were a lot of blue legs in the room and hushed exclamations.

"My God!"

"What a bloody mess!"

"What's the count?"

"Nine dead, three wounded, two not wounded—the Governor and the fat lady."

"Who are you calling a fat lady, you big bum?"

"No offense, ma'am."

From the count, Ralph guessed that Dolin had fled the scene without being able to take Sylvan Brunner with him.

Then Ralph heard a familiar voice, so cultured that Ralph had jokingly claimed that it should provide subtitles so ordinary folks could understand what it was saying. What it said now was, "Sorry, Governor, the casino is hereby closed temporarily until the full committee can make it permanent."

Strange that Roger Meuwssen should be on the scene so quickly, Ralph thought. Ralph was seated with his back to the wall, and an E.M.T. man was putting a bandage on his arm. Ralph's line of vision was blocked by policemen. He called, "Hey, Opal!"

From the far end of the room, she responded in an unsteady voice. "Ralph? Are you okay?"

"In the pink," he replied. "How about yourself?"

"Great! Never better!"

"Hey, Opal!"

"Yeah?"

"On the tapes."

"What about the tapes?"

"Was one of the supporting actors a character named Meuwssen? Roger Meuwssen?"

Meuwssen's fruity voice: "What about Meuwssen? Who is that? Oh, it's you, Simmons."

Opal's voice: "Meuwssen? Of course! Five hundred grand! That's what Sammartino delivered to him. It's all there."

Ralph looked up at the aristocratic face of the chairman of the Casino Control Agency of the State of New York, and a tired grin spread on his own face.

"I should have caught on long ago," Ralph said. "We were being followed within an hour of the time we bumped into you at the club. For a long time I thought it was Alex Burnside who tipped them off. But he didn't know where we lived. You did. So it had to be you, my old friend and neighbor, the great public benefactor, Roger Meuwssen."

Meuwssen said to a policeman. "That's one of them."

Minutes later, Ralph and Lillian Simmons were arrested for aiding and abetting the hijacking of the Staten Island ferry. Toby Ferris was arrested for the actual hijacking. They were taken to Coney Island Hospital where they stayed overnight. Toby said he knew someone who was born there. Opal was also taken to Coney Island Hospital for treatment of a lacerated chest. The Brooklyn District Attorney visited them there.

Sylvan Brunner was taken to Staten Island and delivered into the care of his wife. The only thing he said was that his sinuses were killing him.

Old William Brunner was pronounced dead of a heart attack at Coney Island Hospital.

The Empress of Coney Island was pronounced dead by the head of the New York Casino Control Agency, Roger Meuwssen.

22

THE FERRIS WHEEL, datelined The Tombs, New York City. Well, folks, the Big City has whupped my poor ass again. They call it The Tombs. I call it The Pits.

The judge said, "We can't have people going around commandeering our public transport and directing it to a destination of their own choosing, now can we, Mr. Ferris?" And I said, "No, sir, we can't have that at all!"

He said, "We must make an example of anyone who tries it, don't you agree, Mr. Ferris?"

"It goes without saying, sir," I said.

He said, "What you did was an act of piracy. Do you know what the penalty for piracy used to be, Mr. Ferris?"

"Hanging from the yardarm, sir."

"Right!" he said. "However, since we don't have a yardarm in the New York State penal system . . ."

He sentenced me to six months in Durance Vile, which is another title I've given this hapless hostel for wayward adults. I called it The Tombs up there, because it sounded sort of glamorous to me. Actually, I'm on Riker's Island. I can't seem to get away from islands, all of them prisons of one sort or another.

Captain Andy Anderssen spoke up for me in the courtroom, saying what a fine fellow I was and that it seemed to him the real villain was the wild young man with the gun. Well, I had to straighten them out about Sonny Sammartino. Even a dead man is entitled to his good name. I think he and I would have gotten along fine, if he hadn't done the crazy thing I was aiming to do, namely, die in an attempt to save a brave woman from torture. Of course, he had another motive—to avenge his parents' deaths, but that's not so ignoble, is it?

Anyway, God bless Sonny Sammartino, and God bless Alex Burnside. My friend Ralph Simmons had Burnside figured out pretty well as a man who had broken many laws in getting to where he was in an unsaintly profession, but who was still a man for all that and who drew the line at murder. He killed to prevent mass murder—a noble action by a noble man.

The funny thing about the whole affair is that Everett Dolin was the only other character to end up in jail, despite the fact that he turned state's evidence and donated his own secret tapes to the prosecution's case. He didn't know at the time he made his deal that the district attorney had grave doubts about the admissibility of Opal's tapes into evidence, since they were illegal in the first instance and surely hearsay when presented by a writer who had gotten them from a dead accountant who, in turn, had gotten them from the original taper, also deceased.

The trial of Sylvan Brunner was in progress for only two days when it became apparent to the judge and everyone else that Brunner was not competent to stand trial. His moods changed abruptly. He would leap from a state of deep apathy to the stance of prosecutor cross-examining the judge and everyone else about ancient crimes that no one could understand. The trial was halted, and Brunner was sent to Creedmoor, where he was strangled to death by another inmate shortly after he entered. The inmate thought he was killing the Devil. And so he was.

Thus, poor old Everett Dolin had copped a plea in vain. As it turned out, if he hadn't made his deal, he probably would never have been prosecuted. He's doing five years in Sing Sing.

Roger Meuwssen resigned from the Casino Control

Agency and departed hastily to an island in the Caribbean, where he hopes to live happily ever after. The trouble is, he is not the sort to consort with nubile natives or even with the likes of Robert Vesco. He has been posted for being in arrears at the Stuyvesant Club. This last must have been the most unkindest cut of all.

Ralph and Lillian Simmons were reléased from custody the morning after the massacre, and the charges of hijacking were dropped. The only evidence against them was that they had disembarked from the ferry at Coney Island instead of Staten Island, and the authorities could find no statute on the books that covered the situation. Lillian never was charged with the fatal skull-bashing of Terry Shields, because the authorities never did get straight who did what to whom in the Princess Suite that night. Lillian said she was actually trying to get at old Brunner and reshape *his* headbone to prevent him from shooting Ralph a second time, but Terry Shields was in the way.

The Empress stands majestically empty while the remnant of the Casino Control Agency tries to get its act together. An assemblyman from Harlem has proposed that it be turned into housing for the homeless, but the carnival concessionaries in the area retorted that the last thing they needed was the invasion of hundreds of homeless who didn't have the ready cash to play their games. Graffiti decorates her walls, and some of her windows are smashed. She's beginning to look frumpy.

Opal Wilder isn't a bag-lady anymore. She's working hard on her novel, called *Empress of Coney Island*, based on transcripts she has in her possession.

I get out in two months, and she has promised to wait for me. "I promise not to let someone come along and sweep me off my feet during that time," she said.

She's still a bit skittish, but I'm pretty sure we're going to get married. If you happen to see her, tell her I'm not such a bad sort. Will you do that?

243

FREE!!
BOOKS BY MAIL
CATALOGUE

BOOKS BY MAIL will share with you our current bestselling books as well as hard to find specialty titles in areas that will match your interests. You will be updated on what's new in books at no cost to you. Just fill in the coupon below and discover the convenience of having books delivered to your home.

PLEASE ADD $1.00 TO COVER THE COST OF POSTAGE & HANDLING.

- -

BOOKS BY MAIL

320 Steelcase Road E.,
Markham, Ontario L3R 2M1

210 5th Ave., 7th Floor
New York, N.Y., 10010

Please send Books By Mail catalogue to:

Name _____
(please print)

Address _____

City _____

Prov./State _____ P.C./Zip _____
(BBM1)